CASTLE OF TESKOM

BOOK ONE

Also by Kim Malaj

Ember In Time Series:
Castle of Teskom
Recover or Yield
Protectors of Time
Guide Time Inside (Fall 2022)

Who Is Maggie

The Old Untold

Failed Book Cover Journals (A-Z)

EMBER IN TIME SERIES

CASTLE OF TESKOM

BOOK ONE

KIM MALAJ

Castle of Teskom

ISBN: 9781737493051 (Paperback)

Copyright © 2020-2022 Kim Malaj

Kim Malaj
Haxhaj Nd. 19
Ivanaj, Albania 4306
www.kimmalaj.com

Second Edition: May 1, 2022

For my Grandma Rex

My inspiration to live and enjoy every moment, find love in every human, laugh loud and proud, and smile at every stranger.

N
NW
NE
W
E
SW
SE
S
MONTENEGRO

FORT KELMEND
ALBANIAN ALPS
ASTLE OF TESKOM
BAJZE
LAKE SHKODER

1

Itra's headlamp goes dark, blinding Danae's footing on the rocky terrain. She stumbles forward and grasps the back of his damp shirt for balance. He plays with the switch and shakes the headlamp. He attempts to step through but smashes the bridge of his nose on the stones. He mutters a curse and bends lower, clearing the opening.

Crunch

"What was that?" Danae panics.

"Watch your head," Itra says. "It's low." He interlocks his fingers with hers and thumbs her wedding ring.

She drags her free hand over her head and feels the smooth stones as she steps under.

Crunch

Itra's headlamp flares back to life.

Danae's head snaps up. She follows the beam as he scans the area, revealing a small clearing—a few rocks, grass, and an open space.

"Did we step on glass?" Danae asks.

Itra dips his chin and bathes their feet in light. In contrast with the darkness, his light dances with glints of burnt orange.

"Does it remind you of hot coals?" he asks.

"Or lava?" she adds.

Itra looks up. Danae steps out of his glaring light.

"Careful, watch your step!"

"Ouch!"

Danae rubs her shin.

Itra shines his light on a small wooden post erected on two small pillars with markings along the ridge.

"I think it's a grazing post," he says. "Maybe there is a home nearby."

Danae strains her eyes, but it's still too dark to make out anything beyond the beam of the headlamp. She leans against the post and adjusts her socks and the laces of her hiking boots for the hundredth time in the last six, twelve, eighteen, hell; she has no clue how many hours they've been lost.

It was just before one in the morning when their phones died. They had drained the batteries, using the map, compass, and flashlight apps to find their way down the Mokset hills and back home.

"What time is it?" she asks.

"Close to dawn," says Itra. He stretches and unsnaps their only pack. "Do you want to rest here until we have enough light to see?"

"Sure," she says, trying to swallow a yawn. "Can you hand me a pillow?"

He laughs.

"Is there any water left in the pack?" she asks.

He shakes the silent metal water bottles. He opens the pack and pulls out one apple, two granola bar wrappers, and two rain jackets. They had packed light for a day hike and had finished their water, granola bars, and other fruit hours ago. The headlamp had been a welcome surprise, left in an inner pocket from their last excursion.

Itra hands Danae the remaining apple.

"We've hiked the Mokset hills four times in the last two years," she says, waving the apple around. "We always take different routes. How did we get lost so close to home?" She pauses, taking a bite. "When did you realize we made a wrong turn?"

"Around dusk," says Itra, "but before you get mad, wait until I finish. The lake and mountains on the horizon placed us on or near the same hills before it got pitch dark. I thought once we found a trail again, it would lead us back down."

Danae takes another loud bite of the apple before sharing it with Itra.

"Where do you think we are now?"

"Near the lake? Maybe further north than we planned to go, but on the same hills. I'll know for sure at first light."

As the darkness fades, the air seems to change. The bird song carries a different melody in the early morning hours. Danae's eyes droop as a warm morning breeze lifts her curls away from her cheeks.

"Can you wake me in ten?" she says, yawning.

"Hours or minutes?"

"Ha!" Danae snorts.

He wraps his arm around her, pulling her close.

They're nearly asleep when the clouds part and the sun crowns the horizon, lighting a rocky clearing that abruptly slopes up into a stone wall. The morning glow outlines a tall structure.

"Is that a castle or a fort?" Danae whispers. They stare as the light transforms the stones into an enormous castle. A snort of bewilderment from Danae makes Itra chuckle. They break into exhausted laughter.

Danae catches her breath.

Itra quiets, nudging Danae in the side before he stands.

"Come on."

Danae allows him to pull her to her feet, brushing off the dirt, spider webs, and grass clinging to her hair and clothes.

She shields her eyes, turning to the east where the ground shimmers with shiny, orange-tinted flecks in a half-circle at the base of a stone archway.

"Did we walk through there?" she asks.

"Yes," Itra says. "I think so."

There are four additional archways, each spaced the same distance apart to the north.

"Is this one of those stone circles?" she asks.

"In Albania?" Itra shakes his head. "Not likely."

The landscape beyond the five archways has a few rocky boulders, green and yellow thorny plants and small fruit trees.

Danae turns back to the small grass and rocky clearing with a worn path to the castle.

Itra slowly turns in a circle.

"Where are we?" Danae asks, poking him in the chest.

"I have no clue," Itra says.

Itra hops in place, and his face goes from clueless into a wild grin.

"Oh, no! I know that look," she says. "Did you plan this? Where are we, honestly? Please tell me you know where we are right this minute!"

"Just take a breath," he says, placing his hand on his chest with an exaggerated inhale and loud exhale.

She complies with a loud sigh.

"Good?" he asks.

She nods, but narrows her eyes at him.

"You know the old Mokset Castle remains?"

She nods again, scrunching her face in confusion, crosses her arms, and taps her foot. "We were there today," she says. "Well, yesterday."

"Does the landscape look similar at all?"

Danae spins around, trying to recall the landscape and noticing similar rocky boulders but not enough trees. She turns back, confused.

"The landscape had trees of all sizes," she says, "but I only see a few here and noticed no archways. Do you think we're near the remains?"

Itra turns in a slow circle again, stopping to stare at the castle.

Danae follows his line of sight. The rugged stone steps leading to the lowest wall look vaguely familiar to the castle remains.

"Itra?"

"Hmm?"

"What's going on?"

"Give me your phone."

"Why?"

"I want to hide the phones." He opens the pack and holds out his hand. "It's only a precaution, just in case they search us."

"They? Who?"

Danae glances around for anyone approaching, but they're alone.

"Just playing it safe. We need water, and our best bet is there." He gestures to the castle. "I don't know who or what we will find if we get inside."

"Fine," Danae says, handing over her phone.

"Thank you."

Itra secures the phones and swings the near-empty pack over one shoulder.

"Ready?" he asks.

"Totally, just after I wash my hair!"

He shakes his head, laughing.

Thankful for the morning light, they move along without tripping over the many rocks and roots.

Danae searches for any familiar landmarks. "Itra, do you remember the giant fig tree in the clearing near the remains?"

"Yep!" Itra says, pausing his stride for a moment. "See that small twig of a tree just to your left?"

"That seriously can't—no way!" Danae steps closer to inspect it, and sure enough, it has a few fig leaves and buds. But the top of the tree is eye level.

She stumbles back. "You can't be serious; there is no way that is the same tree!"

"The clearing, the landscape, the steps, the boulders, and we didn't leave Albania overnight," Itra says. "Could be, maybe?"

Danae's head whirls.

"Maybe we crossed over to Montenegro?" she whispers.

He laughs. "Do you remember swimming across a lake?"

Her gaze follows the morning light glistening on Lake Shkoder. "Ugh, no!" she groans.

Danae's fatigue rattles her thoughts. *Am I shrinking, or is the castle growing in height with each step?* A few wildflowers line the path, and one pop of red stands tall.

"Did you see the poppy?" she asks.

"I did," Itra says. "Did you see the snake?"

She quickens her pace to catch up with him, looking around wildly. "Dead or alive, poisonous or harmless?"

"Dead and harmless."

She shoves his shoulder and scowls.

He shrugs and smiles.

They ascend up the familiar rugged steps, follow another path around a curve, and gaze up at the first wall and the towers above. The castle's size is not ominous from a distance, but standing in its shadow—it's slightly terrifying.

The first stone step is tall, almost thigh high.

Itra places his hands on Danae's shoulders. She turns her wide eyes to his anxious face.

"Mui," Itra says.

"Mui?" she asks, tilting her head.

"The almighty giant from the Albanian folk tales," Itra says.

Danae laughs, shaking her head.

Itra explains, "The legend describes the entrance to Mui's home with stairs one meter high." He gestures towards the giant steps.

She looks up the stairs to the castle and back to his grin, expanding the width of his face.

"Ha!" she barks. "And I'm Queen Danae. Welcome to my humble abode!"

"After you, my Queen," he says, still grinning and bows. "I am but your humble servant."

Danae takes Itra's hand, feeling his pulse jump against her palm.

The first wall is nine stones stacked with near-perfect precision. The size is alarmingly huge—each stone is nearly as wide and tall as a billboard. A small decorative stone outlines a large, open arched entry at the top of four enormous steps.

"How did they get equipment large enough to stack these up here?" Itra whispers.

"More like when?" Danae asks, feeling an icy shiver. "Do you think this is a modern castle? I assumed the castle was old."

Itra shrugs as he pulls Danae up the last step.

Itra gazes out at the clearing below. The elevation appears to drop off past the five stone archways down to the lake.

Danae's immediately drawn to the beautiful mosaic tile floor. Too afraid to enter all the way, she kneels at the threshold. A pattern of gold crests and swells of blue waves. The design and colors look very modern in contrast to the thick exterior stone walls. Across the entrance foyer, marble stairs lead to a large landing. Light is shining through a window, and she can see another flight of stairs continuing up. Adjacent walls appear to be a dark descending stairwell on one side and an open archway.

"It's stunning," Danae murmurs, standing.

"Anybody home?" Itra calls out loudly. "We come in peace."

His baritone voice echoes in the stairwells.

"I don't see any cameras or a doorbell," she whispers. "Do you think it's safe to enter?"

"I'll go first," Itra says.

He quietly steps inside, coming back a few steps and motions for her to follow.

"Do you hear a dripping sound?" Danae whispers, cautiously following him across the foyer to a large arched opening.

A whoosh of humid air dampens their skin as they cross through—a conservatory with green-tinted light from the dome glass ceiling. The dripping sound intensifies as they creep along a curving path, passing rows of potted plants and flowers.

Danae's nose twinges with a sneeze, and her eyes water. The sound reverberates off the walls.

"Shh!" Itra says.

"Sorry," she whispers.

He stops at the head of a stone elephant waist high set out from the wall. The trunk is a waterspout with a slow drip into a small stone basin below.

Danae's mouth instantly salivates. She licks her lips.

"It's fresh!" Itra says, catching a drop of the water with his tongue.

"It'll take hours to fill a single container with enough water for one gulp," she says, rolling her eyes.

Itra inspects the spout and finds one stone ear is leaning slightly forward. He gently pulls it, and water gushes out in a quick burst. The noise startles Danae. He smiles smugly as Danae removes the bottles from the pack, filling one in three pulls. She hands over the second bottle. They guzzle down a full bottle each before refilling again. Adequately satiated and slightly waterlogged, they top off the bottles and repack them.

"Now what?" she whispers.

"Explore quietly?"

"I want to sleep in our own bed tonight after the longest shower in history," she says. "A quick look around, and then we find our way down."

He nods with a grin.

Danae follows his lead around the wide arc and rows of plants. She's no garden expert, but she admires the meticulous attention and skill of this caretaker—not a single brown or dead plant. She watches Itra inspect a row of what looks to be cherry tomatoes, and before she can say *don't eat those*, he pops one in his mouth.

His eyes go wide, face goes beet red before swallowing and grinning.

"You should've seen your face, babe!" He laughs as he pops another one in his mouth.

Danae shoves his shoulder before taking a tomato from the vine and cautiously biting into it. She moans in approval and picks a few more.

Itra and Danae continue picking and eating lettuce greens, cucumbers, and strawberries. The sun shining directly over the glass adds additional warmth.

Danae's full stomach makes her drowsy. She yawns and fights the weight of her eyelids.

"I think our quick look around is over," Danae says, trying to hide another yawn. "Do you think it's safe to take a nap in here?"

Itra shrugs. The exhaustion and full stomach make him drag his feet. He motions for her to follow towards another arched doorway in the conservatory's rear. They hesitantly enter a mirror of the first foyer without an exterior door. However, the mosaic tiles are red and silver in a flame pattern. A stairway leads up to a landing with a window and straight ahead, a set of stairs descending into darkness.

"Up or down?" he murmurs.

"Are you serious?" she asks. "Up! I'm too tired for dark and creepy stairs."

They climb the smooth marble steps to a landing with a window. Outside, a view of a wickedly tight hedge maze with a small stone figurine in the center of an open courtyard inside four stone walls.

"Do you see any doors from here?" Danae asks, leaning her forehead against the pane.

"No," Itra says.

They continue up the next flight of stairs to another landing. Two adjacent archways lead to long, wide corridors with marble floors, stone walls, and evenly spaced wood and iron doors. The archway across from the stairs opens to a balcony. From here, they can see the mountains of Montenegro on the other side of Lake Shkoder. They gravitate towards the view. It's stunning, but alarming. They step back, dizzy from the height.

"I think we need to sleep," Danae laughs. "Maybe we're hallucinating from the food?"

"Did you notice any roads, towns, boats, or any movement below?" Itra asks.

"Um, no?" she says. "I've also never seen a sheer drop or cliff of this height on any of our previous hikes. Have you?"

"No, the cliff is a new feature."

"Itra, we need to—"

A clatter of running footsteps from somewhere inside induces a rush of flight, not fight.

Itra grabs her hand and sprints down one corridor, trying each door they pass. One door finally opens. Itra catches the door before it slams against the wall. He quietly shuts it behind them. Danae searches for a place to hide. She opens a second narrow door to a small vacant washroom. They step inside and gently close the door. One giant tear rolls down Danae's cheek. She rests her hand on his chest, feeling Itra's heart race against her palm.

"What now?" she whispers.

2

Itra and Danae hide long enough for the exhaustion to creep back in. He cracks open the door. The room is empty, except the bedroom furniture. They sigh with mild relief. She notices a gold, wing-back chair Itra wedged against the door with their pack.

"Your idea of security?" Danae whispers, nodding towards the door.

Itra shrugs.

The mosaic tile floor matches the entrance foyer's color scheme—blue and gold, but this design with mountains and caves. Danae slides her hands over the smooth silk curtains tied back with a thick gold rope, framing a view of the hedge maze. The room is sparsely but ornately furnished, and there is a notable absence of light, no lamps or overhead fixtures.

A bulky frame hangs on the wall adjacent to the bed. The light from the window casts the frame's contents in shadow.

"Does the headlamp still work?" Danae asks.

Itra flips it on and tosses it to her. He moves to her side as she leans closer to inspect the image. It is a wedding portrait of a couple. The man's strong profile with shaven brown hair, straight, narrow nose and firm chin is gazing at a woman with brown pixie waves framing a heart-shaped face. From the background, the couple appears to be standing on the balcony overlooking the lake.

Danae shines the light on Itra's profile and goes back to the image.

"It's you and me," Danae squeaks out in alarm. "But how? What do you think this means? Have we—"

Itra covers her mouth and puts a finger to his lips. Her rambling continues under his hand until she notices his eyes dart towards the door. She immediately quiets to listen. There is a faint humming sound coming from the corridor.

Itra turns off the headlamp. They crouch beside the bed. The humming stops directly outside the door. The sound of something sliding on the floor has Itra on his hands and knees looking under the bed. Danae leans down to see a royal blue envelope slide to a stop under the chair.

Itra crawls around the bed, staying low to look for feet or a shadow on the other side. He reaches far enough to retrieve the envelope and crawls back.

It is made of heavy parchment with thick cursive writing scrawled on the front—*Itra & Danae*—and a large gold wax seal with a bird on the back. Danae's eyes bulge in disbelief.

"Should I open it?" Itra asks. His voice startles Danae—his first spoken words since their hasty retreat from the balcony.

"Sure, why not?"

Itra clicks the headlamp on and scoots close to her. He breaks the wax seal, and the four corners open with a shower of lavender-scented dust. She stifles a sneeze, holding her nose. The same bold cursive writing in royal blue ink arches across the pale gold parchment.

You have entered the Castle of Teskom. The land and castle are free for you to explore. The wardrobe contains clothes and shoes. A bell will ring for each meal provided on the terrace located directly above this room. The dust you inhaled will induce a restful sleep in ten seconds.

Kind regards, Ivan

She attempts to read the message a second time. Her eyelids are too heavy. Itra attempts to stand, reaching for Danae, but he collapses on the bed. She lies next to him before falling into darkness.

"If you move to the right one more step, I will end you!" a low bass voice thunders.

Danae turns to seek the person speaking. The clearing is empty of people, only the outline of the five archways.

"Who will end me?" she asks.

"Brave and beautiful," the voice booms. "Interesting."

He is mocking her. Irritated, she steps to the right.

3

"Class," Kaly calls from the podium, "settle down and take your seats." She waits until nearly everyone sits before she starts the first slide. "Today, we are going to discuss the family saga of Medusa." She clicks the next slide. "Who can tell me the connection between Medusa and the Grey Sisters?"

"The Grey Sisters gave Perseus the location of Medusa," a student in the second row calls out.

"Correct," Kaly replies. "And who are the Grey Sisters?"

"Dread, Horror and Alarm," a student towards the back answers.

"Correct," Kaly says. "They're also known by their Greek names, Deino, Enyo, and Pemphredo." The next slide shows a family tree with several blank spaces. "The Grey Sisters were also sisters to the Gorgons, one of whom was Medusa. Can anyone tell me the names of their parents?"

"Phorcys and Rhea?"

"Phorcys and Ceto?"

"Phorcys and Ceto are correct," says Kaly, clicking to the next slide to show the complete family tree. "They were known as sea gods or as fierce monsters, depending on the source."

Kaly clicks the slide to an image of the family tree zoomed into the Gorgon Sisters and Grey Sisters. "All sisters, according to this family tree." Kaly advances to the next slide. "This drawing of a haggard, old, hunched woman with stringy hair side by side with the three fairy godmothers from Sleeping Beauty. These are some modern versions of the Grey Sisters."

"Hold up," a student interrupts as Kaly advances to the next slide. "The fairy godmothers?"

Kaly chuckles. "Most versions of fairy tales with three witches, fairies, or sisters have some characteristics of the Grey Sisters, including Shakespeare's Macbeth: The Weird Sisters or the old television series Charmed."

Kaly points to the new slide. "An image of Medusa before the curse and after, the contrast from a dark-haired, pale face beauty to the iconic head of hair made of snakes and green-colored face. These versions have source descriptions dating back 460 BC." Kaly clicks to a drawing of Perseus holding Medusa's head.

"Who can tell me how Perseus persuaded the Grey Sisters to betray Medusa?"

"He stole their shared eye?"

"That is a version of the story," Kaly answers. "According to many written accounts, the sisters shared one eye and one tooth. A recent dig uncovered an ancient vessel containing a perfectly preserved human eye, one tooth, and a shard of unknown origins on any periodic table. The contents made many historians jump to a connection to the Grey Sisters. Can anyone guess the location of this dig site?"

"Greece?" a student calls from the back row.

"Italy?" a second student calls from the front row.

Kaly holds up her hand. "One more guess?"

"Turkey?" another student calls.

"Northern Albania," Kaly answers, advancing the slide to an old map. "Illyria, pre-Roman invasions in 168 BC. The area in red covers what we now call North Macedonia, northern Greece, Kosovo, Albania, and Montenegro. The nation of Albania declared independence in 1912 after defeating the Ottoman Empire. The origin of Albania could easily be a semester block class."

"Does this mean the Grey Sisters are technically not Greek?" a student asks.

"A great question," Kaly says. "Or did Perseus keep and bury the contents elsewhere? The research team released a recent update. They have dated the vessel as third century BC but are still analyzing the contents."

Kaly continues her lecture by discussing Medusa's role as a priestess for Athena, Athena's jealousy of Poseidon's affection for Medusa, and Athena's curse of stone on to Medusa. The Grey Sisters betrayal and Perseus's actions, and how the vessel discovery in Albania make this one of the greatest finds in recent history. She leaves the class with an assignment to research any known Greek Mythology overlapping with Illyrian Mythology for Wednesday's class discussion before ending her lecture.

As the students file out, one of them approaches Kaly with his laptop open. "Have you seen this website?" he asks, turning the screen towards Kaly.

The website heading is *Wandering It Press*, and the tagline is *We are one of three dimensions*. Kaly glances up at the student, trying to hide her skepticism.

"I know, it looks nuts," he says, "but there is a recent post about the dig site in Albania that you discussed in today's lecture."

"I'll look at it, thanks!" Kaly says with a smile. "And good luck with the assignment."

"Thanks!" He shoves his laptop into his bag. Kaly and the student exit the lecture hall and bump into a tall, muscular man.

The student jumps back in alarm. "Sorry, man!"

"No worries." The man steps around the student to kiss Kaly on the cheek.

The student blushes in recognition of Kaly's husband, Leon. "See you Wednesday, Kaly, I mean, professor." The student nearly trips in his retreat.

Leon laughs. "Somebody is hot for the teacher," he teases. Kaly elbows him hard in the ribs. Leon playfully winces, then continues. "Are you ready to go, or do you need to stop by your office?"

"Office first," Kaly says. "I wasn't expecting you for another hour. How was your meeting today?"

"Same as always. They talked about their 'episodes' and how to cope with reality."

Kaly nods, taking his hand.

Leon spent thirty-two hours surrounded by enemy fire, pinned under the remains of a small truck after his envoy hit a land mine. He made it out with minimal hearing loss, dehydration, and some shrapnel wounds. They moved out of their small studio apartment in downtown Kansas City to a ranch with acres of land. Small or crowded spaces trigger his anxiety to near panic attacks. She encouraged him to attend a Post-Traumatic Stress Disorder support meeting at a local veteran's hall. Her husband returned home intact physically minus a few scars, but still has a few demons to conquer.

"My sister hasn't called back with the recipe you ask for," Leon says. "Were they camping overnight on this hike?"

"No," Kaly says, unlocking her office. "Danae made it sound like a day hike, and I think they've hiked that area before. She may have just lost her phone again. Did you try Itra?"

He nods.

"Don't worry," Kaly says. "I'll try her on the way home."

She drops a few items in her bag and checks her office phone for messages. *"One message, today at 3:33 pm. My name is Unis Beard, Wandering It Press. I'm calling to arrange an interview regarding the Grey Sisters. You can reach me at..."* Kaly deletes the message before it finishes. She frowns, hanging up the phone.

"What's wrong?" Leon asks.

"Just an odd message," she says, "and strange timing."

4

Clang, clang, clang, clang, clang, clang, clang

Danae jolts awake, her pulse pounding in her ears. Itra shifts against her, softly snoring. She sits up and moves to the edge of the bed, waiting for her heart to slow. Her eyes catch the morning light reflecting off the glass-framed portrait. A ripple of unease creeps over her as she quietly enters the washroom. A wild person is staring back at her. She jumps, only to realize it's just her reflection in a full-length mirror. She squashes her scream and giggles at her absurd reaction.

The room is no longer dark or narrow but a fully furnished, modern master bathroom. She steps closer to the mirror. Despite her disheveled appearance, she looks lighter, almost radiant.

"Epic bed head," she mumbles, attempting to pat down her wavy curls. The morning crack—that will one day wake the dead—of Itra's neck interrupts her longing gaze at the copper soaking tub.

"Good morning, my dear," Danae says, returning to the bedroom.

One eyebrow raises from his bed-creased face as he stretches his arms overhead.

"Did you hear the bell?" she asks.

"No," he says, his voice is husky with sleep.

"The washroom is through there." She motions to the door. "Fair warning. It looks different from yesterday." She kisses him before sitting to take off her boots. They had both fallen asleep fully dressed. "I have no clue what time it is, but I'm guessing it's morning."

He stands, cocking his head to the side. "Are you okay?"

She returns the look, cocking her head to the side with a smile. "Absolutely not, but here we are. I desperately want and need to shower."

"Hmm. Sure."

Itra goes to the washroom, closing the door behind him. A few minutes later, Danae hears the door unlatch and the shower start. Itra's back is to the door, already soaking in the shower, the glass framing his glorious physique. She takes in his tan skin, round butt, muscular back, and those biceps, *damn*. She bites her bottom lip and continues to stare until he glances over his shoulder, *busted*. She peels off her hiking gear and dumps her clothes near his.

A second water nozzle automatically turns on overhead. The water temperature and pressure are perfect, Danae moans. An intense aroma of lemon and ginger fills the air, awakening her senses. They shower twice before toweling off. She wonders if the inhaled lavender dust is only for sleep. It has the maddening side effect of lust.

The vanity drawer is full of all the essential amenities.

"Bless the fairies!" Danae says, holding up two toothbrushes. After she and Itra brush their teeth, they open and smell the various creams, deodorants, and small jars with bath salts and essential oils. Danae dabs a bit of oil labeled honey blossom on her wrists, rubbing the sides of her neck. Itra leans over, inhales, then playfully bites her neck, hard enough to make her squirm.

Danae bends to pick up their clothes but is distracted by Itra. He swings open the door.

"Seize the day!" he bellows.

Danae watches Itra stride across the room in all his glory. He swings open the wardrobe.

"Hmm, let's see, yes," he says, "definitely this one!" He picks out a blue sundress and gold wedge sandals. He holds the dress up to his chest. "Not sure I can pull this off. Do you think this will be too short for me?"

Danae laughs, taking the items and slipping on the dress. The lightweight softness feels silky against her skin. She sits to adjust the sandals and stands.

Twirling in the dress, she asks, "What do you think?"

Itra is about to pull on a short sleeve cotton shirt and stops with one arm in to admire.

"How quickly can you take it off?" he asks.

"Ha!" she snorts. "Put on your shirt and turn around. Let me see the total package."

He slides his blue shirt on and turns in a slow circle, pausing so she can take in his glorious rear. The pants are denim hugging his butt like spandex—Danae's mouth waters. The shirt is long enough for his long, lean, toned torso, and the sleeves hit mid-bicep. He catches her chewing on her bottom lip as he turns around, and he flexes.

"What do you think?" he asks.

She feels her cheeks flush. "How quickly can you take that off?"

He chuckles. "Remember, my old saying?"

They say simultaneously, "Well rested and fed makes a good man great in bed."

Danae's smile fades as she comes back to the reality of where they are and how they got here. "What do we do now?"

"We go to breakfast. They address the card to us. We need to find out more, but first, we need to eat. Maybe our host will join us?"

She raises an eyebrow. "Always a one-track mind for food with you. And that 'host' drugged us yesterday!"

He shrugs.

Itra removes the chair and leans against the door to listen. He hears nothing in the corridor. He motions Danae to follow. They stride to the landing and up the stairs. The next landing offers three archways, like the floor below, but the view is wrong. Walking out on to a matching balcony just one floor up, they're staring east.

"Yesterday the view from here was facing west, right?" Danae whispers.

The landscape is familiar. It's home, but wrong—the valley of Bajze meets the base Mount Gradec to the east—a thick green forest of wide-trunk trees instead of the homesteads, vineyards, and open pastures of their small town.

Itra shudders out a ragged exhale. "My family has lived in this valley for twelve generations. And now no homes, only trees? How?"

"I have no clue," whispers Danae, equally perplexed.

Itra wraps her trembling hand in his. They attempt to process the unreal scene until his stomach makes the loudest *feed me* growl that Danae has ever heard. Despite the trauma of the situation, he sighs, uttering a small chuckle.

"Should we leave after breakfast?" Itra asks.

Danae nods and turns away from the confusing view.

They find a table set for two with a gold tablecloth and royal blue dome plate covers on the terrace.

"Are we going to discuss the color scheme?" Danae asks.

"That's what you want to discuss?" says Itra irritably. "Seriously Danae, we're in a mind-bending castle with a humming fairy and sleep dust."

"Point taken," she says. "Sit down! You're nearing hangry status."

No further encouragement is required. Itra sits quickly, pulling off the cover—the plate is empty. Danae nearly misses her chair, watching his disappointment unfold. Then, a card with familiar cursive blue ink catches her eye.

"Before you totally lose it," she says, holding the card up. She reads it aloud. "*A house chef to inspire. Imagine the breakfast you desire.*"

He raises an eyebrow and places the cover over his plate again. He grins as his eyes glaze over in thought.

"Are you done, my dear?" asks Danae.

Before he can respond, the aroma of freshly grilled sausage fills the air. He removes the cover. "Oh, wow, it worked!" He looks up at Danae. "Your turn. What are you going to order?"

She lifts her blue cover, revealing her precise thought of bacon and eggs. It smells amazing. She smiles up at him as Itra finishes his last piece of toast.

"Let me guess—you're about to order seconds?" she asks.

"Do you think it will work?"

"No idea. Give it a go."

It works.

Danae slices up her bacon and eggs while Itra inhales a full stack of pancakes, honey, a side of ham, and a mixed fruit bowl. Her breakfast hits the spot—cooked and seasoned to perfection. She waves her cloth napkin in surrender as Itra clears his third round, an order of fresh cherries and figs.

"So, what just happened?" Danae asks. "Voodoo magic, or are we hypnotized to think we enjoyed the most gratifying breakfast of our lives?"

"My waistline will confirm it's very real," he says, waving his napkin and tugging on a belt loop.

A breeze tickles Danae's neck, sending a shiver down her spine. She shudders. Itra squirms a bit in his chair. They stand up and step close to each other.

"Do you want to retrace our steps?" she asks as they embrace.

"Can you walk far in those shoes?" he asks, glancing down towards her feet.

"Far, maybe. Quickly, no. But we should find our way out of here. I would like to get home before dark."

The echo of their footsteps provides the only soundtrack to their walk down the stairs. Itra holds the door as she steps into their room. She immediately steps back out again. Her actions push Itra into a defensive stance in front of her.

"What did you—how?" he asks as he looks inside.

The hiking clothes left piled on the bathroom floor are now clean and neatly folded on the bed next to their hiking pack. Their hiking boots are also clean and placed beside the bed.

Danae feels a rush of tingles up her spine. "What the—oh, my!"

Itra looks her up and down. His face drains of color. While Danae had been wearing the dress a moment before, she now has on her hiking gear, complete with her boots on and tied laces.

Danae can only stammer out a choked, "How?"

Itra pats down his clothes. No change. He takes her hand and gently pulls her into the room, lowering her into the chair before pacing. She is physically shaking so hard that her teeth chatter.

Itra stops pacing mid-stride to look for the original card. He finds and shakes the card while holding his breath before reading the message again. "Ivan? Ivan!" Itra bounds to Danae, kneeling beside the chair so his eyes are level with hers. "Danae, I'm related to an Ivan."

Her ears are buzzing; she can barely hear him. He bounces back up, pacing the room once again.

"Ivan is the first ancestor of my father's line," he explains. "The landscape this morning shows a valley that looks like home but could only be home hundreds of years ago." She nods in acknowledgment, so he continues. "The picture could be us, or it could be my eleven-times great grandfather Ivan and his wife." He grins wider before whispering. "The castle could be in the family, my family!"

Danae swallows hard and says, "Did you forget to tell your wife of five years about some secret, magical kingdom you reign over?"

"It's all speculation," Itra says, "but we're not in the same era, are we?"

She ignores his question and stands. "This is not happening. We were lost, we trespassed, and then we were drugged. Were we fed more drugs at breakfast? Are we prisoners?" She faces Itra. He's still grinning from ear to ear. She sighs. "If we are in the past, how do you explain breakfast and this outfit quick change?"

He shrugs. "I have no clue, but I'm sure they wouldn't serve breakfast like that to prisoners." He folds his hands together, begging. "Can we please explore?"

"No! We're leaving!"

"One-hour tops, I promise, please, Danae," he begs, pouting his bottom lip.

"Fine," she says, "but change your clothes and take the pack. And no solo wandering. I mean it!"

He rocks back on his heels with a low whistle and a mock salute. "Yes, ma'am!"

Before he can reach for his clothes, a tingle runs down his entire body. "Danae, did that quick-change thing just happen?" He dares a glance down. "Oh, that is—freaking cool!"

"Freaky, yes, but not cool!"

She opens the pack to find two extra sets of hiking clothes, two sleep sacks, a second headlamp, and enough food for at least two days. But their cell phones Itra hid are missing.

"Why take our dead phones?" she asks.

Itra brushes off her questions. "We can use the headlamps and explore the stairs that lead down from the first floor."

"Maybe, but only for one-hour Itra, just one."

Danae opens all the drawers in the wardrobe, rummaging through each one before slamming them shut.

"What are you looking for?"

"A pen and paper."

"Why?"

"I want to write a thank-you note to our hosts for a such a wonderful drug induced time."

He laughs.

"Seriously though, this place is enormous," she explains. "I want to map it out. I'm good with directions, but you…?" Danae looks over her shoulder to Itra's attempt to scowl, but he then nods and shrugs with a grin.

A paper flies under the door in a flutter, followed by two pens.

"Your wish is my command!" Itra snorts.

"Funny!" she exclaims. "Magic food, clothes, and paper, check!" She quickly draws the floor plan of the entrance, the curve of the path through the conservatory to the rear foyer. She sketches the hedge maze, the corridors, and terrace level.

Itra checks the corridor. "All clear," he says and bolts towards the landing.

Danae pulls on his elbow, slowing his pace. She feels his anxious energy escalating as they descend the first flight of stairs. She checks the window for any changes. The hedge maze and opposite tower look the same, but she carefully scans the perimeter of the maze—no doors or entries to note. She rushes to catch up with Itra.

"Wait a second," Danae says, pointing at the floor. "We're at the first entrance with the blue and gold waves." She stumbles back and sits hard on the bottom step. Itra looks down and then up. She follows his gaze.

The large wood and iron doors that were open yesterday are now closed with a massive iron beam across the center, barring exit or entry of any kind.

"Are we locked in?" she asks.

Itra gulps. "There has to be more than one door, right?"

They cautiously head towards the conservatory. The mid-morning light reflects off a shiny surface, drawing Danae's attention to a wall of climbing vines. She nudges Itra in the side; he follows her line of sight. He moves vines aside and finds an arched door, but halts before reaching for the handle.

A melody ripples the silence behind them. A delicate female tone sings, "Illyria, ember in time, light…"

Itra panics. Pushing the door handle down, he grabs Danae's hand and bolts through. The melody mutes when the door clicks shut behind them.

They find themselves in a large hall. They creep forward cautiously. Danae's gaze follows the pale gold walls to the high ceiling, vaulted around a stunning dome with three stained glass inserts set at odd angles. She trips over her own feet and steadies her weight on a high-back chair, one of twenty at a long dark wood and iron table.

Itra studies the mosaic tiles covering the floor. The grand design is a giant mural of the castle and the grounds overlooking a raw natural valley. He walks across it, admiring the delicately placed tiles.

He squats to examine a section of the mural.

"Itra?" Danae calls.

When he doesn't respond, she comes to inspect what's capturing his attention. The tiles show the castle, but the top-level is off center, no longer square but a hexagon.

"What do you make of the castle?" he asks.

"I may have a theory," she says, waiting for his eye contact before she continues. "Our view before breakfast was on the opposite side than yesterday afternoon." Itra nods. "And we came down the stairs this morning and found ourselves in the wrong place." She pauses, then continues. "I think the castle, or parts of the castle, rotates with the sun. It moves to harness the natural light. Have you noticed there are no light fixtures anywhere?"

He looks up at the dome, then down at the tiles. "Bravo! You may be right." He frowns, walking outward from the center of the mural. "Do you see a trail down to the valley?"

The mural shows the castle sitting high on a ridge with severe drops on the east, west and south sides. They walk the entire perimeter of the mural.

"Interesting," Danae says. "We can head north once we find an exit."

"Have you marked the doors of this room on your map?" he asks, turning his attention to the three doors on the far side of the room.

Danae scans the hall, noting six doors: a single door on the adjacent walls to the door they came through, and the three evenly spaced doors opposite the conservatory door. "Marked," she confirms after pocketing the pen and folding the map.

Itra tries the far-right of three doors. It's locked. He peers through a keyhole. "I think I can make out a set of stairs going down," he says, "but I can't see very far. There is a slight curve to the wall. I'll check the middle door—you try the one on the left."

Danae hears a faint echo of footsteps as she nears her door before trying the handle. She looks through the keyhole and jumps back. "Itra, a person or a shadow moved as I glanced through the hole," she whispers. She tries the door handle. "It's locked. What do you see?"

"Books," Itra whispers too quietly. Danae moves to his side. He stands allowing her a peek through the hole.

"A small library?" she asks.

The scrape of a key in a lock echoes in the room. Itra and Danae step away from the library door. He raises an arm protectively in front of her as the door swings open. Itra steps hesitantly towards the open door.

"Wait," Danae hisses. Itra pauses, unsnaps, and takes off the pack and throws it through the open door.

Thud

"It's not booby-trapped," he says. He steps closer and reaches for her hand. "Maybe there is an exit?" They barely clear the threshold when the door slams behind them with a loud clunk. Danae yelps.

A faint jingle of keys from outside the door makes them dive towards the keyhole to look through. Itra smashes his chin into Danae's forehead, causing a few muttered curses. He gently kisses her forehead and leans nose to nose with her.

"We're not alone," Itra whispers.

Danae stiffens.

5

"Iana, it's Franc. I live next door to your brother, Itra, and Danae."

"Hi Franc," Iana answers, moving away from the noise of the television to the kitchen.

"Have you heard from either Itra or Danae since Sunday?" Franc asks urgently.

"Is everything okay?" she asks, trying to get her husband Anton's attention. "I spoke to Itra on Saturday," she says calmly, but adjusts the phone, urgently waving at Anton again to get his attention. He catches her waving and mutes the television before joining her in the kitchen. "They were planning a day hike for Sunday."

Iana places the call on speaker mode.

"My wife, Mira, and I have not seen either of them since Sunday morning. Mira was out hanging laundry when they left with a small pack. Danae waved and called out that they'd be back by dusk. She jokingly said if not, release the hounds. I know they're grown and do not need us meddling in their affairs, but Mira will not stop pacing."

Anton steps out of the kitchen in search of his phone.

"We're glad you called," Iana says, pulling her ponytail looser. "We'll try to call them now. And if we can't reach them, we'll head up that way ourselves. Maybe they left a note inside or came back and left again while you two were out?"

"We haven't left home since Saturday morning. Maybe they popped in while we were out in the barn and left before we noticed? Please let me know either way; Mira will wring my neck otherwise."

"No problem, Franc. Thanks again for calling. I promise to let you know once we get a hold of Itra or Danae. Talk to you soon."

"Thanks, Iana."

Iana tries to press end call, but her hand is shaking so much she drops the phone on the kitchen counter. She leans forward to keep from collapsing on the floor.

"Iana, are you off the phone?" Anton says, walking back into the kitchen. "Itra and Danae's phones are going straight to voicemail, and it says their voicemails are full."

Iana sucks in a shaky breath. Anton wraps her in a hug and murmurs into her hair. "I'm sure they're fine, camping, fishing, or extending their hike."

Her eyes blur with tears. "Anton, it's Tuesday. Yesterday morning, just before dawn, I woke with a jolt of panic. I should've known something wasn't right and called Itra to check."

"I'm sure everything is fine, and we cannot assume the worst." He pats her back. "I'll clear my day, and we'll drive up there now. Can you arrange for your cousin Nada to pick up Elis from school?"

She nods. "Can you call Ermal?" she asks. "He works for the local police. Maybe they're out on the lake?"

"Yes, is there anyone else we can call? What about Danae's friends?"

"I'll check for any posts or updates from them or their friends after I call Nada; maybe she's talked to Danae."

Twenty minutes later, they're pulling out of the parking garage and heading north out of the city. Nada agreed to pick up Elis, assuring her that Danae and Itra are probably out enjoying the beautiful weather after their spring prep on the vineyard was complete.

Iana tries to remain calm, but Danae's last post induces her fear meter to near panic status. *"Following this man can sometimes lead to face planting in spider webs, caves, and wrong turns, but he's worth it."* It is time-stamped around seven on Sunday evening. An earlier post was a photo taken of the valley of Bajze from the direction of the Mokset hills. Itra's account is useless, no posts in months.

Anton hangs up the phone for the sixth time in ten minutes. "I postponed my appointments. Ermal is checking with the lake patrol for any vessels registered to Itra or Danae and checking other boats out on the water for any contact or visuals since Sunday. The town people know Itra, but how many know Danae?"

"Danae knows quite a few of the locals, and most will at least associate her with Itra. I'll find a recent photo of them to have on hand just in case we need to print it." Iana swipes through her most recent shots of Itra and Danae. Her lip quivers at Itra and Danae, smiling next to Elis at his sixth birthday party last month. Iana finds another group shot where she can crop the others out to show only Itra and Danae.

Iana scrolls through their mutual friends in her contacts and finds Danae's brother Leon, and his wife Kaly's numbers. Iana fires off a quick group text, *"Hi, quick question."*

Kaly responds quickly. *"Hi, Iana, what's up?"*

"Just curious. Have either of you talked to Danae or Itra recently?" Iana texts.

Kaly responds. *"Not since our family video chat on Friday night. I'll wake Leon."*

Iana's fingers hover over her phone before typing. *"Received a call this morning from Itra's neighbor, Franc. They haven't been home since Sunday morning after saying they would return by dusk. They mentioned hiking on Saturday when I spoke to them, but the neighbor spoke to Danae on Sunday morning. She said if they weren't back by dusk to send the hounds. The neighbor said they were only carrying one small pack."*

A response from Leon comes before Kaly's. *"Danae mentioned the hike in a group text on Saturday, but we've heard nothing minus *a post on Sunday evening. I left a few messages yesterday and never got a response.”*

Kaly responds, *“I’m calling Danae’s two best friends, stateside.”*

Fifteen minutes later, Iana’s phone rings, and she answers.

“Iana, this is Leon and Kaly on speaker. We’ve called and texted everyone we could think of, and the last known contact anyone had with Danae was a late text exchange with her friend Jenny on Saturday night. She confirmed they had plans to hike the Mokset hills on Sunday, but Danae said it would take no longer than six hours.”

Iana fidgets with the car window button, pressing it up and down.

Kaly asks, “Iana, are you there?”

“Yes, sorry, just taking it all in. We have the water patrol out looking for anyone that may have seen the two of them on Sunday or after. I’ll call you once we arrive and check the house for any evidence they’ve returned and left again.”

“I will cancel my morning class,” Kaly says. “Leon will look at flights just in case.”

“We’re about thirty minutes out from their homestead and vineyard. We will notify local authorities if we cannot find any evidence of their return from Sunday’s hike.”

“Keep us posted,” Leon says.

Iana relays the conversation to Anton, who nods and takes her hand. His worry deepens the creases of his brow with each mile. He silently prays for their safe return. *Iana has lost too much.*

When Anton jumps out to open the gate, Iana looks back towards the neighbors’ house. Mira is standing on the porch, holding her rosary, and nods. Iana raises a hand to acknowledge her.

Itra’s one-story house sits at the dead-end of a small gravel road lined with two-story homes. Iana checks Itra’s truck on the side of the small stone house. She checks the other side, and behind the house; both bikes are present. No laundry is hanging to dry and no lights are visible inside.

Anton knocks loudly. "Itra, are you home? Danae? Are you two awake?"

Iana sucks in her breath. He nods for her to try the door. It's locked.

Iana digs through her purse, finding a spare key.

A rotting smell wafts through the door as they open it.

"Oh, god!" Iana shouts, covering her nose. "What is that?"

"Stay here. Let me check the house first." Anton pulls his shirt up over his nose and mouth, checking the living room, bedrooms, and the bathroom. The rooms are all empty, everything is tidy. He enters the kitchen and steps back, almost gagging. A plate with a plastic bag of rotting meat sits near the sink. He tosses it in the bin and ties the plastic bag tight. He quickly washes and rinses the plate.

"Was it meat?" Iana asks, coming into the kitchen.

"It looked like a roast set out to thaw."

Iana shivers. "Danae mentioned a roast on Saturday. This confirms the neighbor's suspicion."

Anton dries his hands before embracing Iana.

"We need to call the police and file an official report," Iana says, her voice shaking. "They're hurt, lost, or worse."

Anton nods and picks up the bag and heads towards the front door to rid the home of the sour, rotting odor. He spots Franc walking up the drive.

Franc hollers, "Are they home?" Anton lowers and shakes his head. "I should've called Monday. I'm so sorry."

"It is not your fault. We found meat left out on the counter that Danae had planned to cook Sunday evening. We know for sure they've not returned and left again." Anton holds up the bag in his hand before lifting the lid of the trash and throwing it in. "Do you think Mira remembers what Danae and Itra were wearing on Sunday?"

"I'll ask her."

Iana joins them outside. "The camping gear is still inside, and I found their car keys in the bowl on the dresser. The house key from Itra's keyring is missing. Have you called the police?"

"Not yet," says Anton. "I asked Franc to get a description of what they were wearing from Mira."

Franc apologizes again and leaves to get the information from his wife.

Anton makes the call.

Two officers arrive about an hour later. Ermal, the older of the two, knows Itra from school, and the younger, Piter, is new to the area. Iana emails the pictures she found on the drive up to the department. Mira gives a statement regarding Itra and Danae's clothing description and the last known conversation on Sunday.

Ermal explains, "Additional officers are out knocking on doors near Mokset to confirm any last sightings of Itra or Danae. Do you know exactly where they were hiking to on Sunday?"

"Danae had a text conversation with her friend Jenny late on Saturday. Danae said it was a six-hour hike." Iana pauses. "They've visited the old Mokset Castle remains a few times." Ermal nods before he radios to the station to start the search from the house towards the castle. Iana shows him the last two posts from Danae on Sunday.

"How well does Itra know the area?" Piter asks. "And do either of them know first aid?"

"Danae is familiar with the basics of first aid," Iana says. "Itra has hiked the Mokset hills a few times with Danae. He also hiked them as a kid, collecting herbs." She sighs. "He's known for not taking the same track twice and has not always chosen the safest route."

"Good to know," Ermal says. "We're assembling a search team and should have a large group here within the next two hours. The lake patrol has stopped every vessel this morning; no one has reported seeing either of them recently. We've called in a K9 unit to assist with the search. Can you grab a few items from inside?"

"I'll check their laundry hamper," Anton says as Iana steps back, sitting on the front porch steps.

"Sorry, Iana," Ermal apologizes. "I know this is overwhelming."

Anton returns with the only items in the laundry hamper: two of Itra's work shirts, a cardigan, and a sundress. He extends them to Ermal.

"Thanks, Anton," Ermal says, bagging the items. "Iana, who should be a contact as Danae's next of kin?"

"Her brother Leon and his wife, Kaly. I forwarded their contact information, along with the photos you requested to the department."

"Great, I think we have what we need. Hopefully, we'll locate Itra and Danae in the next few hours. If anything changes or you hear from Itra or Danae, please call this number immediately." Ermal hands over a business card with a direct line to the officer on duty. "Are you staying here or at the inn in town?"

"Here," Iana says.

"Thanks, Ermal," says Anton.

Anton shakes hands with both officers before sitting down with Iana. As the patrol car leaves the drive, tears cascade down her cheeks. Anton pulls her onto his lap.

"They'll be home by dinner," he whispers.

6

"I mean, someone else is in the castle, not in here," Itra teases.

"We knew that last night!" Danae shoves his shoulder, releasing a long sigh. She jiggles the door handle. It doesn't budge. She pounds on the door.

"Hello!" Danae shouts. Her breath quickens and she pounds on the door harder.

Itra attempts to kick the door open, but it's not budging. "Babe, I know you're mad and scared, but can you look for another exit while I work on this door?"

She sniffles and nods.

Danae examines the dust-free dark wood shelves lining three out of four walls. She moves a few books, knocking on the casing about every other step. She meets Itra in the middle. He shakes his head. She deflates into his arms.

"We might find a few answers in here," he whispers into her hair. She leans back, looking up with her eyebrows raised in question. "Maybe a map or a key to open the door is in a book?"

She pulls out a book from the nearest shelf. "Most of these books look new," she whispers, "but odd, no lettering or other markings on the spine." She opens a book and flips through the pages. It's blank.

Itra pulls down a book from a higher shelf. He finds blueprint and schematic drawings. He gently turns page after page. "I think these are design plans written by an inventor or an engineer for several things, some complex and some simple."

She looks up from her second book, which is blank minus a single page towards the middle. "I found a map of the hedge maze." She turns the book towards him.

They continue to pull out book after book. One has a language that neither can translate and another in Albanian, about native minerals. There are several volumes of handwritten historical, academic, and medical journals.

Danae pulls out a first edition copy of Moby Dick. They audibly gasped at this revelation.

"When was Moby Dick published?" Itra asks.

She scans the title page. "Harper & Brothers, New York, 1851."

The space feels almost claustrophobic as they continue to pull out, read, or skim, and stack the books and journals near their feet.

"I found Ivan's name in a family tree," Danae says.

Itra nearly drops the book he's holding. He ambles around the stacks of books to read over her shoulder. She points out Ivan's name and traces it to Itra's grandfather, Gjeto, on his father's side.

Itra points to the lines before Ivan. "Mui. Ivan is Mui's great-grandson?"

"Did the folk tales give Mui a surname or just Mui the Almighty Giant?" Danae asks.

"I don't recall his last name. Mui was or is real? The stories weren't stories, but our family legacy? It's all real." Itra knocks over a few book stacks in his escalating excitement. "I am a descendant of Mui!"

She laughs at his pure joy and excitement, but then clears her throat to get his attention. "How do you know it is *the* 'Mui'?"

"Where did you find that volume? I'll look nearby. It has—"

Clang, clang

After the ringing stops and their hearts start, they say, simultaneously, "Lunch?"

Clunk

The door swings open. They bolt towards the opening. Itra grabs their pack, and they step back into the dining hall. They head for the conservatory door passing the long table with place settings for two.

"Two rings, two o'clock?" she asks. "We've lost at least five hours of daylight and have found no additional exits."

"Maybe," he says, glancing up at the dome. He opens the pack shoving the family tree book inside.

"Do you think it's wise to steal a book?" Danae asks.

Itra winks, listening at the conservatory door.

Danae gestures to the left when he opens the door. A chill runs down her spine despite the warm air. She shivers.

"Are you cold?" he asks.

"No, I keep feeling a wave of fear, anxiety, or paranoia," she whispers. They weave their way through the many plants to the front foyer.

They stand staring at the massive, locked door. The stairwell down is still dark and uninviting. Danae starts up the stairs, but changes direction. She marches through the conservatory to the rear foyer. Itra wordlessly follows. Still no door.

"Maybe we can order something stronger with lunch?" he says, winking.

"Are you even hungry after the giant breakfast?"

His one eyebrow raises, nearly merging with his hairline. "Do you need to ask?"

"Fine!" She shoves past him. "But after lunch, we need to find an exit!"

They return to the dining hall and assume the same rules apply from this morning. "Ladies first." Itra gestures towards her. They think a few seconds and uncover their plates at the same time. They immediately raise and drain their wine glasses. The food is divine, but it does not lighten Danae's mood. Itra orders an espresso for her and a red velvet cupcake. She sighs and grins at his peace offering.

Itra stands with a yawn and stretches before extending his hand to Danae. She links her fingers with his as they walk to check the other doors in the dining hall and the front entrance—they're still locked in.

Itra snaps the hiking pack in place. "Up or down?" He turns on a headlamp and aims it down towards the stairwell opposite the conservatory entry. "It's a spiral staircase, no ending in sight."

Danae tilts her chin up. "Not ready for dark and creepy."

They walk the terrace level towards a tower. They stop several times to look over the buildings and land below. Danae adds a few domes to her map and points out the domes over the conservatory, dining hall, and library. They can see at least four additional domes to the north.

"It drops off like the other three sides," Danae says, motioning to the north. She hangs her head in frustrating disappointment.

"It looks like the only way down may be under the castle," says Itra. Danae raises her head in question at his statement. He explains, "We've seen several staircases leading down and only one exit so far."

"Possibly?" she answers. They walk to the southwest corner, and Itra pulls her to a stop.

"Ha! Do you see that inlet to the south and west where the lake fingers in towards the valley? We're near or on the Mokset hills." He does a little jig.

"Castle of Teskom," Danae laughs at the absurd realization. "Teskom is Mokset backward."

He sweeps her into his arms, kissing her silly, and twirls her around before placing her feet back down. "Genius!"

They continue a little lighter in step after connecting the name.

"Up to the tower now, my fair genius, or later?" he teases.

"Up, my laird in training," she teases back with a slight curtsy.

The top landing offers three doors. The adjacent doors lead to a perimeter wall with openings for archers—slim buckets with arrows and bows hang near each opening. The door across from the stairs leads to a small spiral staircase.

Danae follows Itra up. It opens to a square, glass-domed room.

"Is this a lighthouse?" she asks, but inspecting the space, she sees nothing to light.

"Possibly. Do you think it lights with magic?"

She laughs until she sees his face. He's serious.

They can see an identical structure on an opposite tower. "Can you imagine trying to explain this to Iana, or worse, Leon?"

7

Leon hangs up with Iana before finding Kaly in her home office.

"It's filed," he says. "Itra and Danae are officially missing." Kaly hugs him. "I booked a flight for tomorrow that will put me there by Thursday morning, pending no delays."

"How's Iana holding up?" Kaly asks.

"She sounds like she's trying to remain calm," Leon says. "But Anton texted after the cops left. She was in pieces." He pauses. "Anton's picking up Elis soon. Maybe he will be a good distraction for Iana."

"Maybe, but Elis is so much like a mini Itra."

Leon laughs. "True."

"I've spoken with the dean's secretary," Kaly says. "We have a meeting in an hour to discuss my leave options. It may be hard for me to leave this close to finals, but I'm almost done writing the last two lecture exams. Hopefully, I can join you no later than Saturday."

"They had better be home by tonight," Leon growls. "I'm not ready for a long international flight in economy."

Kaly finds Leon packing after her call. "According to the emergency leave exception policy," she says. "The dean's meeting went as expected—Danae and Itra are not considered my next of kin." Leon nods. "Therefore, my paid leave is not approved. However, I can fulfill my teaching assignments with my graduate assistants. In that case, I can go but must respond to all forwarded calls and emails during my scheduled office hours. I may be up late a few nights next week if we are still there."

Kaly refolds the contents of Leon's bag.

"Anton called, no additional news," Leon says. "Why do you always refold my clothes?"

She stops mid fold. "Always?"

"Before every deployment, you would unpack and repack my gear."

"Oh dear, I'm my mother," she says, placing a hand over her heart. "She would repack my dad's things before he left for every dig. I remember he got very irritated once and asked her the same question." Kaly's eyes glisten.

"And?" Leon asks.

"Have you ever noticed how I fold your clothes?"

"No, why?"

"My mother wears the same scent my father gifted her on their second date. She has always dabbed a spot under her chin." Kaly picks up a shirt and folds it in half. Leon watches her place one end under her chin to meet the seams and fold it up towards her. "She repacked his clothes for every trip, so every item smelled just a little like home."

He leans over and kisses her nose. "You never say much about your dad. Thank you for sharing." She smiles.

"I see those group therapy sessions are influencing my wild husband," she says. He smirks.

"You want wild? Wait until I get my hands on Itra!"

8

"Today is Tuesday," Itra mumbles. "We have been gone for almost two days." He stares out at the lake below from the glass tower.

Danae whirls, startling Itra. Her eyes bulge and her mouth drops open.

"What is it?" he asks, looking at her shocked face.

"Itra, I left the roast on the counter!" Danae shouts. "Ugh! Can you imagine the smell of our kitchen? And the bugs? We are finding another exit."

Itra cringes at the thought and nods. He adjusts the pack and finds something hard in the hidden pocket. He nearly rips the bag, pulling out their phones and the screens light up. "Danae!"

She takes her phone and holds her breath as she swipes through the home screen to check messages. "Do you have a signal?"

"No signal, no messages, no Wi-Fi, not even a roaming signal." He takes his case off to check that it's his phone. He shakes his head. "Now what?"

"We still need to leave; maybe we can get a signal outside the castle."

Itra shifts the bag's contents to allow more room for the stolen book, but the book flies out, opens and snaps shut. Itra blinks his eyes rapidly. His face is sheet white. Or is that powder? Danae reaches up to touch his face. Her fingers come away covered in white powder.

"Is this sleeping dust?"

"I don't know." He reaches up to wipe his brow.

She guides him down the stairs from the tower and they descend two floors to the blue and gold bedroom.

"Do you feel any different?"

"Not yet," he says, washing his face. He tilts his head from side to side and lowers his chin to check for any remaining white spots. "Danae, my eyes are normally brown, like dirt, brown?"

She steps closer, looking at his reflection. His left eye is green. He turns to look at her directly, but his eyes are brown. She turns his cheek back towards the mirror, and the left one is green again.

"What is it?" he says, reading her alarm.

"In the mirror, your left eye is green, but when you look at me, they're both brown."

"How is this possible?" he whispers, staring at his reflection. He steps back away from the mirror and freezes. "I hear humming. Do you?"

"The sound is close, too close," Danae whispers.

Knock, knock, knock

Itra jumps and whirls towards the door. Danae seems to be frozen in place.

"Who is it?" Danae squeaks.

Itra looks around wildly for something to defend them, opting for the plunger.

A high-pitched sing-song voice answers, "A mark maker."

"A mark maker?" Danae asks.

"Yes."

Danae looks to Itra, shaking her head.

He blurts out, "What the hell is a mark maker, and are you here to harm us?"

A giggle echoes further away from the door before it answers. "No harm, no harm, Ivan would be ever so displeased. Please come out. I'll explain a mark maker and more."

They stare at each other for an eternity before Itra straightens. Danae blinks. He reaches one hand for the door handle and raises his other hand with the plunger. He pulls the door open fast, and they brace their posture in a defensive stance.

The figure in the wingback chair is small, almost childlike. She's wearing a gold cotton dress with blue pinstripes. Dark raven hair cascades past her shoulders, and her wide, green eyes stare up with curiosity and amusement. Her face is bright with a smile. She giggles.

Itra is still holding up the plunger. Danae can see this out of the corner of her eye. She feels a smile tug at her lips. She taps Itra to lower his weapon. He does, but neither of them speak, unsure how to navigate the next move.

The figure stands with a bounce, and they take a step back. She is barely half as tall as Itra. "My name is Teuta. I am Ember's mark maker and messenger. Ivan welcomes you, Itra, son of Nik, an ancestor of Ivan and the Almighty Mui."

Itra is grinning so widely that Danae thinks his cheeks may burst.

"A mark maker teaches a new mark about their gift. Ember marks you, Itra, with the gift to identify. Specifically, the ability to identify any species, plant, or animal."

Itra nods.

"First, who is Ember?" Danae asks. "Second, where and when are we, exactly?"

"Ember is the creator of the Castle of Teskom in Albania. When might be a little harder to explain? Please join me for tea." She turns and walks through an open door next to the wardrobe that wasn't there before.

"Do either of you take milk or cream with tea?" Teuta calls, pulling them forward.

They cross the threshold into a large room with two fireplaces anchoring the long space. Light fills the room through the large bay windows on either side of French glass and iron doors. The mosaic tile floor offers a design that seems to blossom from the center of the room in a petal pattern under another small dome.

Teuta gestures to a modern blue couch and repeats her question. "Milk or cream?"

Danae responds, "Milk, thank you." She nudges Itra to follow her to the couch. They sit. Her hand strokes the smooth, almost-suede-like upholstery.

"Sugar?" Teuta asks as she pours the steaming tea into three cups, topping theirs with a splash of milk. The aroma is a mixture of sage and lavender.

"Is the tea laced with another drug?" Danae asks.

Teuta laughs. "Drug?"

"You delivered a card with a side of dust yesterday afternoon," Itra says.

She nods.

"Why did you drug us?" Danae asks.

"By Ember's request, your health is important. The level of exhaustion and stress showed you needed rest. Did you feel unwell this morning?"

"What is Ember?" Itra asks, avoiding her question.

"The creator of the Castle—"

"No!" Itra shouts. "What is Ember: human, fairy, alien, or what?"

"Goddess."

Itra leans back in surprise. Danae leans forward and asks, "A goddess of what?"

"Knowledge." Teuta holds up a spoon. "Sugar?"

They answer, "No, thank you."

"Why did you or Ember lock us in the library?" Itra asks.

"You were seeking answers. Ember opened the door."

"We were actually seeking an exit," Danae says to counter her point.

"You were." Teuta tilts her chin towards Danae and shifts her gaze to Itra. "However, Itra was seeking answers to his lineage." He shrugs. Teuta offers a blue cup and gold saucer to each of them and sits back with her cup, sipping softly. The chair seems to shrink to her frame because her feet touch the floor despite her tiny stature.

"We're sitting in your suite," Teuta explains.

"Have we been here before?" Danae asks.

"No."

"Why is there a photo of Itra and I hanging on the wall in the next room?"

"The family crested glass door leads to a large balcony with additional seating. The books left stacked in the library are on the shelves directly behind me. You're welcome to any additional books from the library. Ivan and Ember welcome your exploration of knowledge." Teuta smiles, setting her teacup on an ivory table.

"Why are you ignoring my question?" Danae sits on the edge of the couch.

"The entire south wing is for Mui's descendants, including all Itras."

"What do you mean all Itras?" Itra scoots to the edge of the couch.

"There are three," Teuta says.

Itra and Danae are speechless for a solid minute. Teuta smiles and waits.

"Teuta, what year is it?" Danae asks.

She tilts her head. "The year is 2020."

"But the land is all wrong!" Itra growls, his tone deep and ominous. "How can we be in the same year?"

Teuta stands with a twirl. "The land you see from the castle reflects the land as it was when Ember started the castle's foundation."

"How?" Itra asks.

Clang, clang, clang, clang, clang, clang

"Dinner, it's dinner time. You must hurry. No need for details now." Teuta twirls around the couch, ushering them with some invisible force up and towards the door.

"Wait, we need answers now!" Danae begs, attempting to stop. "We need to return home. Please, just explain how we get home from here!"

Teuta sings, "Dinner, it's dinner time. Don't be late." She scoots them out a door into a corridor.

Itra turns to argue but meets a solid stone wall. "Danae, the door! Didn't we just walk through a door?"

"Yes!" Danae cries out, nearly in tears. "Teuta, come out!"

"Where are the other doors?" Itra spins around. "Are we in a different hallway?" The stone corridor is dim, only illuminated by a light from a landing ahead.

"Doors, no doors?" she whispers, shaking with a small shiver of unease.

Itra takes her hand with a reassuring squeeze.

They reach the landing and hesitate.

"Up or down?" Itra asks.

Danae, speechless, walks up the stairs and turns on instinct to look for a table. Itra follows at her heels. A small table for two glows in the evening light.

Itra runs back downstairs. "The doors are back!" He jogs back up with a bewildered expression. "It's like the place hit pause and reset."

"Do you think it's time to go now?" she asks.

"Yes, but how?" he asks with a shudder.

"Itra, we need to figure it out. We can't stay here forever. Iana is probably at the house and has called in a search party—and if Leon knows, he is likely on a flight over." She paces as this statement sinks in for Itra.

"Iana will roast my ass for disappearing like this!"

"Yep! And likely mine, too. Can you imagine the damage Leon will try to inflict on you?" She winks.

Itra visibly shivers. "No, thank you. Leon is scary when he's nice, not sure I can handle his wrath. But Kaly—"

"Kaly will have a team of scholars here to research and dissect the entire place before we blink." Danae leans into Itra. "I'll be in heaps of trouble if Leon flies over. You know how much he loathes confined spaces."

"How do we let the family know we're alive and not dead at the bottom of the lake?" Itra asks.

9

A uniformed officer is standing under a tent assembled at the end of Itra's driveway. He points to the hills and back to the map, instructing a group of local search volunteers. The sound of Anton's car catches the officer's attention. Anton rolls the window down to wave in acknowledgment before driving to the house. Iana is pacing the front porch when Anton arrives with their son Elis.

Elis bounds from the car. "Mom, did you see the cop? Where's Itra and Danae? What's for dinner? I'm starving!" Iana pulls Elis in for a tight hug. "Mom! You're shaking. Are you cold?"

Iana releases her son and makes eye contact with Anton. She shakes her head in response to his unspoken question of any news. She takes Elis by the hand and walks him into the house.

Volunteers have brought trays of sandwiches, chips, casseroles, soups, and more. Elis lets out a low whistle, almost identical to Itra's. Iana's heart squeezes.

"I'll make you a plate. Go wash your hands." Iana watches Elis skip out of the room as Anton enters with their overnight bags. "I've arranged the small trundle bed for Elis in the guest room with us."

Anton drops the bags in the guest room before returning to the kitchen. Elis is pointing out everything he wants; the plate wobbles in Iana's shaking hands.

"How about I take over?" says Anton. "I'm starving too." He winks at Iana. He fills their plates, setting Elis up at the table.

"No news?" Anton asks as he hugs Iana tightly.

"The first K9 unit picked up tracks near the old castle, but it ends just before a large clearing. A local spelunking group went up a few hours ago to inspect some caves. It's nearly dark, and it's been 48 hours. I overheard a volunteer mention that it will change from search and rescue to search and recover after 72 hours. Are they dead?" Iana chokes back a sob, fearing Elis will hear her.

"Itra is resourceful, and Danae is a fighter. They're fine. We'll find them."

Iana pulls back, Anton wipes her tears. "Leon has booked the first available flight that leaves tomorrow afternoon. Do you think your old roommate, David, can make an airport run?"

"No problem. I'll call him now." Anton reaches for his phone. Iana holds his arm.

"Eat first," Iana says with almost a smile. "Elis will want seconds starting with your plate soon if you don't sit and eat."

"Ha! Elis, are you eating my food?" A loud crunch of a chip answers his call. Anton kisses Iana on the forehead before joining Elis at the table. "Hey, where did my chips go?"

A small giggle floats into the kitchen as Iana turns to the sink to fill the kettle. Her mind replays swatting Itra's hand away from her plate when they were kids.

She shakes her head. "I will swat more than your hand if you make it home!" she mutters.

Anton and Elis are busy finishing their second plates when the kettle whistles. "Elis, do you want hot chocolate? Anton, tea, or coffee?"

They respond in unison, "Hot chocolate!"

Anton carries the plates into the kitchen. "With marshmallows?" he asks, waggling his eyebrows and grinning.

Iana snaps him with a dishtowel.

"You know we don't have marshmallows here," Iana says. "Or do we?"

Iana checks Danae's baking cupboard—Danae keeps it stocked with an assortment of baking ingredients.

"Jackpot! Danae has made your wish come true." She holds the sealed bag out of arm's reach of Anton. They grin because their weakness for marshmallows is a joint guilty pleasure. "Five in each cup only. Danae's bag, not ours."

"Fine." He opens the cabinet, pulling out every cup on the bottom shelf. "Five in every cup, my lady."

"Seriously! It's your funeral when Danae can't find the marshmallows next time she bakes." Iana goes pale after comprehending her word choice a few seconds too late.

Elis comes flying into the room. "A man and a dog are coming down the drive! Can I pet the dog, please?"

Iana tosses the bag of marshmallows on the counter before rushing towards the front door. Elis, determined to meet the dog, follows her out the door with Anton close on his heels.

"Any news?" Iana calls as she steps off the front porch. "Did you find them?"

"We haven't found them, but we picked up another track along the west ridge near another clearing. We found traces of these metallic-like shards near the spot where the track goes cold." He holds a small evidence bag out to Anton and Iana. "Have either of you seen anything like this? Does Danae own jewelry with this material?"

Iana takes the bag back to the porch for better light. The contents are almost shiny under the light. "Why is it warm?" She hands the bag to Anton to inspect.

The officer and Anton look at her, confused.

"What do you mean it's warm?" the officer asks.

"Mom, can I please pet the dog?" Elis is pulling on her arm, rocking from side to side. Iana looks to the officer for permission.

The officer calls the dog to sit and shake.

Elis is bouncing up and down. "He's shaking my hand, mom! Look, dad!"

"This here is Daisy."

Anton hands the bag back to the officer. "I don't recognize the material."

"Danae wears a simple silver cross and her wedding ring," Iana says.

"You said it's warm?" the officer asks Iana.

"Yes, the bag felt warm," Iana says.

"And you?" The officer directs his attention to Anton.

"Not warm," Anton says, watching Elis pet the underbelly of Daisy, who is now supine on the ground with her paws in the air.

Iana, distracted by Elis and Daisy, misses the confused look on the officer's face. "Can you hold the bag once more?"

She turns her attention to the officer and takes the bag. The color of the shards changes into an orange glow. She looks from the officer to Anton. "It's getting hot. Do you see it brightening to orange?"

The officer and Anton lean in closer. Iana is now shifting the bag from one hand to another. "It's starting to burn!"

The officer takes the bag and palms it from side to side. "It doesn't feel warm at all?"

Anton takes the bag. "Nothing, no heat at all."

She holds her hands up, surrendering. A bright red raised lump is visible on her right palm.

The officer and Anton stare, speechless.

Anton hands the bag back to the officer, reaching for Iana's hands to inspect the damage. "There is aloe in the garden, right?" Anton asks. Iana nods. Anton calls for Elis to follow.

"I will get this over to the lab right away. Sorry about your hand, Iana. I wish I had more news to share."

"No problem. I know the volunteers and your department are trying to find Itra and Danae. Will you please let me know what the lab finds out about the shards?"

He nods. "Officer Luigi will be here on duty overnight."

"Thank you and please tell the volunteers we have plenty of food. They should come and eat as they return."

"Yes, ma'am," the officer responds. Daisy barks in response to the hand signal he makes as he turns to leave.

Anton and Elis return with an aloe leaf.

Elis calls, "Bye, Daisy."

"Elis, let's take mom inside for some hot chocolate." Anton points Elis towards the front door.

"It was hot." Iana shakes her head, examining her palm before holding it up for Anton. "You saw the red welt, right?"

Anton steps closer, running his fingers over her smooth, pale palm. "Come inside."

Elis is in the kitchen, popping a handful of marshmallows in his mouth when Iana and Anton enter. His full mouth mutes his guilty giggle.

"What do you think you're doing, mister?" Anton chases him out of the kitchen.

The evening light fades to darkness. Iana switches on the overhead light before igniting the flame to reheat the kettle. The dancing flame makes her palms tingle.

"Rocks!" Iana exclaims.

"Paper, scissors?" Anton calls as he walks back into the kitchen.

"No!" Her face is bright, almost manic. "My grandfather told us stories about shiny rocks when we were kids."

"And?"

"Shiny ember rocks are fuel for time; the dull rocks are a fool's dime."

10

"Is Teuta human or something else?" Itra asks, his brow creasing as they walk towards the dinner table after attempting a rash exit by way of the front door—still locked.

"You're the one with the mark to identify any species, plant, or animal," Danae mocks.

"Not sure that includes human-like beings that may be of alien or fairy origin."

She leans into him, and they embrace, taking a moment just to breathe. As he releases her, she pinches his arm.

"Ouch! What was that for?"

She pinches herself. "Nope, not a dream or a nightmare. Just checking." She sidesteps his advance, backing into the table.

Clink—the sound echoes for a beat.

She looks down at the table and finds 'Itra' written in bold cursive handwriting across another envelope. She picks it up and turns it over carefully. The wax seal has the same family crest as the door to the balcony in their suite. She hands the envelope to Itra.

Itra holds it as far away as possible before breaking the seal. He opens it—no powder. He reads aloud, "Dinner for two or only you? Home in speed or time to explore and read?"

"Cryptic poems, so cliché," Danae barks.

He says, "Two and time?"

The plate covers lift automatically—the chairs pull out from either side of the table. Itra and Danae hop back.

Danae raises jazz hands and slowly sings, "Be—our—guest." She stops before she gets to the next line when she feels her skin tingle.

"You—another quick-change—pretty," Itra says, pointing at Danae.

She looks down to find an elegant, flared, knee-length royal blue dress with short sleeves and a pair of gold strappy sandals. She looks up. Itra is in a full blue suit, gold shirt, and tie.

"Nice suit, my dear."

He straightens and spins around for her to check out all sides. She gives him two thumbs up, then he twirls his finger for her to return the move. She slowly spins, the dress swinging out with the movement; the lining of the dress is silky and light. The smile on his face has her grinning back.

The smell of fresh bread and a loud rumble from Itra's stomach breaks their trance.

Itra holds out a chair like a gentleman before rounding the table.

"This is weird, right?" she asks.

"Weird, deranged, twisted, delicious, and more." Itra tries to say over a full mouth.

"Chew with your mouth closed!"

He swallows. "Then no questions during chow time." He cleans his plate before she can even eat half of her salad.

"Seconds?" she asks.

"Only a coffee, you?"

"Yes, to coffee, no to seconds." Two steaming lattes instantly appear on the table. She shakes her head and finishes her plate in silence.

Footsteps echo from the stairwell.

"Teuta?" Danae asks. "Is that you?"

Itra rises, blocking Danae's line of sight.

Danae stands to see over his shoulder, but the tall figure shadowed in the doorframe cannot be the petite Teuta.

"Itra, my name is Ivan." The figure steps forward from the shadows. He is tall and lean, with pressed slacks and a tailored jacket, emphasizing his long torso. His face's contours are soft with a thick white mustache and soft white hair combed to the right. His smile is so much like Itra's father, Nik, that Danae nearly runs towards the man. She can't see Itra's face, but she feels his reaction. He stiffens before relaxing. He can see the similarities too.

Itra struggles to speak, clearing his throat. "Nice to meet you, Ivan."

"Nice to meet you too, Itra and Danae. Now, with the formal introductions out of the way, please join me for an evening stroll. We're running out of light." Ivan motions to the setting sun over the Montenegro mountains. "I know you two have many questions, but I want to share my journey to the Castle of Teskom as we walk."

Itra grasps Danae's hand with a quick squeeze, checking her face for approval. She smiles and nods. They walk towards Ivan. They ascend to the tower's square glass box. The light fills the space, making them squint and shield their eyes from the setting sun.

Ivan turns in a circle. "This, the castle, the grounds, the land beyond, is ours. We are the protectors of the Castle of Teskom and of the goddess Ember," he says, gesturing to Itra and back to himself. "The castle dates back thousands of years before the Greeks, Romans, or Ottomans tried, but ultimately failed, to conquer this land and our people." Ivan pauses, turning back to Itra. "I was born in Kastrat, Albania, in the year 1420. The area of Bajze that you call home is Ivanaj, correct?"

Itra nods. "Yes, sir."

"I was 58 years old when I first discovered the Castle of Teskom. I was looking for a stray lamb, but dusk fell quickly to darkness. The thick cloud cover made it one of the darkest nights in my memory. I rested near a hitching post. At the crest of dawn, the horizon appeared as it did for you, familiar but different. The large landmarks like the lake and the mountains were all there, but the small homes and pastures were not visible in the thick forest."

Ivan motions from the glass walls to the ceiling.

"This room is a reflector. You can think of it as a giant mirror. It mirrors time, reflecting the original landscape from the castle and the grounds. It creates a shield."

Before Itra or Danae can ask any questions, Ivan moves down the spiral staircase. He motions them to follow him further down three more flights of stairs. They follow obediently, stopping at the

52

landing with the red and silver flames near the conservatory's rear entrance. Light is fading quickly. The area dances with shadows from the various plants.

Ivan pulls a small square stone from his jacket pocket. He holds it up with his thumb and ring finger. He taps the middle with his index finger. A small light instantly hovers over Ivan's head.

Itra and Danae step back, blinking.

Ivan chuckles before deepening his voice with a loud, "Let there be light!"

"What? How?" Danae asks.

"Cool," Itra whispers.

"Oh, the details can wait. Come along. It's still story time." Ivan bounds down the steps to their left. The stairs are stone but smooth, with the same stone walls as the upper levels. They curve, never giving way to a landing. Ivan leads Itra and Danae down, possibly five or more stories under the castle. The steps end at a large door.

Ivan clears his throat on the last step. "Ready?"

Light is coming from under the threshold of the wood and iron door. It seems to move side to side. Danae squeezes her fingers around Itra's arm, above his elbow. He flexes his bicep in silent acknowledgment.

"Ready," Itra states.

"Open says me!" Ivan sings. The doors glide inward.

Danae elbows Itra's side, whispering, "Open sesame!" He laughs, but his laugh cuts short.

Teuta appears inside. She is twirling side to side with her arms wide open. A light, like Ivan's, hovers above her tiny frame.

"Welcome to the present," Teuta sings.

The wall to the left is not a wall but a large cave opening, the moon reflecting on the lake below. Itra and Danae gravitate towards the opening, shuffling past Teuta.

Danae cranes her neck to look over the edge. It's a sheer drop to the lake below. Above, the balconies seem to hover in the clouds. The effect is dizzying. She steps back to balance herself and turns.

"Iana!" Danae calls.

Itra spins so fast he falls back, but an invisible barrier bounces him forward.

They move away from the edge, confused.

Itra's focusing on the live video feed projected on the inside of the cavern. The clip shows Iana at the sink. It is as if they are looking at her through the kitchen window.

"Iana!" Itra calls. "How can we see inside our home?"

"The cavern allows time to reflect with the present," Ivan replies.

"Can she see or hear us?" Danae waves to Iana.

"No, but she might sense your presence," Teuta chimes.

"Iana, if you can hear or feel me look up," Itra commands.

Iana stops the running water, looking directly at them. She leans closer to the window.

"Iana, we're safe. Please don't worry," Danae says almost too quietly for Itra to hear, but he wraps his arm around her, pulling her closer.

Iana folds her arms, rubbing above her elbows. Her brow creases. "I hear you, but how and where are you?"

Teuta and Ivan gasp in surprise.

"We're safe!" Itra says. "The how and where are too hard to explain. Please don't be worried. And please call Leon or Kaly—Danae is safe and unharmed."

Anton enters the kitchen. He speaks to Iana, but they can't hear his voice. Iana talks back to him, but they lose the sound. They can only watch as she gestures to the window. Anton's look of confusion only heightens Iana's explanation, her hands flying as she attempts to make him understand.

Iana leans back towards the window, mouthing words.

"It's like someone has hit the mute button," Danae says.

"Ivan, can you turn the sound back on?" Itra asks, sighing in frustration at the silence between him and Iana.

Ivan is quiet. Danae moves into Ivan and Teuta's line of sight. Teuta blinks slowly, and Ivan is slower to react. They both close their mouths, swallowing hard.

"What is going on?" Danae asks. She can see Iana waving in the window. Elis is in his pajamas watching Anton and Iana. Anton looks like he is pleading for Iana to sit down and talk.

"Iana," Itra says. "We're here. We're safe, calm down. You're scaring Elis."

"It's never talked back before," Ivan says, shaking his head.

"Ivan is right!" Teuta says. "In the last nine centuries, it has only been a window to time, never a calling card."

"Is it because she is blood, my sister, your descendant?" Itra asks Ivan.

"Only those who have touched ember have been able to sense if someone is watching," Ivan says. "But they've never been able to communicate."

"Shiny ember rocks are fuel for time; the dull rocks are a fool's dime," Itra chants.

11

"Babe? Who are you talking to?" Anton asks, walking into the kitchen. Iana turns to him with wild eyes.

"Itra and Danae, they're safe. They were right there; did you hear them?" Iana speaks so forcefully, a little spit lands on Anton's shirt.

Anton moves closer to look out the window. "I don't see them, and no, I didn't hear anyone. Did they call?"

Iana moves back to the window. "Itra? Danae? Can you hear me? Are you still there?"

"Please come, sit and talk."

"Mom? Dad?"

Iana and Anton jump.

"Hey, little man, what are you doing out of bed?" Anton turns, bending down to squeeze his cheek.

"Dad, stop." Elis moves to push Anton's hand away. "I heard Itra and Danae say mom's name. Are they home?"

Anton straightens so fast he almost loses his balance.

Iana and Anton lock eyes, the color drains from their faces.

"Elis, dear, you heard me talk to Itra and Danae a few minutes ago?"

"Yep. Itra told you to call Danae's brother Leon," Elis says. "So, where is Itra?"

"Um, he...?" Iana looks to Anton.

"He called. They were on the phone, but not here."

"Cool." Elis nods. "Can I call Leon?"

"No, mister, it is past your bedtime. Come on, and I'll tuck you in again!" Anton ushers Elis out of the kitchen.

"Good night, darling."

"Night, mama."

Iana walks back to the window seeking Itra or Danae, finding only her reflection.

"Iana?" Anton steps up behind her. "I believe you."

Iana folds into Anton, saying into his chest, "They're safe."

He pulls her in closer.

12

Itra anxiously paces the cavern. Danae's chest is pounding. Iana's face through the window looks scared and sad. Ivan and Teuta argue in hushed tones behind them.

The entire scene goes dark.

"What is happening?" Danae asks. "Why is it dark? Are they okay?"

Danae's panicked call stops Itra mid-stride. He turns to see that Iana's image has faded to darkness.

"Ivan, start talking," Itra commands. "We need an explanation! We have too many questions for vague answers. What is this room? This castle? This bubble?"

Ivan folds his hands in a prayer-like motion. "Teuta, will you please take Itra and Danae to my study? I need to retrieve a few items from the archives. Then I will answer your questions and explain everything."

Itra growls in response.

"Yes," says Teuta, "please follow me." The light hovering above her head glows brighter as they enter the darkened stairwell.

They ascend countless steps. Danae and Itra stop in the rear foyer to catch their breath. They examine the foyer with the red and silver flames.

Teuta turns to see why they paused.

"What is this a design of?" Danae asks. "Why the flames?"

Itra points to a small archway and then to another. The silver flecks behind the red flames outline the five archways, but only from specific angles.

"The flames represent the ember of time. Ivan will explain what he knows about the archways and more." Teuta glides away from them. She pauses halfway to inspect their progress before opening the door to the large dining hall.

Itra and Danae turn, expecting to find Ivan behind them but see no one.

Danae's thoughts wander. *Did he take the stairs behind us? No, it was silent, minus the footsteps of Teuta, Itra, and me. Where did he go? Was there another door or exit in the cavern? Just another few questions to add to the growing list.*

Teuta leads them to one of the three doors on the far side.

The door opens to a stone corridor with a small iron spiral staircase leading up to the right.

Danae glances up the stairs, but the space is dark.

Teuta sashays down the corridor a few paces before pushing on a panel.

The wall slides open, revealing an entry.

"A hidden pocket door?" Itra mumbles.

A large version of the floating light hovers in the room above a seating arrangement with two gold chairs, a small blue sofa, and two marble side tables. A desk and chair sit off in the corner. The walls are a deep blue with shelves of various widths built into the wall at random heights.

"Tea or coffee?" sings Teuta, breaking the silence.

"Coffee with milk," Itra replies.

"Tea with milk for me, please," Danae answers.

The cups are rattling on saucers a moment later.

"Please sit. Ivan will be here in a few minutes."

Itra and Danae sit down on the blue sofa. Teuta hands over their saucers with a gentle, efficient swoop.

The tea's aroma calms Danae's nerves.

Itra takes a small sip and sighs under his breath.

"I'm here," Ivan announces. He enters the room, striding with glee. "Oh fantastic, she remembered to get refreshments." Fresh fruits, finger sandwiches, baklava, and a few chocolates appear on the table.

Itra stands in alarm, nearly spilling his coffee and Danae's tea.

"I didn't blink, and the food—it appeared, how?" Itra exclaims.

Ivan chuckles.

Itra sits with less force.

Ivan sits and sips his tea, holding up his finger, gesturing for one moment. "Sorry for the surprise. I thought food delivery would be second nature to you two by now. No bother, I'll explain the connections and delivery. The wardrobe and catering are thoughts. If you imagine an item, it will appear."

A large bowl of ice cream smothered in caramel replaces the refreshments. Danae chokes on her tea in recognition of her thoughts of ice cream. She blinks once, and the smell of smoked turkey fills the space as a turkey leg sits on a platter in front of Itra. She blinks again, and the original refreshments are back. The smell of the turkey still lingers in the air.

"I thought of the ice cream," Danae whispers. "Itra, did you think of the turkey leg?"

"Yes, but how?" Itra shakes his head in disbelief.

"Ember," Ivan says, simply. "I believe Teuta covered that the year is still 2020. The ember archway you and Danae crossed under is in your current time and universe." Ivan pauses casually, taking another sip.

Itra's leg is bouncing so quickly it's shaking the entire couch.

Danae feels his anxiety and finds her voice. "When you say, 'your current time and universe,' what do you mean, exactly?"

"The ember archways act as a pulse in time, fueled by the ember at the base. The five archways are portals to three parallel present universes, one past portal, and one future portal."

"Parallel?" Itra asks.

"Yes," Ivan says. "The year 2020 exists here and in two other universes, which are similar but different to yours."

"Ember created the Castle of Teskom as a central hub joining all dimensions and time," sings Teuta. "A balance of humanity, technology, and knowledge."

"You really expect us to believe this?" Itra asks. "The castle, the food, the clothes—why did you lock us in here?"

Ivan frowns. He looks at Teuta.

"The front entrance was closed," Teuta whispers to Ivan. "I was stalling until you arrived."

"You are not prisoners here," Ivan says. "The front door opens with the same command used on most doors in the castle. Open says me."

"Ivan," Danae asks, "if you were born in 1420, and it's 2020, how are you still breathing and here with us now?"

"Oh, silly old man, how could I forget to explain such a simple fact? Teuta sent me a message Monday morning after you arrived. Tuesday afternoon, I entered my ember archway and walked through the future ember archway to 2020."

"What year is it for you?" Danae asks.

"1482," Ivan answers.

Danae chokes on her tea. She coughs.

Teuta explains, "Ember assigns a host from each bloodline to orient new descendants as they discover the castle for the first time. Ivan is your designated host."

"Let me show you a book." Ivan hands Itra a blue leather-bound book about the size of his hand, but twice as thick. "I found this volume during my first exploration of the castle, or rather, it found me."

The cover has gold embossed lettering in all caps: '*OPEN*.' Itra turns the book over—nothing on the spine or back. Itra hands it over to Danae, turning his attention back to Ivan.

"The book appeared on the bedside table after I slept here overnight. Wait, don't open—"

Danae feels a rumble like an earthquake before the sensation of falling punches her in the gut. She yells, "Itra!"

An echo of her yell answers back. "Itra, Itra, Itra…"

13

"Ivan, where did my wife go?" Itra yells, standing over the spot where Danae disappeared.

"She's gone," Ivan whispers.

"I can see that she's gone. Where did she go?" Itra clinches his jaw, his nostrils flaring.

"Outside of the castle and the grounds." Ivan holds his hands up in defense as Itra lunges for him. "Wait! Let me explain."

Itra steps back only a fraction, trying to catch his breath.

"The book describes the castle and the defense mechanisms to protect Ember, like the archways, knowledge archives, and Ember's magic." Ivan steps back and swallows hard. "I suspect that Danae was a victim of Chapter Nine, a system of checks and balances."

Itra's arm hairs rise. "What do you mean, victim?"

"Danae is likely safe—"

Itra lunges forward again.

Teuta appears between Ivan and Itra, freezing Itra in place.

"Can we take a few seconds to talk rationally?" Teuta asks. "Danae is alive, safe, and unharmed."

"You know where she is? Tell me!"

"A protection portal transported Danae out," she says. "She's now back in the forest outside of the archways. She'll have no memory of her time here in the castle or the grounds."

"Why?" Itra asks.

"Chapter Nine," she says. "Ember assigns a bloodline to protect and serve. The secrets written in the books are a privilege beyond Danae's entrance granted by her marriage to you. Ember has an automated defense mechanism activated to preserve that knowledge."

"Where is Danae from?" Ivan asks.

"She's American. Why?"

Teuta and Ivan lock eyes before answering.

"She is the first person with no Illyrian blood to cross over successfully under our protection," Ivan says.

Teuta chimes, "Gjeto discovered a journal written in Greek in a stairwell in 1994. We can assume that she may be one of two that has crossed over."

"Gjeto, my grandfather?" Itra asks. "He found this place. Is he here?"

"Itra, nearly every generation from our line, finds this place when it's their time. However, we're not the first bloodline to protect and serve Ember." Ivan searches the shelves, pulling out a single book. "Zeus." Ivan hands the book to Itra.

"What will happen if I open this?"

"No consequence," Ivan answers. "How well do you know ancient Greek mythology?"

"Do movies count?"

Ivan laughs. "Zeus had a son, Perseus, who beheaded Medusa."

Itra nods. He hesitantly opens the book, scanning the page. "I can't read whatever language this is." He holds up the book.

"We had the text translated about twenty years ago by your uncle, Vincent," Ivan says.

Itra locks eyes with Ivan. "My Uncle Vincent?"

"Yes! His gift from Ember is languages. He can read, write, and speak any language."

Itra recognizes his Uncle Vincent's handwriting: *Ember, I bind my blood to protect and serve the Castle of Teskom.* Itra turns the page and reads another passage: *Danae, your heir will bind our blood in time. The infinity loop combines. Oh, Ember of mine, our ember in time.*

"Danae?" Itra asks. "What does this have to do with my Danae?"

"Perseus's mother was Princess Danae," Teuta says.

"Mui and Zeus made an alliance centuries ago to secure a legacy to protect and serve Ember," Teuta explains. "The legacy was the union of their lines. If Danae is a descendant of Zeus and we know that you're a descendant of Mui—"

"Stop!" Itra shouts, startling Teuta and Ivan. "Do you hear her calling my name? Danae!"

14

Danae can't see her hand in front of her face. *Where am I?* "Itra?" *Seriously, why am I alone?*

She takes a few deep breaths to calm her nerves. She tries to stand, but the narrow space is too low. She pats around the floor, ceiling, and walls. *The stones feel familiar, but from where?*

"Itra! Itra! Can you hear me?"

She moves to her hands and knees and extends her arm to feel ahead. Her eyes slowly adjust to the darkness, allowing some outline of the space. She crawls until her hand finds a raised stone and then another. *Steps?* She feels above her head. *Space.* She crawls the first two steps before crouching to a stand.

The steps are a little uneven but manageable in the dark. She stops to catch her breath. "Itra?" After eight more steps, a small glimmer of light appears to be dancing ahead. *A firefly or flashlight?*

"Anyone out there?" The light brightens the steps ahead, no landing in sight. Her speed increases with the aid of the light. She climbs another forty steps straight up before stopping again to catch her breath. The light is brighter but wavering ahead. She squints to focus on the source, but a sound startles her attention.

"Danae!" a faint call whispers in her head or out. She shakes her head.

"Itra, is that you? I'm down here! Can you hear me?"

She quickens her pace for another few dozen steps. *What is this thing? A bloody stair master from the depths of hell?* Her calves are burning, and her lungs are tight.

"Itra!"

She feels dampness roll down her cheeks and back. She wipes her cheeks and notices the light bounces off her wedding ring with an almost orange glow. *That's new.*

"Six-hour day hike, my ass," she mutters.

Ugh! Where am I? Where is Itra?

She takes the stairs more slowly but two at a time, up another fifty steps. A shadow looms in the light ahead. *A door or an opening?*

She finally has two feet on a flat landing and turns to give a Rocky impression with her arms raised. She screams. She's alone in a small clearing lit only by the moon and a few stars. The steps are gone. She stumbles back in disbelief, looking in every direction. She only finds grass, shrubs, and trees with a few boulders in the distance. She whispers, "Itra."

15

"Danae?" says Itra. "I can hear you. Where are you?" Teuta and Ivan stare at Itra. "Did you hear her call my name?" Itra runs towards the door.

"Itra, wait," Ivan calls to Itra's back. "Where are you going?"

Itra bursts through the door and hurdles the width of the long dining table before exploding into the conservatory with such force that the plants wave in response.

The front door is locked. Itra skids to a stop, frantically looking for a way to lift the large iron cross beam locking the entrance.

Then he steps back and utters the command. "Open says me!"

A hiss of air escapes the doors as the large iron beam lifts and the doors open with ease. Itra doesn't wait for them to open all the way, squeezing out before nearly falling face-first down the first giant step. He bounds down the last three with more care and sprints back towards the clearing. The path is barely lit by the moon, making it hard to see the stray rocks and roots.

Whack

He rubs his head after running into the ember archway. "Shit!" He scrambles under.

"Itra?" a voice calls in the distance.

"Danae, is that you? I'm coming, don't move!"

"Yes! Itra, I'm here! Oh, thank God."

Itra tackles Danae in a bear hug.

"Itra, I can't breathe!"

Itra releases her, but barely. He smothers her face and neck in kisses.

"Where have you been?" she asks. "How did we get separated? What in the hell are you wearing?" she unfolds from him and his kisses.

"Thank God you're okay! You're okay, right?" Itra ignores her questions, patting her down.

"Confused, tired, lost, but physically fine, except that I might not walk right tomorrow."

Itra visibly deflates, as if he was holding his breath.

"Where have you been? How did we get separated? What are you wearing?" she repeats.

Itra looks down, finding the fancy suit from dinner and back to Danae. She's back in her original hiking gear.

He stares at her with bewilderment.

"Where are we, Itra?"

"What do you remember?"

"We got lost after dark. I don't understand how I ended up at the bottom of those steps."

"Steps?" Itra stands to look around the clearing.

She stands. "It might sound strange, but they vanished the second I climbed to the top."

"If that is strange, I'm not sure how to explain the last 48 hours."

"48 hours?"

"Yes," Itra says. "Can we sit? I'll try to explain?"

"Be my guest," she sings, folding down to the ground. She tilts her head. He smirks. "Déjà vu, or did I sing that a few hours ago?"

"You did, so you remember?"

"Remember what?"

Itra clears his throat. "We found an archway around dawn." He notices her attempt to interrupt, and he holds his palm up, gesturing for her to wait. "We crossed over into an area and time we've never hiked. The surrounding lands looked familiar, but they were slightly different." He takes a long breath. "Does any of this sound familiar?"

"No! I remember our hike, the phones dying around midnight, but that's it before the dark stairwell." Danae throws her hands down in frustration. "Ouch!" She sucks her finger.

"Careful that thorn is from pyracantha, otherwise known as firethorns," Itra says, surprising himself.

"You know the scientific names of thorns now?"

Itra chuckles. "A gift or curse."

"Are you drunk or high?" she asks, adjusting her posture. She feels a poke in her back pocket.

"No. Sober. I think?" Itra nods. "Sober, definitely sober. I will warn you now, it might sound—"

Danae reaches into her back pocket and pulls out a card. She shifts it in the moonlight. It's a gold card with royal blue text: *Do you remember?*

Itra stares at her expression. "What is that?"

She turns the card to Itra.

"Do you remember?" says Itra. "Wait, do you actually remember?"

"Yes," she whispers.

Itra throws his head back, howling in laughter.

"Why in the hell are you laughing? An ancient magic castle? Mui, Ivan, and Teuta? Ember? Really?"

"Sorry," he apologizes. "It's nice to know I'm not insane."

"How did I end up out here?"

"Chapter Nine," Itra explains, "a defensive protection portal from the 'OPEN' book."

"The book opened a portal. Are you bloody mad?"

"Maybe, but it happened. We were really there, right?"

"You're asking me?"

He nods.

"I think I need to sleep before I answer." She yawns.

Itra explains the conversation about Mui and Zeus's alliance, a message to Danae from Zeus about an heir, and his ability to hear her calling his name.

"So, this goes beyond your bloodline. There were others?"

Itra nods.

"What do we do now?"

"Head home. Do you have our pack?"

"No pack or phones, just me got booted out."

"We will need to wait for first light. I have zero intentions of getting lost this time!"

16

A crunch of twigs catches Itra's attention.

"Danae?" Itra whispers.

She looks up to see fear on his face. Itra moves fast, placing himself between her and an approaching man. They scramble to their feet.

"Who is that?" she hisses. They take small steps back.

"No idea!" Itra says out of the corner of his mouth.

The stranger's height grows in size as he moves towards them.

Danae scans the man's tight tunic over a massively muscular physique and flowy dark pants. *He's not from around here.*

A chilled breeze lifts his brown wavy hair away from his chin exposing his smile, but this does not suppress her fight-or-flight response.

"Itra, Danae," he says, stopping a few steps away. "My name is Don."

They're unsure of how to respond.

"The exploration of the Castle of Teskom is your birthright, Itra," Don says. "However, Danae, your ability to cross the archway is troubling. Can I have a word?"

His voice and tenor are familiar, almost ominous.

Danae's grip on Itra's bicep tightens. Itra responds with a quick flex.

"You can say what you need to in front of Itra," Danae says, keeping her tone level. "We have no secrets."

Don grins and tips his head. "The protection of the Castle of Teskom has layers of defense. The knowledge stored inside the walls can revolutionize the modern world beyond this universe." He pauses and his grin falls flat, transforming his face into a menacing glare. "It could also bring countries to their knees in war or cause catastrophic events that end human life."

"It was you I heard in my dream!" Danae exclaims in horror. "Why?"

Don laughs. "Took you long enough."

He retrieves a large dagger from his leather boot, closing the distance between Itra and Danae in seconds. The tip of his blade is within a hair of Itra's chest when a force propels Don away, slamming him into a boulder across the clearing.

"Ouch!" Danae exclaims. An orange glow surrounds her ring finger for a beat as she inspects her hand.

"Danae, we need to go now!" Itra yells. "He is getting up!"

They half run, half stumble down the rocky hillside, turning back every few meters to look for any evidence of Don's pursuit.

The morning sun is not quite over the eastern horizon. The shadows on the path making a speedy retreat nearly impossible.

Danae trips over a large root, falling hard. She shouts, "Itra!"

He sprints back and pulls her up.

A whispered voice echoes. "Watch where you step!"

Hiss

Danae screams, "Snakes!"

"Run! Don't stop, Danae," Itra commands.

She dodges menacing lunges from snakes as she sprints with surprising new agility.

"Enough!" Itra bellows until he loses air.

The hissing instantly mutes.

"That worked?" Danae mutters in between gasps of air.

"For now," Itra says, looking over his shoulder.

Danae pauses at a familiar fork in the path. "Lake or abandoned fort?"

"Lake!" says Itra. "You can swim faster than you can run!"

"Can't argue with that logic!" Danae says, taking his hand.

They continue to look back as they make their way to the lake-level path. Slower than their initial sprint, they navigate a steep descent, pausing several times to gently slide down a few slick spots still covered in morning dew. After righting their near falls countless times, they reach the lake's edge. They pause to splash water on their face and catch their breath. The sprint down felt like minutes, but the sun indicates hours.

Itra's fancy suit is worse for wear, missing the tie and jacket. The once fancy gold shirt is now tied Rambo style on his head.

Danae gently pulls her shirt away from her back to air out, thankful for the shade of the ridge from the mid-morning sun. *This afternoon will be a warm one, folks*, plays in her head.

They pick up pace, now back on level ground. Itra pauses, looking up at a large boulder, motioning for her to stop. She can see two horns poke over first before the long face of a goat. She sighs at the familiar sight of a wandering goat. The threat of Don now seems to be a distant past.

A crackle of a radio chirps loudly. "Roger that. 10-4." They hear before they see Ermal, Itra's schoolmate, in his patrol uniform.

"Did you miss me?" Itra calls.

Ermal's expression is pure joy and relief. "Man, I seriously thought you were a goner. Where in the hell have you been? Is Danae with you?"

"Hi, Ermal, I'm here," she answers.

"Whew, your brother Leon is terrifying. Thank God! Let me radio an all clear. Do either of you need medical?"

"No to medical," Danae says. "Did you say my brother?"

"Water, food, and sleep," Itra answers.

Ermal nods before talking into the radio on his shoulder.

Itra hugs Danae, kissing her head, before whispering into her hair. "How in the hell do we explain any of this?"

She chuckles into his chest. "Not my blood right. I got the literal boot. All you buddy."

A whoop of an ambulance makes them turn.

"Ermal," Danae says. "I said we're fine."

"Simmer down, sister!" Leon calls. "That order came from me."

"Leon!" Danae scolds, looking up.

Leon is standing on a boulder above her head, dressed in military-grade combat boots, tactical pants, and a tan shirt. "Nice to see you too, sis."

"Get your butt down here," she commands.

He makes two leaps before landing in front of her.

She hugs him tightly. "How much trouble are we in?" she whispers.

Leon exclaims, "Heaps!"

"Is Kaly here, too?" Danae asks.

"Not yet," Leon whispers.

After a complete check by the medics, they're cleared to go with an ace bandage to Danae's ankle and instructions to drink plenty of water and rest. Ermal and Leon ride up front. Itra and Danae climb in the back of Ermal's SUV. Itra and Danae feel the exhaustion and fight to keep their eyes open.

Leon's questions, while the medics were checking them over, were unsuccessful. But now, in the same vehicle, he starts in again.

"Where were you?" Leon asks. "What are you wearing?" He turns to gesture to Itra's suit pants and shoes.

"Leon, what day is it?" Danae asks.

"Wednesday. Why?" Leon replies.

"Wednesday, four days. Itra, we haven't slept since Monday night, right?" she asks, squeezing Itra's hand.

"Yep," Itra says through a yawn. The rest of the ride is silent until a few reporters tap on the windows outside the gate to their home.

"What's with the reporters?" Danae asks.

"An American missing in Albania makes local news," Ermal says.

"Seriously?" Itra and Danae groan in unison.

"Iana's going to destroy me," Itra mutters.

Leon laughs.

The officers wave the reporters away, making room for the vehicle to enter the drive. Iana, Anton, and Elis are waiting on the front porch.

Anton has a firm hand on a bouncing Elis. Ermal parks, cutting the engine. He turns to Itra and Danae. "I will need a formal statement for the report in 24 hours, but for now, rest, eat, and good luck with your sister." Ermal winks before opening his door.

Anton loses his grip on Elis. "Uncle Itra!" Elis is now jumping up to look in the window.

"Stand back, make room for the door," Ermal teases.

Itra slowly opens the door. Elis flies to Itra before he has two feet on the ground. "Hi Elis, did you sleep at my house?" He scoops him up for a hug.

"Yes, yes, yes!" Elis sings.

Danae reaches over to tousle his hair, sliding out behind Itra.

"Hi, Danae!" Elis wiggles free of Itra, jumping into her arms.

"Hi, darlin'!" she responds, squeezing him tightly.

Leon jumps out. "Hey Elis, let's go check out the garden. Maybe we'll find some worms for fishing."

Elis's eyes go wide. "Leon! Cool!" He jumps down, skipping to Leon.

"There's a coffee can near the waterspout," Danae says.

Leon waves his hand in a salute.

Itra hugs Iana first. He apologizes, but Iana shakes her head.

Danae hugs Anton. "How bad is it?" she whispers.

Anton's rumble of laughter shakes them both. "You owe me ten dozen chocolate chip cookies bad!"

Danae hugs Iana, whispering, "We're so sorry. He'll explain everything."

"I heard your message," Iana says, squeezing her tightly. "And so did Elis. I knew you were safe."

"Elis heard us too?" Danae asks, pulling slightly apart so she can see her face.

"Yes," Iana says with an amused smile. "To be honest, you two smell something fierce. Go in, get washed up. I'll have supper waiting when you get out."

Itra and Danae inhale their own aromas with disgust before laughing.

"Dibs!" Itra calls, heading inside.

Danae stops in the entry; Iana must have been stress cleaning. Nearly every surface is shiny clean—the floors, furniture, and even the baseboards. Danae turns to say thanks, but Anton and Iana are hugging on the porch. She can see the exhaustion on Iana's face. She hasn't slept either.

Danae enters her room to pull out clean clothes. She peels off the hiking shirt, sports bra, and pants. She pats her pockets down and freezes before dropping them into the hamper.

Itra bounds into the room with a towel draped around his hips, torso bare, and face cleanly shaven. "Your turn!" he says after closing the door. "Danae, what's wrong? Are you okay?"

"I can't find the card."

"The one that says, 'Do you remember?'"

She nods. "What if I forget, again?"

Itra hugs her tightly. "I'll remind you, don't worry."

Inhaling his fresh, clean skin, she sighs. "I need to shower." She takes her robe off the hook and slides it over her shoulders, discarding the rest of her dirty hiking gear.

"Danae," Itra whispers.

She turns. He is standing so close that she rolls on her toes to kiss him softly. Their lips barely break apart.

He whispers, "I love you."

"I love you, too," she says, nibbling his freshly shaven face.

17

The morning light stirs Itra—he moves in closer to Danae. She scoots into snuggle but groans.

"Damn stairs," Danae mutters.

Knock, knock

"Ermal will be here in thirty minutes to take a formal statement," Iana whispers from outside the door.

"Ok," Itra says. Danae snuggles deeper into the pillow. "We're up and moving."

"Up and moving my—"

Smack—Danae feels the sting on her backside.

"How about now?" He leaps out of her reach, laughing, and quickly dresses.

Twenty minutes later, Itra and Danae are sitting on the front porch with coffee—a cluster of reporters call out their names from the gate.

"What do you want to tell Ermal?" Danae asks.

"The truth," Itra says, facing Danae. "We were attacked and if that crazy man is still on the hill, I don't want anyone else hurt or worse."

"True, but the castle?" Danae murmurs.

"I know Ermal pretty well," he says. "He likely won't believe a word. How else do we explain the gap?"

Danae nods, chewing on her thumbnail. "I'll think of something between now and the press."

Iana walks out and leans against the rail with her back to the shouts from the reporters loitering near the front gate. She raises her mug to Itra and Danae. "You two will have to make a formal statement to the press after you meet with Ermal. They won't leave without one."

"Yeah," Danae says and sighs. She sips her coffee. "We're in no hurry."

"I'm curious," Itra asks Iana. "When did you find out we were missing?"

"Tuesday morning after Franc called."

"Wait," Danae says, putting the timeline together. "How did Leon get here so fast?"

"What did I do now?" Leon says his voice still husky from sleep. He joins them on the porch.

"How did you get here so fast?" Danae asks.

"I had a flight booked that would arrive Thursday morning," he says, sipping his coffee. "Do you remember Sergeant Wolfe?"

"Red hair, from Missouri?" Danae asks.

"Yep. He's now a contract pilot for several large international companies. He saw a shared post about you two missing from your friend Paige on his newsfeed and called immediately to offer me a ride over the pond. He already had a flight on Tuesday evening to Greece. An hour later, I headed to a private airport north of Lawson to hop in Wolfe's cargo plane. He made flight plan modifications, and we were wheels up. I landed in Montenegro just before dawn yesterday morning."

"Wow," she murmurs.

The reporters' calls grow louder as the gate opens; Ermal's SUV comes down the drive at a faster clip than yesterday. He kills the engine and hops out.

"Good morning," Ermal says, walking up on the porch. "Are you ready to give a formal statement?"

"Coffee or tea?" Iana asks, patting Ermal on the shoulder.

"Tea," Ermal says.

Itra and Danae stand shaking hands with Ermal. Leon, less formal, waves from his chair, sipping his coffee. Elis's giggle floats out from the kitchen. Danae shows Ermal to their office and the three of them sit on the sectional.

Ermal takes out a small digital recording device. Iana brings Ermal a steaming mug. "Thanks, Iana."

"If you need anything else, just ask," she says. He nods. Iana closes the door to the office, giving them privacy.

"Do you mind if I record this?" Ermal asks.

"No problem," Itra replies, and Danae nods.

"Thursday, 9 am, Itra and Danae. Can you tell me where you were on Sunday?"

"We were home until ten," says Itra. Danae nods in agreement. "And then we hiked up to the old Mokset Castle."

"Did you speak to or see anyone on Sunday?"

"I spoke to our neighbor, Mira," says Danae. "She was outside hanging laundry when we were leaving the house. And I saw two shepherds from a distance."

"And you, Itra?"

"I only spoke to Danae all day."

"Have you hiked that area before?"

"Yes," says Itra. "Three, no four times in the last two years. We've never taken the same way up or down."

"Four times," Danae clarifies. "And yes, never the same way. His idea, not mine."

"Did you make it to the old Mokset Castle?"

"Yes," Danae says, looking at Itra. "Around one o'clock?" He nods. "We made several stops to admire the spring blossoms and we may have made a few wrong turns on the way up."

"And was there anyone up there when you arrived who could confirm this?"

"Just Itra and I, plus a few wandering goats," Danae says. "I think I posted a photo of the valley from the top. That would have been around two. We rested and snacked before I snapped the photo."

Ermal shows Itra and Danae the picture she posted on Sunday to confirm. She nods.

"Itra?" Ermal asks when Itra looks puzzled by the conversation. "Did you know she posted this?"

"She showed me the photo before uploading it. But can I see that again?"

"Sure." Ermal hands Itra his phone.

She looks over his shoulder after Itra mutters, "Son of a—"

"What do you see?" Ermal asks.

Itra hands the phone back, but the picture is zoomed in. "Ermal, do you see a glowing archway?"

"I see a reflection—but a glowing archway?" Ermal squints and shakes his head. "No."

"A reflection would be green," Danae says. "This is glowing orange."

"Okay, but why would that alarm either of you?"

"I didn't notice it from the top that afternoon," Danae says. "But it appears to be the same archway we found before dawn Monday morning."

Itra nods.

Ermal holds up a hand. "Where did you hike after visiting the old Mokset Castle remains?"

They continue to answer Ermal's questions about their attempt to find their way down, the sun setting, the extreme darkness with no moon or stars, and about their phones dying just after midnight. They pause once they reach their discovery of the archway.

"What is it?" Ermal asks.

"We climbed around a large boulder and caught our first glimpse of a stone archway," Itra says. "From a distance, it looked like a door with a light on or a fireplace. We stepped under the archway just before dawn."

Itra pauses, looking at Danae.

She nods, encouraging him to continue.

"At first light, the clearing was familiar, but wrong. There was an enormous castle to the south. Four additional archways, like the one we entered, were set in an equally spaced semi-circle. To the north, rocky, uneven boulders. And to the west, a small clearing with a worn path to a castle." Itra pauses, examining Ermal's expression. "Ermal?"

Ermal reaches down, stopping the recorder. "Off the record, I'd love to hear about this 'castle,' but on the record, I need facts, Itra. We had a lot of resources and boots on the ground to assist with the search for the two of you. Please tell me something I can take to my superiors."

Itra and Danae shift on the couch.

Ermal stands, pacing the small room.

"Ermal, please sit down," Danae pleads. "You're making me nervous."

Ermal finds his composure and sits back down. "Go on, tell me about the damn castle, but I'm not recording this part."

Itra clears his throat, telling Ermal the play-by-play, sharing all the details until the part of Danae's ejection from the castle. Danae explains the stairs, reuniting with Itra, and meeting Don. Itra fills Ermal in on the confrontation with Don, and their flight down the hill with the snakes.

Ermal's face is expressionless. He stands abruptly, leaving the room. Itra and Danae follow him out to his vehicle. Their exit alarms Leon and Iana. They come out to the porch, a piece of bacon hanging from Leon's mouth, and Iana furrows her brow.

Ermal throws open the back, digs in a crate, and pulls out a bag. A series of clicks from the reporters' cameras explode when Ermal holds the bag up.

"Do you recognize this?" Ermal asks.

Itra and Danae can see the contents of the bag. "Yes," they answer in unison.

"What is it?" Ermal asks.

Iana and Leon have joined them, looking like four against one to any onlooker.

"Ermal," Itra says, "this is the ember found at the base of the stone archways."

Ermal drops his arm and opens the bag. "Itra, take a piece."

Itra follows his command without question. He picks up a metallic-like shard. "That's hot!" He throws the shard back in the bag, inspecting his hands.

"Your turn, Danae," Ermal states, holding the bag her way. Before she moves an inch, Leon thrusts his arm across her.

"What is this, Ermal?" Leon asks. "Hot potato, evidence version?" He reaches in and takes a shard. "It's cold, not warm at all." He places a piece in Danae's palm.

"It's hot!" Danae yelps, tossing it back in the bag.

Leon shakes his head in disbelief.

Ermal places the bag in the back of the vehicle and retrieves a paper. He hands it to Itra. "The lab ran every test against this material. It tested inconclusive for what looks like the entire periodic table."

Iana and Danae lean towards Itra to look at the report. Itra hands the report to Leon. Leon shrugs, handing it back to Ermal.

"Iana," Ermal says. "I need to speak with you in private."

"Sure," Iana answers, walking with Ermal towards the garden.

"I'm not sure what is going on here," Leon says. "But you two are going to have so much explaining to do."

He pats their backs before walking inside.

Itra and Danae follow Leon, straight to the aroma of freshly cooked bacon. Anton is managing the skillet, laughing at Elis, giving his best Leon impression when they walk in. Leon ruffles Elis's hair. Itra reaches for the plate of bacon.

Danae swats Itra's hand away from the plate as she tugs him towards the door. "We need to discuss the press statement."

They're about to sit when Ermal and Iana burst through the door. Ermal's face is pale, and Iana is trying to hide a grin.

"A call just came in from a local shepherd," Ermal says. "He says there are close to a thousand snake skins littering a path leading down from the ridge near the old Mokset Castle remains."

Itra and Danae attempt to keep a straight face, but Ermal's shocked, 'I believe you now face,' is too much.

Danae breaks first with a giggle.

Itra barks, "Ha!"

Itra and Danae lose all ability to keep their laughter quiet.

Ermal stares at them like they've gone mad. Iana retreats to the kitchen to loop Leon and Anton in on the latest news.

Itra and Danae try to choke down their giggles, but they keep creeping back up. Danae honks and snorts, trying to hold in the last round of laughter. Leon appears in the doorway, shaking his head.

"Get it together, Danae," Leon scolds.

"Yes, sir!" she says with a salute.

Itra silences his giggles and sits down, but Ermal remains standing.

"Normally," Ermal says, pacing the room, "the press want a statement, but you can't go to the press with this story." He shakes his head. "Just keep it simple. Start by thanking the community—follow with a brief lost and found synopsis. End with a closing statement, expressing sincere gratitude. And you may or may not open this up for questions from the reporters."

"Got it," Danae says.

"What is your lost and found synopsis?" Ermal asks.

"Day hike turns to four-day adventure to a castle, fairies, and giants, oh my," Itra says without skipping a beat, face blank with no expression.

Leon is standing behind Ermal with his fist in his mouth, trying hard not to laugh. Ermal is staring at the floor, shaking his head, and Danae can't stop smiling.

"Well, to be honest," Danae says without cracking into giggles. "It's more like castle, fairies, ancestors, giants, and snakes, oh my." She pauses. "Do you think the snake skins have made the news yet?"

"Only a matter of minutes. It's a small-town people talk. Why?"

"Can Itra and I have a few minutes to discuss the synopsis?" Danae asks.

"Hell," Ermal whispers. "I'll meet you on the porch."

Itra and Danae discuss a few options and land on a nearly plausible scenario.

Itra stands grinning mischievously. "Ready to face the firing squad, Pinocchio?"

"Ha, you think I'm speaking," Danae mocks and bends to roll her pant legs above her ankles. "That's all you, baby."

Itra's grin turns to a scowl. "Seriously?"

"Remember, your blood right, your secret. But I'll express the gratitude and answer the reporter questions at the end. Deal?"

Itra pulls Danae up, hugging her. He whispers in her hair, "Deal."

Itra nods to Ermal as they exit the house—the shouts from the gate grow louder with each step.

Itra steps to the center, waving his hand to silence the questions. "Danae and I want to express our sincere gratitude to our neighbors, community, service people, and dogs for coming to aid in the search for us on Tuesday and Wednesday. We know the resources and effort put into this were expedient and thorough. We are lucky and blessed that we get to sing your praises." He places his hand over his heart and nods. "Danae and I left for a day hike on Sunday and got very lost that evening and overnight. A kind stranger offered water, food, and shelter in an old bunker Monday morning around dawn. No power to charge our dead phones, so we couldn't connect with family or friends. Danae's ankle needed an extra day of rest before managing the hike out on Wednesday morning." Reporters take aim at Danae's feet and snap a few shots. She is still wearing the ace bandage the medics gave her. "The trail down was snake-infested, as you may have heard by now, so we had to find an alternate path, but we made it back mostly intact. The stranger asks to remain nameless. We want to honor this request." Itra steps back. Danae steps forward.

"I know I'm new around here," Danae says in conclusion. "But the overwhelming response to come to our aid speaks to the generous spirit of Albania and is one of the many reasons why I love living here. Please know that Itra and I will be forever in your debt for the efforts you made to bring us home. We're open to a few questions."

"Marie Parker, *Channel One News*. Do you plan to hike the area again?"

"Eventually—but we will not be taking any new trails," Danae says, causing a small ripple of laughter.

"Mark Wayne, *Newsfirst*. Did he mention how long he has been living in the hills? Is he a hermit?"

"Well, Mark," Danae says. "We never told you the kind stranger's gender, but we wish to express our gratitude for the assistance with no further comment."

Mark fires back, "It was a woman?"

"Next," Danae says, ignoring his second question.

"Ruth Rex, *Elmira Press*. Have you seen snakes on the hill before?"

Itra steps in to respond. "Once or twice, but never in the quantity of yesterday."

"Unis Beard, *Wandering It Press*. Did you find any ember?"

"No," Danae says.

"Ermal, what was in the bag?" Unis asks.

Danae ignores his follow-up question. "Thanks again to the community and for your time, but we have no further comments." Danae grasps Itra's hand, walking back to the house. They do not turn to answer the shouts from the reporters.

Ermal manages crowd control, pointing the reporters to their waiting vehicles. Once the area is clear, he returns to the house. Iana and Danae offer him food or a beverage, but he declines.

"I'll be in touch if there are additional questions," Ermal says. "You two handled the press like pros. Impressive. And Unis is a gossip blogger with an ear in the department, so he most likely caught wind of the recent lab tests. I wouldn't worry about him; he has maybe ten followers."

The sound of the gate closing behind Ermal's vehicle is like the starting gunshot of a sprint. Itra is standing on the porch one second and eating a full plate of food the next.

"Slow down," Danae says. "We're home. No need to rush."

Iana laughs. "We'll let you two eat, but as soon as you finish, we need to have a serious conversation about what really happened up there."

They nod in acknowledgment.

Iana refills their coffee cups as they finish. Leon, Anton, and Iana sit across from Danae and Itra. Itra starts from the clearing Monday morning, leaving out nothing except the shower seduction. Leon attempts to interrupt about twenty times. Danae squashes the interruptions with a glare each time. Danae finishes the story with the race down the hill and then allows Leon to start with his questions.

"Danae," Leon laughs. "Did you two find and eat a patch of wild mushrooms?"

"No, brother," Danae says, shaking her head.

"The call from the cavern is what I heard while doing the dishes?" Iana asks.

"Yes," Danae answers.

Leon stops laughing. "You believe this?"

"Yes, because Elis heard them too."

"I can second that," Anton says. "Iana was trying to explain she had heard Itra and Danae. Elis came in, asking for them. He said he heard Itra's voice; that's what woke him up. He thought they were home."

"After that," Iana says. "I tried to call you, to let you know they were safe and unharmed. But Kaly said you had hitched a ride out and would arrive in the morning."

Leon strokes his chin and then grins. "So, we could be descendants of Zeus?"

"Oh, brother!" Danae smacks her hand to her forehead. "That's what you are focusing on?"

"Kaly and I did one of those ancestry swabs last year," Leon says, standing. "It was an anniversary 'gift' from her mother, urging us to use our genes to procreate. I never remember seeing the results. Kaly should be up by now." He walks out of the room in search of his phone.

"Who is going to call Uncle Vincent to ask about his time at the Castle of Teskom?" Danae asks Itra.

Iana and Itra squirm, but Anton stands and flips a coin.

Iana calls, "Heads!"

"It's heads," Anton says, showing Itra the coin.

"Dang it," Itra groans in defeat.

Leon bounds back into the room. "We are…" He pauses for dramatic effect. Danae drums her fingers on the table. "Genuine mutts." He laughs, handing his phone over to Danae. "Kaly emailed the breakdown of my results."

"We are 76% European," Danae says. "Of this, Italian 39% and Greek 14%." Danae passes the phone to Itra, Iana, and Anton to look over the results. "A very slim chance for our line to reach back to Princess Danae or Zeus."

Itra stands abruptly. "Iana, can I borrow your phone to call Uncle Vincent?"

"Yes," Iana says. "It's on the charger in the guest room."

Elis skips in behind Itra's retreat. "I'm hungry. Where is Teuta? Do you have any more marshmallows?"

"Teuta?" Danae asks. "Do you have a friend named Teuta at school, sweetie?" Danae makes eye contact with Itra as he enters with Iana's phone. Itra's eyebrows shoot up in surprise.

"No," Elis says, "she doesn't go to school. Do you have any more marshmallows, Danae?"

"Iana, can you help me check?" Danae asks.

Itra follows Iana and Danae into the kitchen. "Does he have a friend named Teuta?" Danae whispers, opening her baking cabinet.

"Not that I know of," Iana says. "We may have finished your marshmallows on Tuesday evening. Sorry. Stress eating mindlessly, marshmallows took the fall."

Iana is right. There is an empty spot where the marshmallows had been. "How does he know the name Teuta?" Danae closes the cabinet.

"Not sure," Iana says.

"Who is Teuta?" Itra asks, handing the phone to Iana.

Iana and Danae say, "Seriously?"

"Itra, did he pick up?" Iana asks.

"Did who pick up?"

"Uncle Vincent?"

"Why would I call Uncle Vincent?"

Iana places her hands on either side of Itra's head. "Is there a screw loose? We need Vincent to answer questions about the Castle of Teskom."

"Castle of what?" Itra asks.

"Danae, is he playing, or is he having a stroke?" Iana asks, facing Danae.

"Iana, we're out of marshmallows," Danae says, "not sure what Vincent can do about that. Did you visit a new castle?"

Iana gapes. Danae thinks Iana may scream in frustration. Leon and Anton come into the kitchen.

Anton takes one glance at Iana's deep frown. "What's wrong?"

"They've gone mad!" Iana blurts out. "Itra is acting clueless. And Danae thinks I'm crazy."

Leon grabs Danae by her shoulders and stares her down. Danae tries to pull away.

Iana sits down hard.

"Leon, stop!" Danae exclaims. "Iana, are you okay?"

"Danae, look at me," Leon commands. He asks in a slow, serious tone. "Where were you yesterday?"

"Hiking in the Mokset hills," Danae says. "Where's Kaly?"

"You're right," Leon says. "They've gone mad!" He turns to Anton and Iana. "What do we do? Call an ambulance? Is this post-trauma amnesia, shock, or worse?"

"Whoa!" Danae throws her hands up. "Slow down! What are you three talking about?"

Itra and Danae lock eyes with concern.

"You two go to your room," Iana commands, pointing at Itra and Danae from her position on the floor. "I mean it. Go!"

Neither Itra nor Danae question her. They back slowly out of the kitchen.

"What in the hell is going on?" Danae asks Itra as he closes their bedroom door.

"I have no clue, but I feel as though I'm missing something," Itra says with concern.

"Same."

18

"It's been two weeks, three doctor visits, and even head scans," Iana explains to Leon, switching the phone to speaker. "The doctors gave an all-clear, no damage or diagnosis. The last doctor, a psychiatrist, said this reaction is normal. Their memories may come back once they've returned to their day-to-day activities. Neither of them can recall a single moment from Sunday to Wednesday, minus a hike in the Mokset hills. No castle, snakes, stairs, portals, Mui, Don, Teuta, Ember, or Ivan."

"Did your Uncle Vincent confirm anything about the castle?"

"No, he has no memories of anything like what Itra and Danae described. Leon, he said he has never climbed the hills of Mokset."

Leon stands to pace his front porch.

"Are you there?" Iana asks.

"Yes. This is frustrating news."

"Sorry. We're at the 'only time will tell' stage of healing."

"Noted. I will relay this to the family here and check in with Danae more frequently. How is Elis?"

"Elis hasn't mentioned Teuta once. I questioned him this week by throwing the name out and watching for signs of recognition. He would shrug and ask, what is Teuta, not who."

Leon laughs. "Maybe we ate some magic shrooms, and we are the ones who are tripping?"

Iana sighs. "Maybe."

"Kaly has been researching their story since I returned and has come up empty-handed."

"Another dead end," Iana says.

"Give my regards to Anton and Elis, and please let us know of any changes."

"Will do."

"And thanks again for the update, Iana."

"Of course. Please tell Kaly hello. Take care."

"Later." Leon hangs up.

Anton finds Iana chopping carrots with such force, one pings off his chest and lands on the floor as he enters the kitchen.

"Easy, that carrot means no harm." He tosses the carrot sliver into the bin. "How is Leon doing?"

Iana puts down the knife. "He's worried, but okay. Kaly's research has provided no answers. Is Elis still playing over at the neighbors?"

"No, he is washing his hands. He's hungry again. Can you imagine what he'll eat during his teenage years?"

Iana laughs. "If it is anything like Itra, we need to start saving now!"

"Mom, what's for dinner? I'm starving!" Elis exclaims, sliding into the room.

"Dinner is chicken, steamed broccoli and carrots, and snail rolls. Dad will slice an apple for you with some peanut butter until dinner is ready."

"Elis, what are snail rolls?" Anton asks, rinsing the apples.

"They aren't real snails, Dad," Elis says, rolling his eyes. "They're just shaped like them." Elis laughs.

90

Anton smiles, slicing up a few apples and taking the jar of peanut butter to the table.

The front doorbell rings as Iana finishes plating dinner.

Anton calls out, "I've got it."

He returns to the kitchen and holds up a thick envelope. The envelope is royal blue with gold cursive writing. *'Welcome to the Castle of Teskom'* is written across the side facing Iana.

"Anton, we can't open that. Don't even think about it. Who delivered it?"

"A small girl with dark hair," says Anton. His eyes bulge in realization, and he bolts from the room and out the front door. He comes back a few minutes later, out of breath, shaking his head.

"Teuta physically dropped off a note and left?" Iana asks.

Elis calls, "Is dinner ready?"

Anton, Iana, and Elis sit down for dinner. Elis is the only one talking. He rambles on about a new kid at school—the teacher sneezing five times today—and Teuta.

"Elis, honey, did you say Teuta?" Iana asks.

"Yep," Elis says. "She brought us a message today."

"You knew she was coming?" Anton asks.

"Yep," Elis says.

Anton and Iana stare blankly at Elis and then at each other.

After dinner, bath time, and bedtime routines are complete, Iana dials Danae.

"Hi Iana, I just hung up with Kaly. My brother is a bear."

"Hi Danae, is Itra there with you by any chance?" Iana asks. Anton comes into the room, nodding that Elis is asleep.

"He's out in the garden moving the sprinkler. What's up?"

"We had a delivery this evening. Can you go to Itra and put us on speaker?"

"Sure."

Danae finds Itra taking off his muddy shoes near the front porch. He looks up, smiling, but then frowns, seeing the confused look on her face.

"What's up?" Itra asks.

"Iana's on the phone, being very cryptic. I have no clue why, but she wants us on speaker together."

He holds up his dirty hands and heads to the sink to wash up. Danae returns to the line, placing it on speaker as Itra joins her on the couch.

"We're here, Iana."

"Hi. Anton is here too, and Leon and Kaly," Iana says.

"Is everything okay, Iana?" Itra asks, holding Danae's hand.

"A small girl with dark hair dropped off a royal blue envelope with gold cursive writing that says *Welcome to the Castle of Teskom'* as we were about to sit down for dinner. We haven't opened the envelope. Thoughts?"

"Iana, is there any sound when you shake the envelope?" Leon asks.

Anton motions Iana away, and he gently shakes it. They exhale.

"No sound, Leon," Anton says.

"Itra, what do you think?" Iana asks.

Itra clears his throat. "The message was delivered to your door, not ours. Sorry, Iana, not my call, but we're here to support you either way."

"Now you're playing neutral?" Iana scolds.

"Sorry, Iana," Danae apologizes. "We're confused. We still don't have a single shred of memory of those missing days, only what you have retold us. It's hard to offer an opinion."

"Leon, Kaly," Iana says. "Any thoughts?"

"I'd open it," Kaly says, "but only after you have sitter arrangements for Elis."

Leon asks, "Anton, what do you think?"

"Honestly, I would rather not open it. At least not here. I can clear my day tomorrow. Itra and Danae, are you two free tomorrow morning?"

"Sure," Itra says. "Kaly and Leon, we can video chat with you for the grand reveal tomorrow."

"Penciling this in now," Kaly says.

"We will see you soon," Danae says. "Try to get some sleep."

"Good night," Iana says, ending the call.

"Are you worried?" Anton asks.

"Hell yes," Iana replies.

"Itra, have you dreamed of anything in the last few days?" Danae asks. Neither of them have moved since ending the call.

"I think so," Itra says, facing her, "but I can't recall anything when I wake up. You?"

"Three times. I am walking down the same stone stairs."

"Odd. Do you think whatever is in the envelope will have any answers?"

"We'll find out in the morning," Danae says.

"I can think of a few ways to distract us," Itra says with such throaty desire that she moves in closer.

"Oh! Is that right, mister?"

They lie tangled in each other, half-clothed, catching their breath. Danae sniffs Itra's neck. The aroma, a mixture of garlic and mulberries, tickles her nose.

Half groggy, he mumbles, "Round two in the shower?"

She chuckles. "Distract away."

They finally make it to bed. The distracting task completed. Danae moves closer to snuggle; Itra's chest vibrates under her ear.

"What are you humming?" she asks.

"Put our service to the test, be our guest," he sings.

Danae laughs. She closes her eyes. An image flashes into her mind of her twirling in a blue dress. Her eyes fly open, and she sits up so fast it startles Itra to the point that he is now standing on guard.

"What's wrong?" Itra looks around the room. "Did you hear something?"

"Itra that song," Danae mutters. She points to her chest. "I sang the song inside the castle!"

He deflates, lowering his fighting stance. He crawls back into bed. "I don't remember anything," Itra says. "I know we told them you sang this with the magic dinner, but I have no actual recollection of the event. What scared you, forcing you up exorcist style?"

"A dress. I was twirling in a blue dress. The look on your face and a table for two. I closed my eyes, and I could see it." Her bottom lip quivers. "Are we insane?"

"No. We're not insane. We only lost a few days. The doctors say it'll come back. And maybe tomorrow we'll find out more with the envelope Iana is bringing." He pulls her in close and strokes her back.

"Tomorrow," she whispers. She feels his lips kiss her forehead and she burrows deeper into his embrace.

19

Danae rolls over to reach for Itra. His spot is still warm, but he's gone. She opens her eyes to find the room bathed in sunlight. The house seems too quiet. She stretches and stands, reaching for her robe. She hears the front door open, and Itra peeks his head in their bedroom door.

"Good morning, sunshine," she says.

Itra moves into the room, taking her robe from her hands. "Good morning, you." He snuggles her neck.

"What got you up and out of bed first?" She presses against him.

"I left the sprinkler on last night with all the distractions." He kisses her neck, taking off his shorts.

"Oops!" Danae mutters, breathless from his kisses.

He moves her to the bed. "Round three or is this four?"

"Mmm…" She returns his kisses.

Itra's phone rings. He reaches, barely grasping the phone, and slides the screen open. "Hello."

"Good morning," Anton says.

"Good morning," Itra chuckles.

"We're in the car. See you in about an hour."

"Safe travels. See you soon." Itra throws his phone on the pillow and leans to kiss Danae, but her phone pings. He growls. "I'll shower first. Just relax. I don't think we have time for another distraction before they arrive."

Danae pouts but admires her view as he exits their bedroom. She reaches for her phone to check the new message. It's from Iana.

"We just dropped off Elis, bringing food. Couldn't sleep."

Danae responds, *"Coffee and tea will be ready. And booze."*

Iana's response is almost immediate. *"Ha."*

Danae flips through the settings to change the ringtones for notifications. They upgraded to the latest models. Some features are new, including an app for finding a lost phone that would've been useful two weeks ago.

Another message pings from an unknown number. *"Hi, Danae. My name is Unis Beard. I am a blogger and reporter from Wandering It Press."* She can see the text bubbles showing another message is coming, but she blocks his number as spam.

Itra walks in. "You'd better get a move on…" He catches her scowling at the phone. "What is it?"

She holds her phone up. "Just blocked a reporter who tried to text."

"Which one?"

"Unis Beard."

"Really? I blocked his number yesterday. I would like to know who leaked our new numbers to the press."

Danae stands. Itra grins. "Oh, no!" She sidesteps his reach. "I don't have time for that! Put the kettle on and make a pot of coffee. Your sister stress cooked last night."

Danae takes a quick shower and towel dries her hair after dressing.

"Danae, are you dressed?" Itra asks, cracking the door.

"Are they here?" Danae asks, looking at him in the mirror.

"Almost; Iana texted a few minutes ago."

Danae hangs up her towel.

"They stopped for fuel near Koplik. I made your coffee. Join me on the porch when you're ready."

"Ready, thanks." She follows him to the porch and takes the coffee. She sits on Itra's new installation, a beautiful wooden bench. His attempt to stay busy during the last two weeks. And bonus, her honey-do list is finally shrinking. She takes a few sips, gazing towards the Mokset hills, but loses focus when Itra puts down his mug and jogs down the drive to open the gate for Anton.

Anton and Iana exit the car, neither looking well nor rested. Iana opens the back door revealing four covered dishes. She is initially distracted by the food but turns, fully hugging Danae.

"Worried?" Danae asks into Iana's hair.

"Oh well, a mother always worries." Iana releases her. "You look great and rested."

"Thanks. We're trying to stay busy and distracted." Danae smiles. Itra winks.

"Oh, for goodness' sake," Anton says, shaking his head as he catches their smirky exchange. "You two are worse than newlyweds."

Danae ushers them inside and pours two fresh cups of coffee for Anton and Iana. Iana reheats the breakfast casserole. Danae is thankful Itra preheated the oven when he started the coffee. They sit at the kitchen table, and they each take a bite with a collective moan of approval.

Iana lights up at the sound.

"It's excellent, Iana." Danae cleans her plate almost as quickly as Itra, which is a first.

Itra makes a second plate, giving Anton another helping. Iana and Danae decline.

After Anton and Itra finish nearly licking the pan clean, they move from the table to the living room. Anton pulls the envelope out from his jacket pocket.

"Are we ready to call Kaly and Leon?" Iana asks.

"Sure, it's a little after midnight," Danae says, pulling out her phone. She sets it up on a few books so Leon and Kaly can see them and the envelope. Leon's phone only rings twice before his face fills the screen.

"Hey Leon, is Kaly there with you?" Danae asks.

"Yes!" Kaly calls out. "His big head is in the way." Leon grins and sits back. They're on the couch in her home office, dressed for bed.

"Is that the envelope?" Leon asks, leaning forward again, blocking Kaly. She pushes him aside so she can see too.

"Yes," Anton says, moving it so they can see it better in the camera.

"Wow," Kaly expels in a whisper.

Itra and Danae lean forward, but neither reach out to touch the parchment.

Anton turns the envelope over, popping the wax seal on the back. He slowly slides out a gold card. He turns it over. There is an image of a maze with a circular center.

They all lean forward, nearly colliding heads and blocking Kaly and Leon's view.

"What is it?" Kaly asks.

"A drawing of a maze," Anton answers.

"Iana, can you take a photo and send it to Kaly?" Leon asks.

"Sure." Iana snaps a few pictures. "That's odd." She takes a few more before she turns the phone towards Itra and Danae. The photo is not of the maze but of three words in royal blue cursive: *Do you remember?'*

Itra and Danae gasp in unison.

Itra whispers, "I remember everything."

"Me too," Danae answers.

"Everything?" Anton asks.

Itra and Danae nod.

Iana smiles with relief and turns the phone towards the camera so Leon and Kaly can see the message. They cover their mouths in disbelief.

Anton moves the card around, seeing if the light changes the maze.

"It's the hedge maze in the center of the castle," Danae says. "I saw this image in a book I picked up in the library. The same message was on the card I found in my pocket after my ejection. Kaly, can you run the image through the university archives?"

"No problem, if you can get me a clean copy," Kaly answers. "Also, I came across something odd I need your input on. The Monday you two were missing, a student showed me a site called the *Wandering It Press*. I received a message from Unis Beard, the editor, the same afternoon requesting an interview. He has left three messages over the last two weeks, but the last one was super creepy. He said he knows Ember and her weakness."

Itra and Danae stiffen.

"Unis Beard was at the press conference after we returned and asked about Ember," Itra says.

"He was physically there?" Kaly asks in alarm.

"Yes, Ermal said he was a conspiracy theory blogger with an ear at the police department," Danae says. "He's attempted to text Itra and me, but we blocked him as spam."

"Didn't you get new numbers with the new phones?" Leon asks.

"Yes," Danae answers. "We wondered how he got our new numbers. We haven't even given the phone numbers to other friends yet."

"Itra?" Leon asks. "Can you ask Ermal to investigate this guy for harassment? I'll have an old buddy of mine run a background check on him."

"I'll call Ermal as soon as we hang up."

"I promise we'll call or text if any new developments occur," Danae says.

Leon and Kaly say, "Us too."

They all take a collective breath after ending the call.

"I'll make another pot of coffee," Iana says. Itra follows her out of the room to call Ermal.

Anton hands Danae the card and steps out to answer a work call.

Danae attempts to scan the image on their scanner connected to their printer. The scanned image of the maze finally remains a maze on her third try. "Got it!" She blows up the image, prints a few copies, and sends the image file to Kaly and Leon.

She joins Iana and Itra at the kitchen table. They each take a copy of the maze and study the pattern. Itra traces a route in pencil, and Iana folds hers in half twice to examine a fourth of the maze at a time.

Danae looks at the image as one piece and tries to recall the book she found. She places the original next to the scanned image and notices one fine detail. "There are stairs in the center."

Itra and Iana's heads pop up and say in unison, "What?"

She holds up the original, pointing to the center. "Do you see the shading here and here?" They each take turns looking it over again. Itra shakes his head, but Iana nods.

"You mentioned the hedge maze had a small figurine in the center, right?" Iana asks, handing Danae the original. "A shaded outline outside the stairs shows a small figure, right here." She points out the shaded area.

Danae traces the outline of the shaded area, turning the paper vertical.

"Does it look familiar?" Iana asks.

Itra and Danae nod.

Danae makes a few additions based on what she can recall from the window.

She texts Kaly and Leon. *"We found shaded lines showing steps in the center and an outline of the stone figure in a shaded area just off-center."*

Kaly responds. *"I got a hit when I ran it through the database. Check your email."*

"Checking now, thanks!" Danae responds. She opens her email, but she has two unread emails. "Itra, I have an email from Unis Beard. Did he email you as well?"

Itra checks. "No new emails."

Anton walks back in, joining Iana at the table.

Danae opens Kaly's email first. An image almost identical to the maze with a description: *King Agron's ship manifest, a hand-drawn map of the canals or shallow reefs near the Bojana River.*

"Who is King Agron?" Danae asks, turning the phone to the group. "Where is the Bojana River?"

"Queen Teuta's husband," Anton answers. Danae and Itra stare at Anton. He shrugs. "While Iana was up cooking, I went down a Google rabbit hole with the keyword Teuta."

"Sorry, my history of this region is rusty. What was Queen Teuta, queen of?" Danae asks.

"Illyria, pre-Roman invasion," Anton says.

Itra asks, "What else did you uncover in your search?"

"An old tale of Queen Teuta's treasure that was buried by her servants before she conceded to the Romans," Anton says. "The servants were killed to keep the location a secret."

"Dark," Danae mumbles.

"Buried treasure," Anton adds with a mischievous smile.

Iana elbows Anton in the side. "We've had enough crazy adventures." She points to Itra. "No wild ideas, brother. Do you hear me?"

"Fine." Itra hands Danae's phone back with the map app zoomed in on the Bojana River. "It runs into Lake Shkoder and the Adriatic Sea in northern Albania," says Itra.

"So, all of this points back to here, or near here," Danae says.

"So far." Itra holds up his scanned copy of the maze. "I've found four connecting routes that all lead back to the middle. I think there is a fifth, which would tie into the ember archways."

"If you end up with five," Danae says, "we'll include that as a connection, but will wait before jumping forward. Iana, do you see any other shading?"

Iana nods. She points to each corner and a spot near the middle. The letters are a hair darker than the shading. Iana has four words written on the page next to the figurine's traced outline: *Illyria, Ember, Time*, and *Fire*. "I think the middle word is *Dawn*," Iana says, writing the word.

"Really?" Danae says. "Anton, do you want to go down another keyword rabbit hole?"

"Sure. Can I borrow a tablet?"

Itra heads to the office to retrieve their tablet.

"The subject line for Unis's message says Urgent: Uncover the Maze," Danae says. She opens the email from Unis Beard in a ghost browser when Itra returns. She reads aloud.

"Illyria ember in time, light the fire at dawn, o'treasure of mine. Illyria ember in time, discover the haze the army will raise, o'treasure of mine. Illyria ember of mine, uncover the maze you will embrace all treasures in time."

"Keyword search void," Anton says.

"We need answers," Danae says, "not riddles." She forwards the email to Kaly and Leon with the added details of the shaded words found in the maze. Kaly calls immediately.

"Hey, Kaly. Sorry, we've kept you up with all of this!" Danae puts her on speaker.

"I live for this," Kaly says. "Don't apologize. I checked my university email spam folder and found four emails from Unis Beard. All with cryptic messages, stating that time is near with separate verses of the poem you forwarded. Itra, did Ermal have any intel on this guy?"

"I left a message with Ermal," Itra answers. "He hasn't called back."

"I've requested some archived documents not in the digital library related to Queen Teuta," Kaly says. "They should be ready by this afternoon my time. I read summaries for a few of these when you two first returned from the Castle of Teskom. Nothing stood out, but I recall one with a notation about the river. I will keep you in the loop."

"I think it's time we try to talk to Uncle Vincent again," Iana says. "Maybe the same message will make him remember."

"I hope it works!" Kaly says. "I'm fairly sure sleep is a no go for me tonight, so keep me updated. I will update Leon in the morning."

"Sounds good!" Danae says. "Thanks, Kaly!"

20

"Can you text the image of the phrase to my phone?" Itra asks Iana. She nods. "I want to confirm the image comes through as the phrase and not the maze." He holds up his phone. "It works."

"Do you think I should send this to Uncle Vincent?" Iana asks.

"Worth a shot, right?" Itra asks.

Iana sends the image with no explanation. "Done."

"What's done?" Danae asks, as she tops off the other mugs with fresh coffee.

"Iana sent the image to Uncle Vincent."

"I hope Vincent opens that while sitting down." Danae jokes.

Itra and Iana exchange a worried glance.

Itra calls Uncle Vincent.

"Hello?" Vincent answers.

"Hi, Uncle Vincent, it's Itra."

"Who died?"

"Nobody died."

"Then call me in two hours. The roosters aren't crowing, and neither am I," Vincent says before hanging up.

"Ha! I love that old man," Danae says, laughing at the expressions on Itra and Iana's faces. "He has a point. It's only four in the morning stateside."

Itra's phone rings, making each of them jump.

"Hi, Uncle—"

"What do you think you're up to, Itra?" Vincent shouts, making Itra move the phone from his ear to speaker mode.

"Do you remember the castle?" Itra asks.

"It's my blood right. What is so important?"

Itra says, softening his tone, "We woke you because Danae and I found the castle two weeks ago, but lost all the memory of it until a few hours ago. We have so many unanswered questions."

"Very well. I need to make a pot of coffee and take Duke out for a walk. Call you back in twenty minutes." Vincent hangs up before they can ask anything else.

Itra's phone rings twenty minutes later, almost to the second.

"Hello," Itra answers.

"Duke, sit," Vincent says. "Hi. Where do you want to start?"

"Can you tell us when and how you found the castle?" Danae asks.

"Who is us?"

"Itra, Danae, Anton and me, Iana," Iana says. "We've got you on speakerphone."

"Fine," he says. "I was 22 the first time I found the ember archway. I was setting up a few traps for eels in the lake. It was before dawn to avoid the Communist patrols. I tried to return home but lost my way. Clouds covered the moonlight and the stars."

Itra and Danae nod.

He continues. "In the darkness, I stumbled out near the patrols and two charged towards me. I came around a bend in the path, and I ran under the archway."

Itra and Iana's faces lose all color and shift in their seats.

"I turned back to see the five archways, and the sun cresting the eastern ridge. The pursuing officers were gone, but my forward momentum did not stop until I was standing in the middle of a clearing, trying to catch my breath. I turned in a circle, waiting for the command to stop or else. But I only heard the song of a morning dove and, to my surprise, saw a castle." He laughs. "I may have shat a little because I thought I was staring at a secret Communist bunker, and my death was certain." He coughs.

Iana and Itra shiver.

"I heard Teuta humming before I saw her walk into the clearing. She raised her hands in surrender and spoke my name. 'Vincent, I mean you no harm. Ivan is waiting for you. You are safe.' You can imagine my confusion. I was looking at a tiny fairy-like woman in the woods outside an enormous castle after being pursued by communist officers, and she knew my name." He sighs. "We stood there for probably three full minutes, neither of us moving an inch. I finally asked her how she knew my name. She said, 'Vincent. Your father is Gjeto. You are a descendant of Ivan and live in the village of Ivanaj.' She had me. I didn't understand how to respond, so I followed her to the castle. She floated up the enormous stone steps."

Vincent laughs at the memory. "I never asked who she was until we were standing at the entry. She said, 'I'm Teuta, follow me.' I followed her through the conservatory, the dining hall and into Ivan's study. There, Ivan explained the bloodline to the castle and the knowledge it held. He looked so much like an older version of your father, Itra and Iana. I wasn't sure how not to believe him. He gave me a book with the word 'Open' on the cover, served me tea and sandwiches that appeared out of nowhere, and he left. I read the book cover to cover."

"We're not only descendants of Mui." He pauses. "Iana and Itra, we are the protectors of knowledge. The book details our family tree, the origins of the castle, the technology, science, the evolution of life beyond humans, including artificial intelligence, and so much more." He pauses again when Duke barks in the background.

"Beyond…" Itra says, starting to speak, but Iana kicks his shin under the table and cuts him a look. He winces and shrugs.

"I stayed for four days during my first visit," Vincent says. "I scared my parents to death when I walked through their front door. They thought the communists captured me, or worse. I tried to tell them about my discovery but was hushed and sent to my room. When I woke the next day, I couldn't recall a thing. I found a card years later in a cave behind the house, wedged beneath an ember rock. The message said, 'Do you remember?' and I nearly jumped out of my skin when the memories flooded back. I planned my route, and crossed under the ember archway, without alarming any officers. I spent two weeks reading everything I could, and I received my gift. I can translate, speak, read, and write any language at first sight or sound. Itra, did you receive a gift?"

"Yes, I can now identify any species, plant, or animal."

"Did you mention Danae crossed over with you?" Vincent asks.

"Yes," Danae says, "but it booted me out via a protection portal into a dark stairwell."

"That you crossed and entered at all is surprising. We thought only the bloodlines could cross under the ember archways. I'm sure you made Ivan and Teuta very uneasy."

"Well," Danae says, biting her lip. "I have recently discovered that…"

She looks at Itra and blushes before continuing.

"… I may be carrying part of your bloodline."

"You're pregnant!" Iana exclaims.

Itra stands so fast he knocks over his chair. "Are you?"

"I've only taken a home test, but it came back positive. I would say I'm barely five weeks or so."

Itra pulls her up out of her chair and into his arms, smothering her face in kisses.

"I love you too," she laughs. "Now put me down."

Iana is crying but smiling. She hugs Danae almost as tight as Itra. Anton gives Itra the biggest guy hug Danae has ever seen.

"Vincent, are you there?" Danae asks.

"Yes," he sniffles. "Itra, I wish your dad was there to share the joy in the room right now." They all swallow hard.

"We miss him too," Iana says through tears.

Vincent clears his throat, asking another question. "Itra, did you see any caverns during your brief visit?"

Itra explains their visit to the present cavern, and Elis and Iana's ability to hear them, and vice versa.

"Remarkable," Vincent says. "I made four total trips to the castle, at the ages of 22, 29, 36, and 45. My memory of the experience would fade within a day or two. A small twinge of feeling like I was forgetting something, or a strange dream, would make me wonder. The only way to trigger my memory is a message written on the parchment from the castle. What I can't figure out is how Iana and Anton remember what you told them?"

"We were hoping you could answer that mystery," Iana says. "They had no memory until the delivery of the maze."

"What maze?"

"The card has a drawing of the hedge maze in the inner courtyard of the castle," Itra says. "Iana tried to take a photo, but only the words showed up. Fancy ink or tech, we're guessing?"

"I've only received words, never drawings. There was a book in the library with the maze—"

"I found that book during our visit," Danae says. "It was blank, minus the middle page with the map of the maze. Have you ever walked the maze during your previous visits?"

"I never found an entrance," Vincent says. "During my third visit, I spent three days and nights searching for a way in and never found it. On the fourth day, I found Teuta shelving a book in the library. When I questioned her about entry to the maze and its purpose, she quoted a rhyme. 'Illyria ember in time, light the fire at dawn, o'treasure of mine.' Ivan even quoted the same rhyme. And on my last visit, I didn't even see Teuta or Ivan."

"We found five words in the drawing of the maze: Illyria, ember, time, fire, and dawn," Itra says. "And Danae received a poem with that verse and more from a man, Unis Beard. Does that name sound familiar?"

"No, I can't recall anyone with the name Unis Beard," Vincent says.

Danae recites the entire poem for Vincent.

"Uncover the maze, huh?" Vincent asks.

"When Danae and Itra were missing, the police recovered ember shards," Iana says. "Why do they heat for some and not others?"

"Ember shards are slivers of her essence. They are conductive to those that protect and serve."

"The police ran diagnostics on the shards," Itra says.

"What did they say it was?" Vincent asks.

"The tests came back inconclusive."

"Where are the shards now?"

"Still in police custody, I presume." Itra answers.

"Any chance you can retrieve them?"

"Maybe, why?" Itra asks, raising an eyebrow to Iana and Danae.

"We must protect Ember," Vincent says. "The shards are powerful, and if in the wrong hands could be dangerous."

"Dangerous!" Danae blurts out. "We haven't told you about the man that attempted to kill Itra." She explains the encounter with Don, including the echo of his warning and the snakes.

"The description of the attack feels oddly familiar," Vincent says. "Danae, what are the chances you are related to Zeus or Princess Danae?"

"It's possible," Danae says, "but it's a very slim chance. My brother Leon confirmed that we have some Italian and Greek roots."

"I'm not sure," Vincent says, "but I think we need to return to the Castle of Teskom soon. The attack in the clearing sounds like an image I saw in the cavern of the future. This is the first part of several events that leads up to a battle between the true protectors and rogue descendants."

"What do you mean, battle?" Iana asks. Anton stiffens.

"I'll explain more once I arrive."

"How do we keep our memories?" Danae asks.

"We will need to read that message about every ten hours," Vincent says. "So we don't forget until we get back to the Castle of Teskom."

"Done," Danae says. "I'll set up a group message every ten hours with the image from Iana's phone."

"See you soon, and Danae, congrats," Vincent says before he ends the call.

Itra stands too anxious to sit. Anton's brows are creased with worry and Iana's eyes water with fresh tears.

"Sorry," Danae apologizes, "this is all very overwhelming." She reaches to comfort Iana, who is wiping a few tears away.

"Overwhelming, and you're pregnant, Danae."

"We'll see next week," Danae says. "Home tests can be wrong. I made an appointment with the clinic to confirm. Itra, can you sit in on the conversation with Kaly and Leon just in case I miss something?"

"Only if I get to break the news that we're expecting to Leon."

"Fine, but you'll feel the wrath of that announcement when he realizes I was pregnant on the hike when we were missing and attacked."

"Ugh!" Itra groans. "That balloon of joy just burst."

Itra hugs Iana before running down the drive to open the gate.

Anton nodded his farewell in silence.

"Is Anton okay?" Danae asks, hugging Iana.

"I think he'll need more time to process this news," Iana says. "I'm sure the silence will only last past the driveway before he explodes into twenty questions."

"Call us when you get home," Danae says. Iana nods and hops in the passenger seat.

Itra closes the gate and nearly sprints the length of the drive. He scoops up Danae with glee. "I can't believe you're pregnant, and you didn't tell me first." He takes her straight to the bedroom.

"Itra, I love you. I know this is most likely the worst timing for this, but I'm over the moon, excited."

"The timing is always right for us to start our family," he says, kissing her stomach. "I love you, too." He tickles her side. "Are you ready to call Leon?"

She laughs and squirms away from him. "Are you?"

"Hell, yes, I impregnated—"

Danae throws a pillow at Itra's head.

21

Danae is waiting on the porch when Anton's SUV pulls down the gravel road.

"Itra, they're here," Danae hollers.

"I'll get the gate," Itra shouts back, tying off the last vine in the garden.

Anton pulls in and Iana, Anton, Leon and Vincent disembark with a chatter of hellos and hugs.

"The office is set up for Leon and Vincent, and the spare bedroom for Iana and Anton," Danae says, waving them towards the house.

They follow her inside.

Leon waves Danae over after setting down his bags. She walks over and bumps her hip to his. He opens his suitcase. "Kaly sends her love!"

Danae laughs. Sitting on top of the clothes are a few pregnancy books covering yellow bags. She shakes her head. "There are at least a dozen bags of butterscotch chips. How Kaly managed to cram this many into your luggage is sheer talent?"

Leon smiles and shrugs.

"Kaly had two more finals to administer this week?" Danae asks. Leon nods. Danae sends Kaly a quick text. *"Hey Kaly, thanks for the goodies. Sweet treats will be ready on your arrival in a few days."*

Kaly responds, *"Yum! See you soon!"*

Leon pulls a folder from his backpack. "Kaly also provided copies of her research of Teuta," he says. "And the vessel found with the human eye, tooth, and a shard that could be ember."

Danae takes the folder and thumbs through the papers. She sighs. Leon and Danae join the others in the kitchen.

Danae winks at Itra. He nods in response. "I moved up my doctor's appointment by a few days to confirm our status," Danae announces as the group settles at the kitchen table. "We're officially expecting our first child."

Another round of hugs and congrats to Itra and Danae occur before they settle back at the table with tea and coffee. Vincent clears his throat. They all turn to face him.

"I received this from a small, dark-haired flight attendant while exiting the aircraft." Vincent opens his jacket and pulls out a royal blue envelope from his inside pocket. The gold cursive handwriting reads *Welcome Back.*

Vincent places the envelope down with great care. "I looked down at the envelope for just a second and I looked up to find a blonde flight attendant." He chuckles. "I'm pretty sure the blonde thought I was about to ask for her number."

Leon laughs. "I was a few people behind him when we were exiting the plane. I saw you pause. I thought maybe you were hitting on her, too."

Vincent winks. "The switch was fast. I barely had time to blink. I nearly forgot about it, but then I found it again while looking for my glasses. Shall we open this now?"

Vincent waits to make eye contact with each of them for approval, and they nod. He opens the envelope carefully. A familiar gold card inside has a three-dimensional drawing of a dome; it is a bird's-eye view. The three stained glass panels are not odd from this viewpoint.

"It's an eye!" Danae points to the drawing. "The dark glass is a pupil and the three pieces curve, connecting to make the shape of an eye. This is the glass dome in the dining hall, right Itra?"

"Maybe," Itra says. "We only saw this looking up from inside during the day and only a portion from the terrace level. I do remember three oddly angled pieces of colored glass. Vincent?"

"The dining hall holds many tales of the future, present, and past. The murals on the floors and the glass domes all have a significant purpose, not art for the sake of art. I believe this is the dining hall, but it is not exactly an eye. Can I get a pen and paper?"

Danae steps out to the office to grab a pen and paper—her computer dings with an email. She wiggles the mouse. Another email from Unis Beard. She almost moves it to the spam folder, but the subject line stops her cold. *FW: GLASS DOME*. "Seriously?" she grunts.

"What is it?"

Danae jumps. Itra is standing in the doorway.

She shakes her head. "Unis Beard." Danae points to the screen.

"Did you open it?"

"No."

Vincent and the others are now hovering behind Itra.

"Is everything okay?" Iana asks.

"I received another email from that blogger Unis Beard," Danae says. "But look at the subject line. Is our house bugged?"

Leon springs into action. He pulls a device from his bag that looks like a smartphone. He immediately sweeps the house. They stand frozen in place, watching him methodically move from room to room.

"It's clear. No bugs."

"Did Ermal come up with anything on Unis Beard after the first email?" Leon asks Itra and Danae.

"Nothing good," Itra says. "He said one of the lab techs found broken glass two days ago near a ventilation window. The evidence bag with the ember shards was the only item missing from the lab. He also said the station received frequent calls from different people, including Unis, trying to find out more about the shards. They have moved Unis to suspect number one. He was already on the list of people to question."

"Danae, humor me," Leon says. "Open the latest email from him on a ghost browser."

She hovers over the email. "Ready?"

Leon leans over her shoulder and nods. She opens the email.

112

Danae, if you're reading this, please don't delete till you read everything.
The Castle of Teskom is real.
Mui was real.
Ember provides energy to parallel universes.
You're related to Zeus.
Please come before the haze.

"Seriously?" Danae asks, pounding her palm on the desk. "I think he's been listening in on our private conversations."

"Can I check your phones?" Leon asks.

Itra brings Leon their phones. He scans each of them. They are clean, but then he checks the application settings.

"Gotcha! Mother F! Where did you buy these?" Leon says, disabling both phones, removing the SIM cards, and taking the batteries out.

"At the shop in town," Itra says.

"Both phones had a listening app running in the background," Leon says. "Did either of you accept a system update notification in the last few weeks?"

"Yes," Itra and Danae say in unison.

"Itra call Ermal. Unis has been listening and likely recording all of your conversations for the last few weeks. Danae, please forward the emails to Ermal." She nods. "I'll run a system check on your computer to make sure nothing is afoot there. And I need to check everyone's devices."

Itra steps out to make the call to Ermal from Leon's phone. Danae moves away from her desk to let Leon take over. She's physically trembling. The intrusion on their privacy is shattering. She doesn't realize she is crying until Vincent hands her a hanky.

Itra comes back in with a grim expression. "Ermal is sending an officer over to pick up our phones as evidence for the tech team to trace the origin of the update message and, hopefully, narrow down a location. But they've confirmed Unis Beard is definitely an alias, no known records or accounts with that name."

"My buddy," Leon adds, "hit the same roadblock with Beard's alias, but he confirmed his site, *Wandering It Press*, was created six months before you two went missing. It's registered to a God of Water, LLC." He hands their phones over. "These three are clean, but do not accept updates until they catch this guy."

"Vincent," Danae says, "you asked for a pen and paper before this all went sideways. Can you show us what you were about to explain?"

"Sure," Vincent answers, taking the pen and paper from the desk to the table where they left the drawing. They follow him and take their previous seats.

"The castle rotates with the sun during the day," Vincent says. "The domes also rotate in a few rooms, one being the dining hall. The mural on the floor shows the Bajze valley with no homesteads or roads, only a forest untouched by settlers. There are three colored panels: purple, orange, and gray. The panels' alignment changes the mural on the floor with tech not invented here in our timeline but from the future. It's a similar concept to showing a black light on a surface."

He draws two other shapes using the three oddly angled pieces. "I have seen the mural change only twice, once to our current timeline showing the various homesteads, highways, and town buildings. The other was to a similar time, but the structures and forest looked different. The building materials looked more futuristic, less square, more spherical, and the trees and plants looked healthy and thriving. I found several references in the library to a world that adopts a low carbon footprint in the early 1900s, changing the landscape. Communism never happens—the big natural trees and vineyards remain."

"I never understood that logic," Danae says. "Why did the Communists destroy mature trees and vines?"

"They 'claimed' it was for firewood to make bread," Iana answers.

Vincent nods. "I think the card's drawing is documented, by my grandfather, Gjon, in the library. He referenced a battle scene on the mural with lakeside attacks and soldiers on horseback from the mountains."

Iana centers the card under her phone. Danae catches a slight change with the flash of her camera. "The image remains the same." Iana turns her phone to the group.

Danae stands quickly, killing the lights. "Iana, turn the flashlight app on and scan the image." Her light hits the card, and the image transforms into a battle scene.

"That's it!" Vincent exclaims. "It's been almost twenty years since I last saw the text, but that is the battle scene Gjon describes."

"Elis asked for three specific markers two days ago," Iana says, turning to Anton. "Did you see what he drew?"

Anton nods. "I took a picture because I thought it was an odd, random pattern." He swipes through the images. He pauses and turns his phone to Iana before showing the others.

"It's identical to the card," Itra says. "How?" He holds the drawing next to the phone.

"After we received the message with the maze," Iana explains, "Elis has been more creative. He's spent more time drawing, building complex buildings with his Legos and magnet toys. I've also overheard him talking to himself, always quietly, when I'm near his room. I never made out the words, only the noise of talking."

Itra shows Vincent and Leon the image of Elis's drawing next to the card.

"How?" Leon whispers.

"My goodness," Vincent says, fighting a yawn. "I'm going to go lay down for a few hours. Jet lag is real, folks." They watch as he exits.

"Do you think he is okay?" Danae asks the group.

"I think I know the feeling," Leon says, yawning loudly. "Kaly mentioned that Vincent's house was clean from top to bottom. The aroma of cleaning chemicals still hung in the air when she picked up Vincent and Duke. I don't think he has slept much since your first call. Anyway, I think I'll turn in for a few hours, too."

Leon messes up Danae's hair as he stands to leave the room.

"Will you ever stop?" she chides. "We're grown, you know!"

"Old habits never die, sis." Leon laughs mid-yawn and leaves the room.

"Do you think we could ask Elis if Teuta has a message?" Danae asks.

Anton and Iana look at each other for a few seconds.

"I need to call to check in with him soon," Iana says. "I'll try to ask a few questions related to the dome and Teuta."

Anton rises, taking Iana's hand as they head to the front porch.

"Are you feeling, okay?" Itra asks when they're alone.

"We're fine," Danae says, placing his hand over her abdomen. "A little overwhelmed thinking of the conversations that creep Unis Beard listened to. Why would he target us?"

"No idea," Itra says. "I promise, we will press charges against him or whoever sent the listening app to our phones."

Danae nods. "Help me with dinner?"

Itra nods, clearing the mugs from the table.

Anton and Iana sit quietly together on the front porch for several minutes, processing the conversation with their son Elis.

Iana asks Anton, "How do we explain this to Itra and Danae?"

"Honesty is our only option. We can't sugarcoat this just because Elis is a kid. It may be accurate, it may not, but they deserve to know either way."

Iana leans on Anton. "How are you doing with all of this? Facts and figures are not part of this equation."

"It's hard to put into words. The logical side of my brain is screaming bull shit; however, the other side is saying… believe!" Anton sings the last word.

Iana chuckles. "Do you believe?"

"In life after love?" he says, grinning. "Yes, I do."

"Cher? Really?" Iana teases.

Itra pops his head out the front door. "Did I hear Cher? Danae is setting the table. Are you two hungry?"

Iana stands stretching. "Yes to Cher, and yes to hungry. What's for dinner? It smells delicious."

"Pulled pork, roasted sweet potatoes, green beans, cornbread, and warm chocolate chip cookies for dessert," Itra says. "And I'm about to wake Leon—so if you want a serving, come quick—it's his favorite."

"Too late, bro," Leon yells. "The smell of Danae's pulled pork would wake me from my grave!"

"You can wait two minutes for the others!" Danae scolds Leon as he reaches for fresh cornbread.

"What's all the fuss about?" Vincent emerges from the office, his white hair standing on end.

116

"Nice bed head, Uncle Vincent. Dinner's ready." Itra pats Vincent's head as he ambles towards the dining table.

"Beer, water, or lemonade?" Danae asks, as they all sit down.

The men shout, "Beer!" making them roar in laughter. Danae looks to Iana; she is rolling her eyes at their antics. Danae sets down beers for the men and lemonade for Iana and her.

"Enjoy!" Danae laughs as the others watch Leon. He catches on that he has everyone's full attention. His plate was full, brimming over the edges. He sets down the serving tongs for the pork, raising his fork and knife in surrender.

"And I thought Itra's ability to eat surpassed all," Anton says, letting out a whistle. "I stand corrected."

Leon eats his way through any chance of leftovers.

After dinner, they sit down in the living room except for Leon and Itra. They're laid out flat on the floor, groaning in a too-full moan of discomfort.

Anton and Vincent clink mugs in a toast-like motion before sipping their coffee.

Iana and Danae smile, taking in the scene.

Leon half sits up. "Did the police pick up the phones?"

"Yep," Itra groans.

"How was Elis this evening?" Danae asks Iana.

Iana and Anton make eye contact before she speaks. Danae notices the worry on her face and braces for the news.

"Elis had a lot to say." Iana stops to clear her throat. "This evening, we questioned Elis about his drawing. His response was startling. Elis said he drew the colors after Teuta showed him in his dream. The next night, he dreamed of a painting with ships on a sea, a castle, and soldiers with swords riding horses coming down the mountain. He ran out of paper to draw every scene."

"He also mentioned a message from a man," Anton says. "Elis said he knew it wasn't his Uncle Itra, but it sounded like him. He asked Elis to warn his family of a battle that would happen soon. And this is where we nearly fell out of our chairs. Teuta sings him to sleep nearly every night, but the only line he can remember is

'Illyria ember in time, light the fire at dawn, o'treasure of mine. Oh, Illyria ember in time.'"

"Itra," Leon says, "what kind of game are you playing and with a kid, no less?"

"Hang on," Anton says, "Elis hasn't seen Itra since the Sunday after they returned from the castle. And we pressed him further, asking him how he spoke to Teuta and this man. Elis said he could only hear the two of them."

"I believe he is sincere," Iana continues, "and he believes that he speaks to Teuta and this man. My guess is that they're communicating the same way Itra and Danae spoke to me while they were at the castle."

"Itra, you went back?" Leon stands over Itra.

"No," Itra states.

"It's not this Itra," Vincent says. "It's the other one."

"Other?" Leon asks.

Vincent raises his arms, motioning to Leon to sit down. "There are two portals to other similar but different planes of this universe. Itra exists in each plane. The Itra communicating with Elis is not our Itra but an Itra from one of the parallel planes."

"Why would they speak to a kid and not to the adults of this family?" Leon asks.

"We're busy in our everyday lives," Vincent says. "We may miss the signal or cue to listen to their call. Iana, when you heard them call out, you were focusing on Itra and Danae, right?"

"Yes, I was praying for any sign that they were alive and safe."

"Children are more perceptive to the other realms of physics," Vincent states. "They pick up a sixth sense without often trying. It's not a new theory or fact. Just more complicated."

"What are the five dimensions?" Anton asks.

"Communist dimension," Vincent says, "is our timeline and history of Roman Empire, the Ottoman Empire, World Wars and Communism. The Ottoman dimension is a timeline where the Ottomans maintain their control and reign over all of Europe. The Revolutionary dimension is the ideal timeline for peace-loving hippies. They've never fought with any enemies: no wars, empires, or communism. It is true, world peace does exist. They also adopted a green Earth movement back in the early 1800s. The Past and Future dimensions are what they sound like. If you are from the communist portal, you can only go to the future or past in your dimension."

"Did you ever try the past or future portals?" Itra asks.

"No," Vincent says, shaking his head. "But your grandpa, my father, Gjeto with my mom did travel to the future once. Mom was pregnant with your father."

"Wow," Danae whispers, wrapping an arm around her middle.

"Vincent, what can you tell us about the battle?" Iana asks.

"Only what Gjon described in the mural," Vincent responds. "Like Elis's dream, there were ships on the lake and soldiers on horses coming down the mountain towards the castle. The archives may have additional details, and the significance of the maze is still a big mystery for me."

Leon's phone rings. "It's Kaly," he says, holding up a finger. "Hey, Kaly."

"Leon!" Kaly yells into the phone. "There is a large man following me on campus! He fits the description of Don!"

Leon stands. "Campus police? Have you called them?"

"I called you on first instinct," Kaly says. "There is an event in the quad this afternoon. They are likely tied up with the crowd there."

"Can you get to your office?" Leon asks.

"I'm almost there," she says breathlessly. "But Leon, there is no exit from my office."

"Stay on the phone with me," Leon says. "Danae's calling the campus police. How far away are you?"

"Running up the steps now," she says. The keys jingle through the receiver. Leon hears the click of her lock. "I'm in, but I can hear him running towards my door."

"Put me on speaker!" Leon shouts. "Hi Professor, thanks for agreeing to meet with me last minute."

"No problem. Take a seat." Kaly plays along, moving the chair out. "How can I help?"

"Can you help me understand my final paper?" Leon stumbles for a conversation topic that may be believable.

"Sure, the topic you selected was on modern-day heroes with old-world similarities," Kaly responds, keeping her tone light. "Is that correct?"

"Yes," Leon stalls looking at Danae. She holds up two fingers. "It's two minutes for the hero—I mean, the presentation is two minutes."

"Yes, a two-minute synopsis of your paper," Kaly says. "I think I hear; I mean, I think I have examples to show you." Kaly opens and closes a few drawers. She whispers, "Campus police are in the building."

"Great, is there someone at your door?" Leon asks when Danae nods.

"Leon! It worked. I could see his shadow at my door, but he moved away once you started speaking. I'm going to talk with the officers and have them walk me to my car. I'll call you once I'm secure in my vehicle."

"Thank God," Leon whispers, kneeling on the floor. "Love you, woman."

"Talk soon," Kaly says before ending the call.

Danae kneels next to Leon. He is shaking.

"What does this guy want?" Danae asks the room.

"How did he even find Kaly?" Iana asks.

Anton's posture goes from slumped to upright and rigid.

"Is Elis safe?" Anton whispers.

Iana slaps Anton's knee. "Don't scare me like that!"

"He's right," Itra says. "If this guy found Kaly across the pond, are any of us safe?"

Vincent clears his throat. "What if Don is short for Poseidon?"

22

Kaly calls Leon from the car. "Campus police didn't catch him, but they got a clean shot of him on a security camera near the building. I emailed a copy to Danae for her and Itra to confirm if it is the same whack job that attacked them."

Leon relays the message to Danae. "She's opening the email now," Leon says. "I don't want you to head to the farmhouse alone. Can you stay with a friend in town tonight?"

"I'm actually heading straight to the airport," Kaly says. "I made my last class submit their final papers online. I can grade my last two classes on the flight over and submit their final scores shortly after I land."

"We believe it's the same guy," Danae says, showing Leon.

"Did they say the same guy?" Kaly asks.

Leon switches his phone to speaker mode. "Yes."

"What does that mean?" Kaly asks.

"Vincent made a suggestion we can't ignore," Danae says. "He thinks Don may be short for Poseidon."

"Poseidon, God of Water," Kaly mumbles. "Why come after me?"

"Whoa!" Iana exclaims. "Repeat that again?"

Leon catches on a second later. "Kaly, you said Poseidon, God of Water?"

"Yes," Kaly responds.

"Unis Beard's blog is registered to a God of Water, LLC," Leon states.

"What the actual…" Itra mumbles.

"Can you send us your flight information?" Leon asks.

"Sure," Kaly says. "My first flight isn't for another two hours. I'll try to find what I can on Poseidon from our database before I board."

"Kaly," Leon says, taking the phone off speaker. "Valet the car. I don't want you isolated in the parking garage. I don't care how much of a rip off it is."

"Yes, sir, love you too," Kaly responds. "I won't be there till late tomorrow. Try not to climb the walls. Maybe you can help pull some weeds in the garden?"

Leon barks out a laugh. "I will be fine. Stay safe and no headphones until you're on the flight!"

She laughs. "Good night, see you soon."

"Night," Leon says. He plugs his phone into the charger in the kitchen, taking a cookie from the pan. "Ouch!"

Danae laughs. "Grown man, ha, you saw me pull them out of the oven five seconds ago."

"Anyone up for a round of dominos before calling it a night?" Leon says, trying to sound calm.

Danae shakes her head. His need for a diversion is evident.

Vincent asks, "Are you any good?"

"He thinks he is," Danae says, "but he gets distracted."

"Hey, that's not true! You beat me once, and only because you and Kaly were playing two against one."

Anton responds, "I need to make a few calls and send some work emails. Iana is rather good. Just a warning."

"I will keep the refreshments coming." Danae winks at Iana because she has played her in chess and dominos. She will smoke Leon.

Itra says, "And I'll call Ermal to give him a head's up on Kaly's encounter with Don. And check for any updates or developments with the case."

122

Three hours later, they all say good night. Leon grumbles about his massive loss to Iana. Vincent laughs because he is the one who taught Iana to play as a child. According to Vincent, Itra could never sit still long enough to learn. Danae has no problem believing that.

23

By late afternoon, the following day, Itra and Danae's living room is covered in stacks of papers and a small whiteboard is leaning against the wall.

"After a full day of research, the only lead we have is the shards?" Danae asks Iana pointing to the whiteboard. "The description of the shards in the vessel found with the eye and tooth matches the shards the police found, and we held." Iana shrugs. "Maybe Kaly will have come up with something new?"

Leon enters the living room covered in dirt. "Kaly just texted. Her last connecting flight has been delayed for mechanical issues. It could be nearly midnight before she takes off."

"So, another day gone," Danae says. "No new answers, just more questions."

"I do have some good news," Leon adds, stepping back in from the kitchen and drying his hands. "Your garden is weed free!" He gestures to dirt still clinging to his clothes. "If no objections, I am calling dibs on the shower."

"Thanks brother," Danae says, nodding her head towards the washroom. "All yours!"

Vincent and Itra come in a few minutes later. They ran to town to get a few items from the store.

"Vincent," Itra says, "may have found a clue."

"I ran into my cousin's son in town," Vincent says. "Forgive me, I don't recall his name, but he said his father has dementia and has been attempting to leave the house. He shouts to the neighbors. 'The battle is near!' Coincidence? I don't think so."

"Do you think the message you and Elis received are the same that this old man is shouting about?" Danae asks.

"I do," Vincent says. "I am making an executive decision. We are heading to the Castle of Teskom tomorrow afternoon. Agree?"

"Agree on what?" Anton asks, entering the living room.

"That we are hiking to the Castle of Teskom tomorrow afternoon," Itra says.

"Disagree," Anton responds.

"Anton, wait a minute," Iana says. "We have spent every waking minute of the day trying to connect the pieces and are still no closer to solving this puzzle. We need answers and the only answers are at the Castle of Teskom." Anton looks at the mess of papers and the whiteboard before looking at Iana.

"Why is this our puzzle to solve?" Anton asks.

"Teuta has been talking to our son, Anton!" Iana states. "We are knee deep in this, like it or not."

Anton sighs. "For the record, this is a terrible idea!" He turns abruptly, leaving the room.

"Sorry," Iana apologizes, following Anton out to the porch.

Itra and Danae turn to Vincent.

"He'll come around," Vincent says, "but we need to be prepared for just about anything. This does come with risks if this battle is truly near."

"Did I hear battle?" Leon asks as steam follows his exit from the washroom.

"Yes," Danae says. She fills him in on the conversation.

"What if Don is there and ready to attack?" Leon asks. Danae shivers.

"A risk we have to plan for," Itra states.

They spend the next hour going over the topography of the Mokset hills and the best route to reach the archway. Anton and Iana rejoin the group. Anton is still visibly agitated, and Iana is somber. They all turn in early after prepping the hiking gear after dinner.

The others are asleep when Kaly arrives just after two in the morning.

Leon explains that the group has decided the only answers are inside the Castle of Teskom. They plan to hike up the following afternoon and cross under at dawn.

Kaly nods in response with no objection.

"Are you okay?" Leon asks.

"Just exhausted," Kaly says.

Ermal pulls into the drive just as they are about to hike over to the Mokset hills. His arrival sends a wave of worry over Danae. She has been trying to shake off a feeling of doom all morning.

Ermal hops out, grinning from ear to ear. "Unis Beard is in custody. He's not admitting to the listening app. But he admits his source provided intel for the contents of the email communications he has been sending over the last few weeks. We charged him with harassment with harmful intent. I have a feeling the evidence we collected from his place will provide a few more charges."

"That's great, Ermal," Itra says. "But you could have just called."

"Dude, I took your phones, remember?" He moves to the back of his vehicle. Danae notes his apparel; he is in hiking gear. "And if you think I'm coming to look for your ass again, you're wrong. I have a few days of comp time to burn, thanks to some recent overtime." He winks. "I brought my gear, food, and water. Plus, a police radio and sidearm, just in case we run into trouble." He pulls out his pack.

Danae laughs. "I need to tell the neighbors we're going for another hike—this time with a cop—and don't expect us back for a week." She jogs over to the fence to talk to Mira and Franc.

Leon and Ermal shake hands, and Leon introduces Kaly. Then Iana introduces Vincent to Ermal.

"Are your parents well?" Vincent asks.

Ermal nods. "Doing good. My parents moved to the city near my sister three years ago."

"Are there any old-timers left up here?" Vincent asks, shaking his head.

"A few," Ermal laughs. "But mostly the stubborn ones."

Vincent laughs.

Returning from the neighbors, Danae asks the group, "Okay, are you ready?"

Anton's head is buried in his phone, but otherwise, their response is forward motion towards the gate.

"We plan to hike to the clearing near the giant old fig tree," Itra explains to Ermal. "It should take around two hours, maybe longer, with Vincent."

Danae's mind wanders back to the clearing and the attack.

"You are a million miles away," Iana says.

Iana's statement breaks Danae's thoughts. "I'm here," she says. "I can't shake the worry. How is Elis?"

"He is beyond distracted with grandma and grandpa." Iana loops her arm through Danae's.

"And how are you doing?" Danae asks.

"I'm coping. The worry never goes away, just increases tenfold. And you? Any morning sickness?"

"No actually," says Danae. "I have more energy than usual after starting the prenatal vitamins. Is that normal?"

"My grandmother gave me a useful note when I got pregnant with Elis. There is no normal pregnancy. It varies from woman to woman." She looks at the pace of their male companions. "If Itra starts his rapid pace, I'll remind him to slow it down for you and Vincent."

Danae laughs. "Itra has a few concerns of his own. I'm not sure he'll be in a hurry to face that clearing again. The attack from Don was very real. We do not wish to repeat that adventure."

Kaly falls back in step with Danae and Iana. "Do either of you get a feeling that we're being watched?"

Danae nods. "I feel like I could crawl out of my skin."

Iana shudders.

They walk in silence past the first row of homes before the road turns from gravel to grass. Anton falls back, taking a business call just before the path narrows to a game trail between large boulders and thorny plants. Navigating the terrain is slow and methodical to avoid any turned ankles or snags from shrubs. Vincent, surprisingly agile, keeps pace with Itra, Leon, and Ermal.

The definition of the path later widens into an old road. They pause, sipping water, waiting for Anton to catch up. The sky is clear, allowing a stunning view of the valley below and the layers of mountains to the east.

"It sure is pretty," Vincent says, placing his water canteen back in his pack.

"Iana!" Anton calls.

"We're around the bend," Iana responds.

The worried expression on Anton's face when he moves into sight makes Danae stiffen. Iana notices the grim look, too.

"What is it?" Iana steps closer to Anton.

"Snakes! I saw at least twenty, maybe more." Anton shakes his legs, looking wildly down around his and her feet.

"We haven't spotted a single snake," Itra says with concern. "Did you notice what color they were?"

"Dark, maybe grey, mostly," Anton says, fidgeting from side to side.

Ermal and Itra make eye contact before moving past Anton.

"Are they venomous?" Anton asks.

"Could be," Danae answers. "I think they're checking."

Leon, Kaly, and Vincent move around Anton to look down the trail for Ermal and Itra. They part ways quickly as Ermal sprints up the path.

"Move!" Itra yells, running behind Ermal.

"I take that as a yes to venomous," Leon says, taking Kaly's hand.

They hustle behind Ermal and Itra for another ten minutes. Vincent has lost pace with them.

Danae calls ahead, "Itra, wait for…" She takes a deeper breath. "Vincent."

Itra jogs back. "Danae, keep moving. I'll find Vincent."

His panicked expression tells her 'this is not a drill'. Danae moves without hesitation. The nice wide path abruptly stops near a few rocky boulders, slowing their progress, but allowing enough time for Itra and Vincent to rejoin the group. They're all breathless after climbing the last boulder onto a rise of the ridge. An anxious

Ermal is first on his feet, but Leon grabs Ermal's pack, gesturing for him to sit, tossing Ermal's water bottle towards his head. Ermal catches the bottle with a wicked grin.

"Itra, what did you see?" Leon asks.

Itra and Vincent join the group overlooking the rocky path. Itra takes a long swig from his water bottle. "Vipera ammodytes, otherwise known as a horn viper. They are rare in Albania, but they are deadly, venomous snakes. The evidence suggests that the number of snakes could be close to a dozen or more."

Iana, Kaly, and Danae eye each other and shiver.

"The number of snakes makes it unsafe to make camp," Itra says. "We all may need to enter the castle, bloodline, or not." He looks at Vincent for his opinion.

"We can try," Vincent responds. "I have no idea how the archway will react to Leon, Kaly, Ermal, or Anton."

"Itra, the report of the snake skins found after your return, has made the rumor mill in town theorize about an old omen," Ermal says. "Did you know that the people abandoned Bajze because of snakes?"

"Twice, actually," Vincent says. "And a third time because of heat. A mural of the snakes invading Bajze is in the future cavern stairwell in the castle."

Danae stands to stretch.

"Danae, are you okay?" Itra stands to check on her.

"Just a cramp. I need to walk it off." Danae paces back and forth. A light over the next ridge catches her eye. The sun is still up, but the glow is like a spotlight moving to stay in her line of sight. Itra follows her gaze.

"Holy hell," Itra whispers.

Leon catches their fixed gaze. He stands, moving to Danae's side. "What do you see?"

"A spotlight is following my movements." She walks two steps to her left, back to her right. The light follows.

"I don't see a light," Leon says.

The conversation catches the group's attention. They stand facing the ridge above. Iana, Vincent, and Itra all point as Danae walks back and forth. The others shake their heads.

"Is it the ember archway?" Danae turns to face Vincent. He is grinning ear to ear.

"Teuta, you are clever," Vincent responds.

The group spins, expecting to see Teuta. He laughs. "She is using the reflection tower to say hello." Vincent raises his arm, waving back up towards the light. He snaps his pack into place, taking the lead as he climbs up the next boulder.

"Wait," Itra says, scrambling to secure his pack and follow Vincent. "How do you know it is, Teuta?"

"On my second visit," Vincent calls over his shoulder. "Teuta used the reflection tower to blind the communist soldiers when I made my way down the hill back to the valley. She told me it's useful for defense and offense when needed. One story written before the Ottoman Empire in the library tells two tales. The light will follow a mark, sending an 'all clear'. The defensive tactic would send pulses of blinding light to any approaching intruders. If she is following Danae, it's an 'all clear'. Clever, right?"

"You could see it?" Anton asks Iana helping her up the next boulder.

"Yes. It was like a spotlight on Danae as she moved from one side to another."

Leon clears his throat with a loud, "Bull shit!"

"Leon, language!" Kaly scolds.

"Danae," Leon says. "I can see the next ridge. There is no light coming from up there." He points up. "It's just the sun in the sky."

"Get a hold of your manners, brother," Danae says. "Doubt is not a shade that suits you."

"I saw the snake skins but not the light," Ermal says, patting Leon on the shoulder.

The group continues moving up the ridge—with no further comments from Leon. The path widens again over the next ridge. Itra and Danae recognize the path to the old Mokset Castle remains. The sun is slowly descending as they take the ancient stone steps to the old communist bunker centered on the rise.

"This is or what was Mokset Castle," Itra announces to the group as he removes his pack to stretch.

The dusk light offers a bright, unobstructed view of the Albanian Alps, an outline of the Montenegro mountains, and the lake, with the sun glittering on its surface.

"My backyard never looked so stunning," Ermal says in surprise. Itra and Danae grin at each other as they take in the faces of the group. Iana and Anton are beaming, slowly turning, taking in the view. Vincent sits quietly on top of the round bunker, eating a snack, taking in the setting sun over the lake.

Leon and Danae make eye contact. His expression turns from cold to warm.

"How do you like the view?" Danae asks, walking up to him.

"It's something." Leon deflects an honest answer. He takes out his phone, snapping a few shots of the surrounding landscapes. His eyes go wide when he reviews a shot. "Danae, what is this?" Leon turns the phone towards her.

She smiles in recognition. "The ember archway."

"You're kidding," Leon says.

"Nope!" She waves to Itra.

Itra walks over, grinning at her expression of triumph. "Do you have a believer?" he asks. Danae turns Leon's phone towards Itra; he glances at the photo, looking from her to Leon. "The ember archway!"

Itra's baritone voice carries over to the group—they gather around Leon's phone to see the picture.

"Which direction is this?" Ermal turns, scanning the area. Leon looks defeated before pointing to the north. "Did you take this?" Ermal asks. "I don't see it. Itra, do you?"

Itra hands the phone back to Leon. Itra places his hands on Ermal's shoulder, turning him slightly west, pointing with his other hand. "Just to the right of the large boulder. Do you see it?" Ermal leans forward, following Itra's finger.

"Holy shit, it's real!" Ermal exclaims.

"Yes, my friend." Itra slaps Ermal's back. Anton approaches with a gaze of wonder. Itra points in the same direction for Anton.

"Wow," Anton mutters.

Vincent chuckles. "Who knew we had some serious doubters on this venture?"

Iana and Danae raise their hands before bursting into laughter. Leon, Anton, and Ermal turn, glaring at their outburst.

"Sorry," Danae says, trying to rein in her laughter. "But I should've snapped a photo of your faces." She mocks changing her smile to wide eyes and a mouth hanging open. "It was classic." They attempt to scowl back, but they end up laughing too.

"Where's Kaly?" Iana asks.

"What did I miss?" Kaly peeks out of the bunker.

"Just a chance to see Leon put his foot in his mouth," Danae teases. "Did you find anything interesting?"

"It's too dark to make out much," Kaly says, pulling a spider web from her ponytail. Iana squints, looking Kaly over. "What? Do I have a spider on my head?"

"Have you always had a grey patch in your hair?" Iana steps closer to Kaly.

Kaly pats her head and nods. "My grandmother called it a kiss from my ancestors. I normally braid it in with my other hair." She pulls her hood up before rejoining the group.

"We're losing daylight, let's get moving," Itra calls out, taking his and Danae's headlamps out before securing his pack. The others do the same. "Vincent, do you still think we need to wait till dawn to cross?" Itra leads the group away from the old bunker.

"We got an all clear from Teuta. I believe it should be okay to cross when we get there, but crossing with all of us—maybe? Hell, I don't know."

"So, are we going to be teleported somewhere?" Leon asks.

"Well, technically," Vincent says, "the Castle of Teskom is a dimension of its own."

Leon turns back to Ermal. "Are you down with traveling to another dimension?"

"Seize the day, seize the dimension." Ermal shrugs.

"Anton?" Leon asks.

"I hope to decide in the next few minutes," Anton says. "Elis is my primary concern. Will we come out?" He squeezes Iana's hand with the last question.

They nearly have to crawl through a low narrowed path of thorny bramble bushes. Itra pops up, leaving Danae eye level with his behind. She snickers in appreciation before pushing through the last bush. He catches her snicker, reads her coy smile, and laughs with a little booty shake.

They wait for the group to stand upright on the path, removing the bramble, snagging their packs and clothes.

"Kaly?" Leon turns his face towards her light. "Is there a scratch along the side of my cheek?"

"Your face is bleeding."

"Thought so," Leon says.

Iana goes into mom mode, pulling the first aid kit from her pack. She cleans the scratch, placing two butterfly adhesives over the cut. "It's clean, but it may leave a tiny scar."

"One of many," Leon and Danae say in unison.

The last light of dusk dissipates, making the glow of their headlamps dance across the boulders ahead. A rise of anxiety flutters in the pit of Danae's stomach as she maneuvers towards the last curve of the path. An ominous feeling grows with each step.

Itra reaches for Danae's hand. "Geez!" She jumps and stumbles. Itra steadies her.

"Oops, sorry," he apologizes.

"What's all the commotion back there?" Vincent calls over his shoulder.

"I accidentally startled Danae," Itra calls. "We're good."

"Good, my ass!" Danae mutters. "You nearly gave me a heart attack." She shines her light in his face. The guilty grin lets her know the 'sorry' was just words. "Can you even pretend to be sorry?"

"Danae, may I please hold your hand?" Itra gestures with a sarcastic bow.

Danae frowns but laughs, extending her hand. "Why, yes, kind sir?" He kisses her hand, pulling her in for an actual kiss.

Walking by with Iana, Anton mutters, "Get a room."

Smack

"Ouch, what was that for?" Anton rubs the back of his head.

Iana laughs. "I tripped."

"We made it," Vincent calls out.

The ember archway glows, the light dances like a lit fireplace just behind Vincent.

"Vincent making his age look undefined and our slacking redefined," Danae says. "A bunch of thirty somethings to be out hiked by a sixty-year-old, sad."

Vincent laughs and turns to walk under.

"Wait!" Leon calls.

Vincent stops.

"If Don is on the other side of this thing," Leon says, pointing towards the archway. "Should we go in armed to be safe?"

"If Don is on the other side—game over," Vincent states.

"Hang on," Itra says, raising his hands in peace. "The signal from Teuta earlier convinced Vincent this was an invitation, not war. I believe we can cross as a group." Itra turns to Iana and Anton. "Anton?"

"My gut says all for one, one for all," Anton responds.

Vincent nods and takes two steps back, disappearing under the archway.

24

"Where did he go?" asks Ermal, stumbling forward.

"It's okay," Itra says. "But to be on the safe side, cross with a bloodline. Leon and Kaly hold Danae's hand as you go under. Anton, you can hold Iana's hand. Ermal, you can walk with me."

Leon and Kaly take Danae's hands. Kaly is trembling; Danae squeezes her hand. They step under the archway.

Crunch

They find themselves alone in the clearing for a few moments before Anton and Iana emerge.

"Where's Vincent?" Iana asks, looking around the clearing.

"Nature called." Vincent's voice carries from a distance. Itra and Ermal enter as Vincent emerges from the bushes.

Ermal draws his gun.

"Whoa! It's me, buddy!" Vincent freezes, with his hands in the air.

Itra lowers Ermal's arm. "It's cool, my friend."

Ermal exhales. "Sorry." He slides his sidearm back in the holster.

"No worries, good reflexes," says Vincent, chuckling.

"Wow," Iana says, looking beyond Vincent to the dark outline of the Castle of Teskom.

Danae elbows Leon. "Point one, Danae. Leon zero."

Leon grumbles, "Ha, ha."

"Vincent, do you want to lead the way?" Itra asks.

"Sure thing. It feels like I was here yesterday."

Vincent moves with a youthful bounce.

Itra and Danae follow his lead down the same path they took only a few weeks ago. She catches Itra's glance as she turns to look back towards the furthest archway. He turns to follow her line of sight. The shiver that has been running down her spine seems to have moved to Itra. He tries to shake it off, but she feels his anxiety. They let the group continue a few paces ahead.

Danae asks, "You good?"

"Surreal," Itra answers. "You?"

"Same, minus the nonstop spine shiver," she answers flatly. Itra moves her in for a long-overdue hug. She settles in her favorite nook of his shoulder. She inhales after a long sigh. "Ugh!" The smell of garlic is strong, almost overwhelming. She tilts her head back to look up at him. "Are you wearing garlic?"

He playfully smashes her face down towards him, laughing. "I finished my last one right before we walked through. Natural pest repellent, and if vampires were waiting—I was ready." He releases her after kissing her forehead.

"Vampires, really?"

"You never know, my dear, we are dealing with ancient gods and fairies." He takes her hand. "Why not vampires?"

She pushes him away, wrinkling her nose. "You may have to sleep in another room tonight."

They take one last look at the archways before catching up with the group.

"My phone has no signal or map," Leon growls, shaking his phone. "And the camera app is missing. Useless!"

"Dude, we are all in the same boat." Ermal shows Leon his phone.

"Cell phones didn't exist during my last trip here," Vincent laughs. "You're worse than teenage girls without Snapgram for a day."

"It's Snapchat and Instagram," Iana says, laughing.

136

Vincent shrugs. "Who cares? I don't."

"Holy…" Anton whispers as the group comes to the base of the first giant step.

"How did we do in our description?" Danae asks Ermal.

"Dead on," Ermal nods. "Seriously, I remember stories of Mui, but never thought I would stand in a fairytale."

Iana cranes her neck, looking up at the large wood and iron door ahead. "Where is the red-carpet welcome? The door is closed. Wasn't it open when you two arrived?"

"It was open for us," Itra answers. "Vincent, was it ever closed for you?"

Vincent shakes his head. "No, always open."

Panic shoots through Danae's limbs, springing her into action. She climbs the first step. Itra helps her up the next few steps. The group follows their wordless actions.

"Open says me," Danae says breathlessly after reaching the top. "Opens says me!"

Itra takes her hand, repeating her words. "Open says me." A whoosh of air makes Itra and Danae step back into the group.

The interior is still dark, minus the glow from their headlamps. Vincent moves between them, blocking the threshold with his back to the entry.

"I suggest we move through the conservatory to the dining hall." Vincent holds his arms out wide.

"Come along." Vincent walks into the conservatory. The light from his headlamp creates alien-like shadows from the plants. He marches to the climbing vines and finds the door, pushing it open with ease. "This way!" He waves his arm towards the entry.

Itra and Danae shuffle in the front foyer last after staring down at the entry mural with their headlamps.

"The blue and gold waves seem to roll and crash in the light," Danae whispers.

Itra tugs Danae's arm. "We should go." She follows him.

Vincent walks to the door on the adjacent wall to the left. Iana, Kaly and Danae follow. The door shuts with a loud thud behind them. Kaly jumps.

"Where are we going?" Iana asks.

"It's a new door for me," Danae says.

Vincent adjusts his headlamp to shine on one of the pictures hanging in the stone corridor. "Do you recognize her?" Vincent asks Iana.

"Is that grandma?" Iana asks.

Vincent beams. "Yes! She was pregnant with your father when this photo was taken."

"But it's in color?" Danae asks.

"Funny thing about having access to a future portal," Vincent says, winking at Danae's dumbfound expression. They carefully examine each photo in the corridor.

In the dining hall, Ermal and Leon scan the floors, walls, and glass dome with their headlamps. Itra removes his pack, leaning it against the wall near Anton.

Anton sips his water, taking in the room.

"Are you okay?" Itra eyes Anton's stooped posture.

"Ask me when we're in cell range again or in roughly nine months when your parental instincts are clanging loud and clear."

"Elis is safe and sound with your parents," Itra says, patting him on the back. "We'll only stay long enough to get answers."

A door on the opposite wall opens, causing Ermal and Leon to take a defensive stance. A glow hovering over a figure's head startles Leon into action. He moves instinctively over to the door Vincent led the ladies through. Ermal's posture is rigid, with his hand resting on his sidearm. Itra and Anton creep closer to the room's center.

The light orb expands from the doorway to the center of the hall under the glass dome. They blink, taking in the hall. The door closes as the door behind Leon opens.

"What the actual—" Leon jumps.

"Oh good," Vincent says. "We have light."

Danae observes Ermal, Leon, and Anton's startled faces, staring up with a look of horror. "What did we miss?"

Anton moves quickly over to Iana, checking her over. Ermal and Leon stare up at the light and back to Danae like that's enough of an explanation.

"The light came from a person standing in the shadows of that doorway." Itra points to the closed door on the opposite wall. "The door closed right before you came back in the room."

Danae marches over and shoulders the door near Ivan's study, causing it to slam. "Honey, we're home. Teuta! Ivan! Come out now!" Her voice echoes back.

"I think mama bear is hungry," Iana whispers to Itra. He looks proud and concerned at Danae's forceful, take-charge attitude.

"They'll come when they're ready," Vincent says. "Teuta has never rushed greetings except for my first trip." He pulls a chair out and sits down at the large table. The sudden appearance of a proper steak dinner sizzles on a plate in front of Vincent.

"How?" Ermal asks.

"Really?" says Anton.

"Steak?" Leon bolts for the table and takes a seat.

Iana covers her mouth in surprise.

"Ember," Kaly whispers.

"Go ahead." Itra pulls out a few chairs. "Maybe our host will appear after we eat." He raises his eyebrow with a smirk in Danae's direction.

"Fine!" she says. Itra pulls a chair out for her. "Itra?" Her gaze is fixed on the floor beneath the chair. "It's the battle scene."

"Hell," Itra whispers.

"Sit, order, and eat," Vincent mumbles between bites. "We can discuss this after dinner."

Vincent's dessert arrives with flare, literally, a flaming torte. This startles Leon mid swallow, causing him to cough up a bite of steak.

An hour later, Ermal, Leon, and Vincent are nearly passed out on the floor, groaning with how full they are while Anton and Itra are still sitting upright but have loosened their belts twice. Iana and Danae walk the hall, checking the mural from every angle.

"Is Kaly okay?" Iana whispers to Danae. Danae looks from Iana back to Kaly's rigid posture sitting at the table focusing on the chair in front of her. Her hood is still up and tied.

Danae shrugs. "Jet lag?"

Iana shrugs, too.

The room goes quiet for a few beats. Then a soft snore from Vincent creates a ripple of giggles.

"I see the chef has completed the task," a voice says.

The group's laughter quiets at once.

Danae spins around looking at each door. "Teuta, is that you?"

"Hi, Danae," Teuta says, tapping Danae's elbow.

Danae jumps. "Holy hell! Where did you come from?"

"Oh, the answer to that is too long for this evening. I'll show you to your rooms. Come along." Teuta twirls in place, waiting for the group to stand and gather their packs. Vincent wakes and smiles from ear to ear.

"Hey there, Teuta!" Vincent grunts while Ermal and Leon help him to his feet.

"Hi, Vincent," Teuta sings back with a trill that sends a shiver up Danae's spine. "It's been a long time. I see you received my all clear message."

Vincent nods.

"No sleeping drugs this time," Itra says. "We have questions that need answers. Is Ivan here?"

"He'll be here by morning. I've notified him of your arrival. No drugs, I promise."

Teuta twirls away after passing out small, square stones to each guest. She demonstrates how to turn on the light. She holds the stone between her thumb and ring finger, then taps the center with her index finger. The stone illuminates and hovers above her head. She snaps. The stone goes dark and lands in her open palm. She repeats the process and waits for them to mimic her actions.

They follow Teuta, moving to the rear of the conservatory. The landing is on fire.

Danae stops. Itra runs into her. She points down.

"It's not an actual fire," says Teuta. She laughs and dances in the space to show them it is safe to enter.

Danae feels a tremble through Itra's hand to hers. She squeezes his hand before they follow Teuta upstairs. The illusion of fire dissipates. They pause to peer out the window on the first landing. The hedge maze is still intact. Anton and Iana linger for a while, taking in the shadows of the maze in the moonlight.

Vincent clears his throat on the second-floor landing, garnering their attention. "The first door on the left will be Kaly and Leon's, first door on the right Ermal's, fifth door on the left Itra and Danae, the seventh door on the right Anton and Iana, and eight doors down on the left is my suite."

"The bell will ring for breakfast," Teuta chimes. "Rest well, talk soon." Her light goes dark. She vanishes.

"She is odd and ridiculously small," Ermal says. "I'm going to check out my room." He laughs. "I feel like we're in school with a curfew."

"Tomorrow," Vincent says, "we'll meet here after the bell. Good night, kids."

"Night!" they call back as he turns, not waiting for a discussion.

Iana and Leon come into Itra and Danae's room to check out the wedding portrait. Leon physically shivers at the sight.

"Sis, this place gives me the creeps," Leon mumbles.

"I didn't hear any creepy comments at dinner," Danae teases.

His stomach makes a loud growl of satisfaction.

"Never complain about the food!" He rubs his stomach. "Rule number one."

"Danae," Iana says, "the picture is of you, but the hairline on Itra is off. Maybe the alternate dimension has better nutrition, reducing his hair loss."

Itra walks in. "What's this about my hair?"

"Or lack thereof," Leon teases. He steps out of Itra's reach. "Good night!"

They call in unison, "Good night."

Iana points out the hairline difference to Itra. "You may be right, Iana, but we may have more important battles to win than my fading hairline." Iana and Danae harden at the mention of battles. "Hey, now, I didn't mean to imply anything." He hugs Iana. "We'll get you and Anton home as soon as possible. I promise."

"Make sure you can deliver before you promise." Iana hugs him back, whispering, "Good night, you two." She pecks them on the cheek before joining Anton in the corridor.

Itra and Danae respond, "Good night."

Danae closes the door, their old pack hanging on a hook. "Itra, look!"

She dumps out the pack: two headlamps, her hand-drawn map, and their useless phones. Danae sighs. Itra reaches for her, pulling her in with a firm embrace.

"We did the right thing coming back." His tone is less positive, more question. She pulls back to look at his face.

"You doubt this decision?" she asks. He shrugs. "I won't argue. The fear factor is at a seven out of ten." She leans nose to nose with him, meeting his eyes.

He swiftly lifts her into his arms, moving them towards the shower—her attention occupied by his mouth and wandering hands. She doesn't recall undressing as the water hits her back. Itra turns off the shower and reaches for her towel.

The high-pitched giggle of a child echoes in the room.

"Is that Elis?" Itra tosses her the towel, bolting out of the shower towards the bedroom door.

"Itra, you're naked!" She watches his perfectly bare butt run out the door. She quickly covers herself in a towel before following him. Her legs are still jello, slowing her pace.

Their room is empty, but the door to the adjoining room is open. She quickens per pace to a jog. She passes the wardrobe wishing she had time to dress. Her towel vanishes and she's fully dressed in sneakers, stretch pants, and a long-sleeve tee-shirt, and her hair is dry. She enters the lounge fully clothed.

She gasps. Itra, clothed, is talking to Elis over the balcony.

"Danae! Go wake Iana and Anton," he says, keeping his eyes on Elis standing in the middle of the hedge maze.

Danae sprints from the room, releasing her loudest whistle and shouts, "Iana, Anton!" She hears a door open; it's Anton. "Come now! Elis is here!" He registers what she says, but Iana bolts past him.

"Where?" Iana yells.

Danae points to her suite. She runs in. The sight of her son nearly makes Iana go over the edge, but Itra holds her back.

"Elis!" Iana's voice trembles. "How did you get here?"

"Teuta sang me a new song." He sings with a clarity that instantly chills them to the bone. "Illyria ember in time, light the fire at dawn, o'treasure of mine. Illyria ember in time, discover the haze the army will raise, o'treasure of mine. Illyria ember of mine, uncover the maze, and you will embrace all treasures in time." He grins ear to ear at their open-jawed expressions.

"Elis," says Iana, her voice hoarse with tears. "How did you end up here?"

142

"Dreamland?" Elis shrugs. "I don't know, Mom. I was in bed at grandma's house. Teuta sang me the song, and I felt ticklish. And then Uncle Itra came out to say hi. Am I dreaming?" Elis yawns, stretching his arms overhead. "Mama, I'm sleepy. Can I sleep in your room?"

"Yes, baby, but we need to get you out of there first." Iana looks from Anton to Itra. "How in the hell do we get him out of there?"

"He's gone!" Anton yells.

Iana looks frantically around, shouting down, "Elis! Elis! Are you hiding?" She glares at Anton. "What do you mean, gone?"

"Elis closed his eyes, stretched, yawned and poof, he vanished." Anton rubs his eyes. "Are we dreaming?"

"Poof, Anton, poof?" Iana screams. Anton flinches.

25

Vincent joins them on the balcony. "We can check on Elis in the cave of the present." His voice is wary with worry and sleep.

"Now!" Iana takes Vincent by the arm. "I need to know right now that my boy is safe." Itra, Anton, and Danae follow Vincent and Iana out into the corridor.

A confused Ermal and anxious Leon are standing near their suite door. Danae shakes her head. She explains the event as they descend the stairs several stories down to the cave of the present.

Vincent clears the sleep from his voice. "Open says me!"

The air changes as the door opens. Iana bolts through and Itra sprints forward, reaching for her as she teeters near the open edge.

"Easy." Itra turns Iana to face the interior wall. They stand with their backs to the opening.

"Show us, Elis," Vincent whispers.

A close up of Elis, with his eyes closed, widens to show him half under the covers of a bed.

Anton mutters, "That's my mother's guest room."

"Elis," Iana cries. "Baby, are you okay?"

Elis stirs. He rolls over and mumbles, "Yes, mama." Iana collapses in a heap of sobs as Anton quickly takes her from Itra. "Shh, don't cry," says Elis, his voice filling the cavern again. She cries louder.

The image of Elis fades.

"Where did he go?" Iana urgently asks.

"It's normal for the image to fade," Vincent says. "We know he is safe."

Ermal taps Itra, gesturing with his head towards the opening to the cave. Ermal quietly asks, "Have you ever seen large ships on the lake before?"

Itra looks down at the lake. He can see the outlines of at least four large ships floating on the far side of the lake and a few smaller canoes following in their wake.

"Shit!" Itra exclaims. His outburst causes a stir of attention towards the view.

Danae gasps, looking down.

"That can't be good," Vincent states.

Leon looks down before stepping back quickly. "How high are we? Are those ships?"

Anton asks, "Did you say ships?"

Iana raises her puffy red eyes. "Ships?"

Itra nods.

"Leon," Danae whispers. "Where is Kaly?"

"In bed," Leon answers. "Years of sleeping next to this snore monster have made her a champ at sleeping through almost anything. I didn't even attempt to wake her when I heard you whistle in the corridor."

"You left your wife alone in a magic castle with enemies at the ready?" Danae points towards the ships.

"Well, now that you put it that way." Leon heads for the door, but it closes.

The shouts of confusion and shock quiet with the sing-song tone of Teuta. "It is time." They find Teuta near a new door on the side opposite from where they entered. "Ivan, along with a few other familiar faces, are waiting. Please follow me this way."

Vincent sends a calming look to their group, attempting to reassure them that this is a good thing. He is the first to follow Teuta. Obediently, they fall into line. Danae tugs on Itra's sleeve to pull his gaze away from the ships below. Her face creases with worry, mimicking his deep worry line between his eyebrows.

Teuta leads them down a curved stone corridor to another cave, with four people facing away. Danae recognizes Ivan almost immediately, but stops dead with an unobstructed view of a familiar backside.

"Itra?" she says. Beside her, Itra watches Danae's face drain of color before the four people in the center of the cave face them. He jumps back at his mirror image, who turns at Danae's call.

Itra is staring at himself.

"What's going on?" Itra asks, moving in front of Danae.

"I see the gang is almost all here," Ivan says. "Shall we begin?"

"We may want to start with introductions," Vincent says, stepping forward to greet Ivan with a familiar embrace. "My group has not slept yet." Ivan nods before stepping back to gesture to the three strangers.

"I'm Ivan. May I introduce Itra, Ana, and Gjeto?" The three raise a hand as Ivan calls their names.

Vincent steps forward. "May I introduce Itra, Danae, Iana, Anton, Ermal and Leon. And I'm Vincent."

Leon bursts out with a loud, "I'll be damned!"

Ermal calls, "I second that."

Iana and Itra move towards the strangers. The smiling man introduced as Gjeto looks no older than Itra.

Anton and Danae stand back, looking back and forth between the new Itra and Ana and their Itra and Iana.

Iana is the first to reach Gjeto. "Are you our Gjeto?" Her puffy eyes are filling with tears again.

Gjeto places a loving hand on her cheek to wipe her tears as he answers, "Yes, my Edona."

Iana gasps hearing her nickname.

Itra and Iana tackle him in a hug.

Danae moves closer to her Itra. The doppelgänger, Ana and Itra, watch the exchange with Gjeto while Vincent and Ivan huddle together in a quiet but intense conversation. Iana and Itra step back from Gjeto.

Iana motions for Anton. "Grandpa, this is my husband, Anton."

Gjeto grins, gripping Anton into a firm handshake.

Itra wraps his arm around Danae. "And this is my wife, Danae." Gjeto tilts his head to the side, looking her over. He takes her hand in his with a gentle shake.

"Do you know Zeus?" Gjeto teases. Leon and Danae stiffen.

"Just a coincidence, maybe?" Danae answers.

"Mui and Zeus said our lines would one day intersect," Gjeto says, nodding his head towards Ermal and Leon. Itra and Danae turn to make the introductions, but Gjeto beats them to it. "And you, Leon, are Danae's brother and Ermal, a school pal of Itra's." He says this with confidence. "Ermal, I believe your grandmother and I were classmates; her name is Beta?"

Ermal nods. "A small town, not too surprised."

Ivan clears his throat, and all eyes shift towards him. "This is the cavern of the future. We only know what it will show us. You've seen the incoming ships heading towards our shore as we speak. A battle has played out in pieces here in this cavern, but the ending has never been foretold. We've tried to document every detail in our library and murals, but today's message could bring something new." He turns, gesturing to the interior wall. "We are here. We are open. We are present."

The wall flickers like an old movie projector, fuzzy, and then clears to arrows raining down from the castle down to the lake, piercing the boats rowing to shore. A bright white light flips the scene to an army on horseback coming from the north and east. Ice and wind topple the riders from their horses. The scene drops into a major battle of swords near the ember archways. It pans over to a tiny figure near the archways. The figure extends their arm and points to a misty veil falling over clusters of people in blue tunics. A second image appears like a split screen, to a giant man with brown wavy hair holding a massive dagger lunging towards two shadowed figures.

The group reacts with a collective inhale.

Danae grasps Itra's hand in a tight grip.

The last scene shows the hedge maze and the figurine in the middle. The figurine suddenly animates and twirls, revealing stairs beneath before the cavern goes dark.

The energy escalates from stillness to mass conversation in seconds. Gjeto lets out a loud whistle, bringing the chaos back to order.

"Teuta, will you please show our guests to the dining hall?" Ivan asks.

She nods and heads to an open door. The doppelgangers Ana and Itra officially meet Iana and Itra as they climb the stairs immersed in conversation. Ermal regards the snake mural on the wall in the stairwell—Vincent winks back at him. Leon and Danae hang back.

"Can you find your way back to the room to fetch Kaly?"

Leon looks at the entry floor, the stairs, and the conservatory. "Head to the rear of the conservatory up the stairs and to the left?" Danae nods. He turns to jog away, but Danae pulls his arm.

"The castle rotates so your door may not be in the same spot," she says. He nods.

Danae is the last to enter the dining hall. She notices the table is set for twenty. *We are only a party of thirteen.* She surveys the hall for any new arrivals.

Anton chats with Iana and Ana. His expression goes from bewilderment to laughter.

Iana and Ana laugh as they finish each other's sentences.

Danae's Itra and his double are chatting about the other Danae. Danae's cheeks go pink as the other Itra talks about his wife with such love and adoration.

Ermal is at the table draining a pint of beer.

Vincent, Gjeto, and Ivan are missing.

Danae steps over to Itra.

"Where is Leon?" Itra looks around the hall.

"He left Kaly in their room."

Itra's double barks in laughter. "You sound just like her."

"Is your Danae's brother as dense as mine?" Danae asks, shaking her head.

"He is rather burly and snarky," Itra's double states.

Danae laughs.

The conservatory door swings open. Danae spins, expecting Leon and Kaly, but four unfamiliar faces emerge.

One is so tall, the group physically tilts their chins up.

Ivan walks over to introduce the group. "You're just in time. I'll start with the introductions. This tall man is our fearless guardian, Mui Junior." Ivan watches the group's jaws drop before continuing. "His sister Dita, a healer, and their cousins Geri and Nordi, illusion artists, all from the communist portal."

Vincent gestures to begin his introduction, but Mui Junior holds his hand up for him to wait. "Just call me, Junior. Please wait for further introductions. We have a few late arrivals that will join us soon. Ivan, a word in private?"

Ivan nods.

They step inside the library for privacy.

"How tall do you think he is?" Ermal asks Itra.

"At least seven feet?" Itra answers.

They exit the library, and Junior takes his place at the head of the table. His presence causes the rest of the lingering group to move towards their seats. The conservatory door opens again, and four men dressed in blue and gold battle gear enter.

Itra moves a protective arm in front of Danae.

Junior nods to the men.

Itra relaxes, but still sizes the men up with concern.

"Gentlemen, just in time," Junior says. "Please join us for formal introductions." The four men sit at the opposite end of the table from Junior. "My men were assembling the archers and prepping the towers. We expect the additional support units to arrive in the next hour. It's two hours until dawn. My first in command is Altin. His second is Glendon. Both are from the communist portal. Berto, our strategist is from the Ottoman portal, and Rudolfi, the weapons master, is from the revolutionary portal." Each of the men semi saluted at the call of their name. "Ivan, please introduce your guests to the group."

Ivan stands. "Ana, oracle, and Itra, species master, from the revolutionary portal. We have Gjeto, trap master, Itra, species master, Vincent, communication master, Iana, Anton, Danae, and Ermal are from the communist portal. And the former Queen Teuta is also from the communist portal."

The tiny figure that has always been Teuta is now a tall, curvaceous woman dressed in a formal blue and gold empire waist silk gown. Her hair waves down her back in thick raven curls, with a few curls pinned back under an ancient gold crown near her flawless tan face. She stands at the opposite end of the table from Junior.

Ermal lets out a low whistle of approval. Danae slides his fourth beer out of reach.

"Thank you, Ivan," says Teuta. "We are here at the precipice of a battle we've been anticipating for nearly nine centuries. To fully understand our enemies, we need to understand the stakes."

Teuta flicks her wrist, causing the lights to dim.

A three-dimensional image of a throne appears centered above the table.

The group gasps.

"The grounds here at the Castle of Teskom date to 1 BC. The knowledge, power, and technology held within these walls were bestowed to your bloodline to protect and serve by the goddess Ember."

The picture wavers to a woman inserting her hand into the ground and releasing a warm ember glow.

"The five ember archways are an extension of her hand and power. The archways provide a portal to five dimensions. Over the last century, the portals have earned the nicknames revolutionary, communist, Ottoman, past, and future."

A series of pictures of the caverns, the castle's construction in various phases, and the finished castle appear.

"The knowledge stored here will rival any historical collection across the world. We hold the keys to every past and current monarchy, ruler, dictator, government, and empire. The documentation here could easily rewrite history as you know it."

Danae raises her hand, but Teuta shakes her head.

"Why are we harboring knowledge?"

Danae nods.

"Balance."

Itra raises his hand.

Teuta shakes her head again. "Ember has given many protectors gifts that have changed the past, present, and future. The documentation here shares accurate descriptions of battles, war, and peacetime. We've created a narrative to only mock the gifts through fairytales, legends, or myths."

Another picture flares to life. Two men fly above the destruction of the Berlin Wall. Then another scene where a man appears on a beach, delivering a message to a woman and child, and disappears moments before bomber jets descended on Pearl Harbor. Another is a large hovering ship causing a tsunami soaking an entire village. The last is the destruction of an entire nation with the breath of a single person.

"Wow," Ermal stammers. Iana elbows him in the side. "Sorry."

"Ember has had four bloodlines serve as protectors to the Castle of Teskom. The battle we're expecting at dawn is from rogue descendants of the previous bloodlines. My lineage dates to the second bloodline of protectors. We served Ember for ten generations before we were overpowered by the greed for the knowledge stored within these walls, and we broke our vow to protect and serve. I know there are many tales of my treasures hidden somewhere in the Balkans, but the truth—Ember buried our treasure as punishment for our disloyalty. After the fall of my kingdom, I sought refuge here, begging for forgiveness. Ember assigned me as the eternal messenger and mark maker. I'm only allowed to leave the grounds for message delivery."

Teuta turns her focus towards Danae and continues. "Danae, your presence here is not by accident. You're a direct descendant of a previous protector, the bloodline of Zeus. The man you encountered with Itra in the clearing is Poseidon, who goes by Don these days. He is seeking vengeance for your ancestor's murder of his love, Medusa."

"Hold up," Danae stands. "If I am who you say I am, why was I booted from the castle?"

"Chapter Nine protects the current bloodline," Ivan answers.

"How did Poseidon find us in the clearing?" Itra asks.

"You were technically off the castle grounds when he arrived, correct?" Ivan asks.

"Yes, I ran under the archway to Danae and then we encountered Don." This news causes a stir of conversation.

"If the castle and grounds are only accessible by the archways," Iana says. "How are the rogue descendants arriving by land and water?"

"Over the centuries," Junior explains. "Ember has enchanted several items, now considered rare artifacts. Several of these have been stolen and never recovered. The energy stored in the artifacts could draw enough fuel to create a portal large enough for an entire army to get through, including ships."

The room falls silent.

Suddenly, Leon barrels through the door, red-faced and dripping in sweat. "She's gone!"

Every person stands in alarm at his loud entry.

"Who's gone?" Junior asks.

"Kaly, my wife!" Leon yells. "I've checked every room on the second floor."

<h1 style="text-align:center">26</h1>

Kaly struggles with her restraints, but her ankles and wrists are bound and tied together behind her back. It's too quiet and dark.

"Leon!" she screams, but she can't hear her own voice. *Am I deaf? Why would Leon just leave me?*

She rolls from her right side to her stomach. A cool dampness seeps through the fabric of her shirt, sending chills down her spine. *Where is my hoodie?* She attempts to bring her knees in close to her stomach but has to arch her back as the restraints bite into her wrists. The movement makes her head spin for a moment. After she catches her breath, she tries again and makes it to her knees. Years of yoga finally paying off with some flexibility in her shoulders, she finds a semi-comfortable position.

"Leon! Danae! Anybody?" She can feel the breath and vibration of her words, but no sound. *Why?*

A breeze tickles the back of her neck, and she feels the earth tremble under her knees. She looks for any sign she is no longer alone, coming eye to eye with a man. She flinches and blinks rapidly. He is kneeling beside her, grinning. The darkness makes it hard to see, but she knows in her gut it is Don.

He cuts the restraint binding her ankles to her wrists. Kaly rolls her shoulders in relief and immediately attempts to stand. She falls forward, unable to break her fall with her wrists still restrained. She panics, but Don catches her with ease.

Now standing face to face with Don, Kaly can clearly make out his features. His tan complexion, firm jaw, long narrow nose, brown eyes, and wild brown hair all look menacing but somehow handsome at the same time. She feels a pang of guilt for feeling any attraction to this psychopath. She tries to break free from his grasp. He shakes his head with a firm grip on her arms. He leans his forehead to hers, and the ground falls out beneath her. She screams, silently.

Kaly lands with a thud and coughs hard upon the impact. *I can hear!* She tries to assess up from down fighting a wave of nausea. She manages a position back up to her knees and takes in the surroundings for the first time.

A dim light hangs from the cement dome and a man, huddled in the corner, is smiling at her confusion.

"Ha!" he exclaims. "You have no idea where you are right now. Do you, Kaly?"

Kaly bristles at the use of her name. This is not Don. His stature is too small, and his voice is too high.

"Who are you?" Kaly asks.

"Unis Beard."

"But you're in jail. Is that what this is?"

"I wish!" Unis mutters. "Don took me and left me here."

"Where is here?"

"A bunker, but where is a good question."

Unlike other Albanian Communist era bunkers deserted on the hillsides and roadsides, Kaly notes that there are no lookout holes. This one is closed in, or maybe further underground than most?

"How long have you been here?" Kaly asks.

"Hours, maybe an entire night."

A door latch screeches in the small space.

Kaly and Unis cringe at the sound.

Don walks in with a woman. Her face veiled, but she is wearing a long flowy white gown, and her hair is loose with wild dark curls.

"Have you two formally met?" Don asks Kaly and Unis.

Unis nods.

Kaly glares at Don. "Where are we?"

"Mokset, Albania," Don answers. "When is the fun part? Any guess from the professor or the blogger?"

Unis and Kaly make eye contact before asking in unison, "When are we?"

"Poseidon," the woman says from behind the veil. "*When* will be revealed, when I find it necessary." She moves under the light, but the veil still hides her eyes. "I have chosen you two to bring down the bloodline of Mui and take back what is mine."

"And you are?" Unis asks with a sarcastic tone.

"Your death," she says with a malevolence that rattles Kaly to her core.

She gestures to Poseidon, and he holds up documents that were once in Kaly's pack. "It appears you have documents that may help your claim, but I can provide you one better." A worn document appears in her open palm. "Kaly, you will take these to your husband and convince him and Danae to leave the family ties of Mui's descendants and take back the Castle of Teskom."

"I will not harm Itra or his family," Kaly says.

The woman hands the papers to Poseidon and floats over to Kaly. "You will do as I command!" She clasps a chain around Kaly's neck.

Kaly tries to knock her hand away but freezes. Every muscle goes rigid. The woman steps back, and Kaly can feel her muscles release as if they were stone.

"Medusa!" Kaly exclaims.

"Very good, Professor," Medusa says.

27

"Kaly never arrived," Teuta says.

"What do you mean, Kaly never arrived?" Danae asks.

"The woman you brought under the ember archway was Pem, not Kaly," Teuta says.

"I think I would know my own wife!" Leon growls.

"Leon," Iana says, "her hair after the bunker."

"What are you talking about?" Leon yells.

"Does Kaly have a grey streak in her hair starting from the right temple?"

"No!" Danae and Leon answer in unison.

"When she came out of the bunker, I noticed it right away. She pulled up her hood and tied it. She said she had the grey patch since birth, something about a kiss from her ancestors." Iana shakes her head. "I'm sorry. I wish I had said something sooner."

"She left her hood up during dinner and didn't explore like I thought she would," Danae says.

"Who is Pem?" Anton asks.

"Pemphredo," Ivan answers. "She is one of the Grey Sisters, the betrayers of Medusa. Perseus persuaded the sisters to give up the location of Medusa."

"Where is Kaly now?" Leon asks.

"Where is Pem?" Danae asks.

"We don't know," Ivan responds.

Leon turns for the door, but it slams shut with force and locks. He turns, eyes bulging. "You're locking me in here when my wife is god knows where and Don is still on the loose? I don't think so!"

Teuta moves between Leon and the door, changing back into her fairy form. He only slows in surprise but doesn't stop until Junior bellows, "Enough!"

"We don't have time for hide and seek," Junior says. "Kaly can wait. We have a battle at our door."

"Like hell!" Leon charges the door but bounces off an invisible barrier. He struggles but can't break free. "Danae!"

"Let him go!" Danae begs.

"Can we please discuss this?" Anton asks, attempting to negotiate.

Junior ignores Anton and Danae. "Anton and Ermal, you'll leave in a few minutes. Anton, you're the keeper of Elis, an important descendant of the bloodline. Ermal, should no one else return, we'll need your full cooperation to make this transition for Anton and Elis."

"Please send Iana and Anton," Itra objects. "Elis deserves both of his parents." Iana is sobbing into Anton's arms. "Please."

Ana stands. "I'm here to fulfill any need of Iana. I have the gift of vision. I will share this gift with her as the goddess instructed, but she should be free to leave."

"Very well," Teuta says, walking back to her chair. The images overhead dissipate, and the light brightens in the space.

Leon is still struggling to break free, but he can't move in any direction.

Ermal stands looking wildly around from Itra to Vincent and back to Anton and Iana huddling together. Ana takes Iana by the hand. She whispers something so softly Danae can't hear over the curses Leon is muttering under his breath.

Iana and Ana touch forehead to forehead for less than a minute before they break apart. Iana looks over to Itra and Danae with fear-filled eyes. Itra jogs to her with his arms open.

"Itra!" Iana exhales loudly, hugging him.

Ana steps back, trying to give her space, glancing at Itra's double.

"Please come with us," Iana begs.

"What did you see?" Itra asks.

"Please trust me, brother," Iana says, leveling her tone. "We all need to leave now."

"Tani," Teuta sings.

Itra's arms are vacant. He spins wildly around, scanning the space. Anton, Iana, and Ermal are no longer in the hall.

28

Itra charges towards Teuta. The four guardsmen stand in defense. "Where did my sister go?"

"Stop fussing," Junior says. Itra stops mid-stride, turning to glare at Junior. "We don't have time for this. They're safely returned to their homes and are nowhere near the clearing."

"Was that necessary?" Itra says with his jaw clenching, causing a vein to bulge on his forehead.

"Yes," Ana answers. "Unfortunately, the gift of vision is complex. Iana will see flashes from five minutes and five centuries from now, all jumbled together. Her fear is genuine but complicated. It is not possible to train her before dawn."

Itra's furious glare turns on Ana.

"Then why bother at all?" Itra asks.

"Enough," Teuta calls. "They're safe, as Junior stated."

Gjeto stands, moving to Itra's side. "Itra, it's okay. They are together and near Elis."

The four guardsmen and Ana take their seats.

"The future cavern has shown us the coming ships, the riders from the north and east, and an enormous battle in the clearing near the archways. If the enemies destroy the archways, the Castle of Teskom will remain, but no one will return to their families or said dimensions. Do you understand what is at stake?"

Everyone nods, except Leon and Danae. Danae raises her hand. "What roles are Leon and I supposed to play in this battle?"

"Danae," Teuta says, "the child you're carrying is the first descendant from two bloodlines of protectors. The protection of this asset is second to that of the archways. Danae is carrying an heir more precious than any jewel, relic, or knowledge here at the Castle of Teskom."

Danae's spine tingles. "What do you mean?"

"Time," Teuta explains. "Danae, your child, holds the key to time. When you arrive here, time continues to move on in your dimension. When your child enters the archways to the Castle of Teskom, time will freeze in all dimensions."

Itra squeezes Danae's hand. "So, our child will play freeze tag with time?"

"We won't know for sure until she gives birth," Ivan answers. "But the invasion at our door indicates the heir foretold for centuries is with you, Danae. Leon's role is to guard you in the archives below."

"I can't leave Kaly out there!" Leon exclaims.

"I'll protect Danae," Itra says, wrapping his arm around her.

Junior shakes his head. "Leon, we will send a unit to look for Kaly. Itra, you're needed with the other Itra and Dita in the conservatory, making weapons and medicines. Your knowledge of plants will provide an added layer of defense. Understand?" Junior raises his eyebrow.

Itra glares back.

Junior stands, commanding, "The rules of engagement, capture and question, no harm if possible. Does everyone know and understand their posts?"

"Yes!" A unison call from the family rings back.

"We have less than an hour until dawn," Ivan says. "Please fuel up with plenty of caffeine and food. The next meal may be hours or days away."

"Teuta, Ivan, and Gjeto," Junior says. "Please join me in the library for a few minutes."

When the door closes, Leon turns to Itra and Danae. "Help me! I can't leave her out there."

Clang, clang, clang, clang, clang

"Three vessels are approaching," Altin, first in command, calls. "We need to move to our posts now."

"How—" Leon asks. Then Leon and Danae are falling.

Leon and Danae land in a lit corridor with a door at the opposite end. Danae bends over with her hands on her knees.

"Danae, are you okay? What the hell just happened?"

"Guessing, but pretty sure the answer is Teuta," she says between gasps of breath. She straightens, assessing her heart rate, and the room tilts to the right before she catches her breath. "I assume we're near the archives." She loops her arm around his, tugging him towards the door at the end. "Let's go check out what is behind door number…well, only one." Her voice is light, but she can feel every ounce of tension Leon's trying to contain.

Their footsteps echo in the space, making them pause and check behind them to ensure they're alone. In the center of the large wood and iron door before them is a family crest in colored glass and iron. "Teuta told us this is Itra's family crest on our first trip." She reaches to touch the bird in the center, but the door swings open from the middle.

Leon steps in front of her. The room is wide and long, more like a banquet hall with vaulted ceilings, and a stained-glass dome in the center. Large paintings hang on nearly every wall. The floor is covered with bookshelves laid out in a maze-like pattern.

Leon takes Danae's hand as they wind their way through the bookshelves. Danae stops to pull a book down and read the cover, but only finds blank pages inside. After twenty blank books, she stops inspecting. She follows Leon to a sitting area directly under the dome. Her gaze floats up to the figures on the stained-glass.

"What are you doing up there?" she asks Leon. A man with his shape, size, and facial features is standing with a glowing staff in his right hand.

"Well, if that's me, that one is you." She follows his finger to a stained-glass panel to the left. A woman with pixie waves around a heart-shaped face is holding a bundle that looks like a swaddled baby. They examine the dome, discussing names for the images portrayed. The middle, they assume to be Ember's hand.

Danae stretches her neck from side to side, catching movement to her right. A man is striding towards them. She moves behind Leon.

Leon shifts his position, ready to pounce towards the noise of the stranger's footsteps.

The man stops with a slight bow. "My name is Zarek. I'm the keeper. How may I be of service to you?"

His formal introduction relaxes Danae, but Leon is still on guard.

"How do I know you are who you say you are?" Leon asks.

Zarek shimmers, transforming into Teuta. "Excellent, Leon. I knew you were the right guard for this role."

Leon charges her.

Danae grabs his arm to stop him from punching her in the face.

"Where is Kaly?" Leon demands. "I'm not here to play games."

Teuta is stoic, not moving an inch at his menacing stance. "We have sent a unit to look for your wife. We'll keep you updated if they find any leads." Teuta smiles. "These are the archives. No passage leads here. The only ways in or out are through well protected portals. The first time is always mind-bending. The second is not so bad."

"I beg to differ," Danae says. "My second ride was worse."

"Sorry, Danae, pregnancy factors are not included in my experience," she says before continuing to explain the space. "The doors in this room all go to different portals except for that one." She points towards a small door on the opposite end. "There are living quarters there with three bedrooms, a living room, a kitchen, and two full bathrooms. Zeus created this space to keep his Danae safe after her father tried to harm her and their son. It's fitting his descendants would be here for nearly the same purpose." Teuta pulls a book from the shelf.

"Why are the pages blank?" Danae asks.

"Ember protects the contents of the books," Teuta says before showing them the blank pages and stops at one page. She whispers over the page, "Hapur." Words and images fill the page. "Take your time to learn what you can about the history, the maze, or any other events you may question. The catalog is thought provoked. Think of a topic, and the books will assemble in your direction. If you whisper, 'Hapur,' and the pages remain blank, there is an added layer of protection to that knowledge. It will automatically move back to the shelf. Questions before I leave you two?"

"Yes," Danae says. "What is happening up there?"

29

"Danae!" Itra yells. "Where, what?" He turns to Gjeto and the rest of the group. No one makes eye contact with Itra. "Where are they?"

"Secure in the archives," Ivan says. "They're fine. It's time." The room goes into full action, with everyone moving towards different doors.

"She's safe and with Leon," Gjeto says, patting Itra's shoulder.

Itra shrugs off his hand. He follows his double into the conservatory. "What do we do now?"

"Start with this row," Itra's double says, pointing to a row of plants, "and grind these down to a powder. It creates a temporary nerve agent that stops an intruder's progress with a brief inhale. They recover, but it will give us enough time to transport or restrain them."

Itra examines the row, looking over each plant. He quickly identifies each one down to its scientific name. "This gift is incredible, but scary. I know exactly what each plant is and how to use it as a weapon." Itra looks at his double.

His double nods. "Now look at the row directly behind it. Think remedy or health."

Itra turns to survey the plants. His mind calculates the method, dose, and medicinal purpose or treatment for each plant. "Wow.

After I finish grinding the nerve agent, I can work on the remedy in case someone suffers from friendly fire."

"It is incredible," says Itra's double. "I believe we have everything we need here. Dita is around the corner if you run into questions. She's been doing this for centuries."

"Centuries?" Itra asks. "She is no older than forty!"

"I'm 42," Dita says as she rounds the corner. "I started weekly studies here when I was fourteen. Ember gave me the gift of healing on my eighteenth birthday. I've studied the medicinal use of plants, osteopathic practice, eastern and western medicines. I even spent one year with a shaman in a South American rainforest. The knowledge stored here has saved millions of lives."

"Fourteen?" Itra says. "How did you find the archway?"

"My father, Mui, brought Junior and me before a battle with the Ottomans who crossed the borderlands in the northern village of Hot. We stayed inside the castle for two months on our first visit."

BOOM

Itra, his double, and Dita cower in response to an explosion from outside the castle walls.

"Less chat, more work, gentlemen," Dita says. "Time is not on our side." She straightens to her full height. Like other women native to northern Albania, she is tall.

Itra studies her for a moment. Her broad shoulders, slim waist, deep brown wavy hair is half tied back, her profile sharp but still feminine. Itra suddenly recognizes her as for what could only be a direct ancestor to his deceased aunt. The resemblance is striking.

BOOM

"They're attacking the lakeside caverns; prepare to sink immediately," Altin commands.

Glendon responds, *"Copy. Sinking in 3, 2, 1."*

A massive suction sound causes the plants to sway.

"Can you hear these conversations?" Itra asks.

"Yes," Dita answers. "Ember's magic, Junior calls it eDrum."

"Received a message from a northern rider," Vincent says. *"The message says, 'Surrender now, and we'll spare the bloodline.'"*

"Geri, ensure the rider doesn't find his company ever again," Junior responds.

"I created an endless loop in the rider's path," Geri says.

"Ana, what do you see?" Junior asks.

"The eastern riders split in the valley," Ana says. *"Two groups will pass through the future archway in less than three minutes, and there are only four targets left in the water."*

"Nordi, stall the invasion," Altin commands. *"Provide cover near the future archway until the units can establish proper coverage."*

"Copy," Nordi says. *"I created an illusion of a smooth cliff face with a large waterfall and pool near the ember archways, hiding the assembling units just beyond the clearing."*

"Traps are armed to the east," Gjeto calls.

Altin commands, *"Rudolfi, fire when ready."*

Rudolfi calls, *"3, 2, 1."*

A ripple of explosions of water, ice, and wind mark the riders charging through the valley. The riders to the east fly into the air.

"Archers, fire!" Altin commands.

The guided arrows find their targets in the few men and women that made it past Rudolfi and Gjeto's defenses.

Teuta calls, *"132 men and 160 women."*

"Dead?" Itra thinks and says aloud.

"No captured," Teuta states. *"Dita, fourteen major and six minor injuries."*

"Ready in two minutes," Dita responds. She turns to Itra. "We're not killing them, only transporting them to a locked cavern, stripped of any armor or weapons."

"The assembled units are ready in the clearing," Berto states. *"Gjeto, retrieve the gas from the conservatory."*

Rudolfi and Gjeto enter the conservatory a moment later. Itra double packs the glass bulbs into a giant weapon after coating them in a second dust that Rudolfi brought along. Gjeto and Rudolfi completed this task, never exchanging a word. Gjeto throws a look back to Itra of reassurance and winks as they exit. A chorus of battle cries can be heard as the door closes.

Dita loops her medical bag across her body and places rolled bandages in every pocket of her jacket until they are full. *"Teuta, now."* Dita blinks out as if she was never standing there at all.

Itra watches Dita vanish, and his knees give out. He crumbles to the ground.

"Itra, can you hear me?" Itra's double is snapping his fingers and clapping in his face, but Itra's eyes are wide and unblinking.

His ears ring with a loud thud of pulses until he hears Danae.

"Itra, are you okay?" Danae asks. *"Babe, can you hear me?"*

Itra stands frantically, looking around, causing his double to stumble back. *"Danae, where are you? I can hear you."*

"We're safe. Leon is here with me, remember?"

Itra takes in a ragged breath. *"Yes. Okay. I'm okay. Just a lot going on."*

"We can hear," Danae says. *"But we can't see anything from down here."*

"Archers," Altin commands. *"Fire!"*

"All clear," Berto calls.

"Ana?" Junior asks.

"Incoming unknown aircraft hovering to the south," Ana says.

Altin commands, *"Rudolfi, activate drone surveillance with an option for attack."*

"Copy," Rudolfi responds.

"Geri and Nordi, build a reflection illusion over the shield barrier," Altin says.

"Copy," Geri responds.

"Troops in the clearing collect weapons and return to stations to await further command." Junior barks.

"The triage bay has 34 injured and stable," Dita reports.

"Drone approaching target," Rudolfi calls. *"Ivan, do you have visuals? Can you identify friendly or foe?"*

"Foe," Ivan calls. *"Take it down."*

"Copy," Rudolfi commands.

The walls rattle, and a few plants knock over in the conservatory at Itra's feet. The barrier holds any impact from the falling aircraft.

"Clear," Berto calls.

"652 captured," Teuta calls. *"33 injured but stable, and one critical. Dita is working fast, should be stable soon. No fatalities."*

A book hovers in front of Danae. She reaches for the book and whispers, "Hapur." The text is the history in Albania without empires, war, or communism. Albania rapidly grew and developed like many western European nations, thriving on exports of minerals and wine. Descriptions of the digital age start in the 1940s, with one of the first artificial intelligence computer programmers noted in the 1960s. She turns the page. A picture of a young Itra is staring at Danae next to a small robot. The picture is captioned with Itra's father's name, Nik. "Leon! Look at this." She walks towards him, shoving the book in his face.

"What am I looking at?" Leon asks, studying the image, then turning the page back. "Nik, Itra's dad?"

"Yes," Danae says. "In this history of the Revolutionary dimension, he is one of the first in AI tech. How cool is that?"

"You would nerd out over that," Leon jokes, shaking his head.

Leon hands Danae the book, taking another that is hovering near him. He whispers, "Hapur." He opens the book, and it is blank. It's the fourth book he's attempted to read that remains blank. He hands it to Danae. "You try."

She whispers, "Hapur." It remains blank. She reads the spine of the book. "Defense and Strategic Studies Advancement. Sorry, Leon, no luck."

Leon sits in an oversized chair and sighs. "What's the point of being locked in a chamber of knowledge with no access to the knowledge?" A book moves within a hair of Leon's nose. "Shit! I was not asking for another book." Five more fly in his direction.

Danae laughs at his confusion. She squats to the floor to miss two additional volumes flying in his direction. "Stop thinking!"

Leon clears his mind except for one question. *Where is my wife?*

All but one book moves away and back to their shelves. He breathes in a sigh and reaches for the volume. "Hapur." The book opens to a passage about a sensory deprivation chamber. The captives lose their ability to hear or see inside the space.

Danae sits on the arm rest reading over his shoulder. "What kind of thought provoked this?"

"Where is my wife?" Leon says. *"Is there any sign of Kaly?"*

"Nothing yet, Leon," Ivan responds.

"Which dimension has a sensory deprivation chamber?" Leon asks.

"Future," Rudolfi answers.

"My wife is likely in the future," Leon mumbles.

"Copy," Ivan responds.

"How did this get so messy?" says Danae, settling in the other chair. A book lands in her lap. She turns it over to read the title. "Medusa."

"Sound defense: ready, aim, fire," Altin commands.

GONG

The vibrations rattle the castle's interior as a pulse defense weapon sends a round of sound waves towards the second round of riders.

Teuta calls, *"No injuries, 52 captured."*

"Weaponized sound?" Leon asks.

Danae shrugs. Another book falls in her lap and opens. She watches a book land on Leon's lap. "What were you thinking?"

"Weapons. I was wondering what other non-lethal weapons they use to portal people." He says the word and the text is revealed. He turns page after page. "This stuff is incredible and could have saved so many lives during my last tour." He looks up with glassy eyes. "Danae, if this is real in any dimension, it would change modern-day warfare altogether." He clears his throat. "What is your book about?"

"Time. I want to learn more about the freezing of time and the heir they keep referencing."

Leon stands, walking towards the living quarters. "Will you be okay out here for two minutes?"

"Of course, no way in or out, remember?"

The door closes behind Leon with a suction sound in the vast space. The book Danae is reading only repeats the story that the descendants of Mui and Zeus will merge creating the heir of time. She stands and stretches, gazing once more at the glass panels of the dome. The sunlight is pouring through the pane that resembles Leon. The new lighting changes his glowing staff to a scythe.

"Well, this just got ominous," she mutters.

A whoosh of air sends a chill down her spine.

"Leon, you need to see this," Danae says without turning towards the door.

"Danae," a deep voice calls from the opposite direction of Leon.

She jumps, screaming in surprise. "Who's there?"

A hand grips her shoulder, turning her around. She raises her hands balled in fists and swings.

"That's the best you got?" Leon laughs, catching her swinging left hook. "Why are you swinging?"

"Someone just called my name," she whispers, looking over her shoulder. Leon releases her fist, changing their positions, placing her behind him.

Leon whispers, "Back quietly towards the living quarters."

A book flies off a shelf a few rows over, directly towards the direction Danae heard the voice.

Danae squeezes Leon's arm. "Do you see anyone?"

He shakes his head.

The book stops and lowers between two rows of books.

Leon quickens their retreat, nearly reaching the door.

The voice calls, "Leon. What a fine blade you have?"

They freeze.

Leon looks back at Danae, his eyes searching. She points up towards the dome. He turns his head, straining to see the image from their position.

"Is that the grim reaper?" Leon whispers. She nods. He mouths a few curses.

She reaches for the handle of the door, fumbling with the mechanism.

"Push!" Leon says. The air-seal releases a second before echoing footsteps rush towards their position. Leon shoves her inside, slamming and locking the door behind them.

Leon turns to assess Danae. "Are you okay?"

She's shaking and holds up one finger.

Leon leans close to the door, listening for a beat. "It's clear, I think. The door's sealed. It may be soundproof too."

"Teuta, Ivan, or anyone who can hear me," Danae calls. *"Leon and I are safe and locked inside the living quarters. An unknown man was in the hall a moment ago. Do you copy?"*

"Can you identify or describe the man?" Ivan calls back.

"Never saw him, only heard a deep voice and chasing footsteps."

"I've found tampering near the north portal entrance to the archives," Ivan calls. *"Sending a unit now."*

"Danae?" Itra calls.

"I'm fine. Leon got us out before anything happened."

Danae leans on the counter near the sink, closing her eyes, counting to ten, slowly inhaling and exhaling. She reaches for the faucet but finds air. She opens her eyes to a black abyss. She turns and can't even see the door or her feet. She blinks a few times, trying to get her eyes to adjust. A tiny light flickers in the center of her vision. "Leon!" The light grows to a large projection. Danae shields her eyes, nearly losing her balance. She squints to focus on the image. It's Elis. He is standing outside a glass enclosure, making faces at a gorilla.

His laugh echoes, startling her senses.

"Elis, can you hear me?"

Elis turns away from the gorilla. "Hi, Danae." He scrunches up his face, dropping his chin, pointing his finger towards her. "You need to go under the maze."

"Elis! What do you mean?"

The image fades to light. She blinks, only to see her reflection. She takes a step back. The washroom is intact. She splashes her face with the coldest water possible. "I'm losing my mind."

She finds Leon pacing outside the door. "Leon, I just saw Elis! The room went black, and Elis appeared with a serious look. He pointed at me, saying, I need to go under the maze."

"And we're officially tripping," Leon responds. "Follow me." He pauses at the next door on the left. "Kitchen," he says and continues walking, pointing at the next door on the right. "A bedroom."

The bedroom door is open. Danae assesses the large mahogany framed bed with matching side tables and a chair off to the right. *Almost modern?* She quickens her pace to catch up with Leon. He's frowning at the next open door.

170

"Oh my! Is this a—No! It cannot be, but why?" Danae's eyes travel over the delicate, tiny contents of the room. She turns to Leon. "Is this a nursery? How long are we supposed to stay down here?"

Leon lowers his chin. His eyes narrow before he pushes her into the nursery and pulls the door closed before she can react.

"Lock the door!" Leon sprints towards the main door.

She locks the door, listening for any further action before slowly turning. There is a dresser, a crib, and a plush blue rocking chair.

A door slides open. Danae searches for something to use in her defense, but everything is plush and soft. No intruder enters, but the door remains open. She moves cautiously towards the opening, flattening herself against the wall, before peeking in. It's another bedroom. At first glance, it appears vacant, but there is movement on the opposite wall. A mirror shows a figure, shuffling papers, standing in front of a desk.

"Danae, I know you can see me. Come in." The voice is smooth, melodic, and female.

Danae flattens her back to the wall. "Who are you?" Her chest is heaving. *Where is Leon?*

"Come on in. Let me show you." The voice is calm but commanding.

"Where is Leon?"

"Securing the door, I may have tripped some alarms on my way in."

"I'll wait for Leon."

"You can never be too cautious in your state."

Bang, Bang

Danae's knees buckle.

"Danae, are you there?" Leon yells.

Danae stumbles to unlock the door—but the woman is standing between her and the door.

"Allow me."

Danae steps back in surprise. The woman is Kaly, well, a version of Kaly. Her wardrobe, a white gown, gold chain, and wild hair are all wrong, but she is Kaly. Danae tries to find her voice before the woman swings the door open. Leon reaches for the woman but stops, stepping back in surprise.

"Hi Leon," the woman says, stepping towards him.

"Kaly? How did you…" Leon's confusion of wanting to go to her versus keeping his guard alert is heartbreaking to watch.

The woman nods and glimmers back into Leon's version of Kaly in jeans and a hoodie, with her hair pulled back in a ponytail.

"What the hell is happening?" Leon spits.

"We're the protectors of time," the woman says, pointing at Leon and herself before pointing to Danae's abdomen.

The room goes sideways. Danae feels the cold tile floor press against her cheek before darkness.

30

"Iana, my mom just called on the landline," Anton says, walking into the kitchen.

Iana is standing hunched over staring out the window.

"Did you hear me?" Anton asks, stepping up beside her.

She nods. "What did your mom say?"

"They're at the zoo. Elis was making faces at the gorillas for a few minutes before he had a one-sided conversation with Danae."

"Wait, Danae and Itra are at the zoo, too?"

"No. I mean, I don't think so. My mom just said Elis was giggling, and then he abruptly turned with a serious expression and started talking to the air as if Danae was there. When my mom asked him about it, he just giggled and continued playing. She found it odd enough to call me." Anton scratches his head. "What do you think this means?"

Iana walks past him into the dining room. She paces back and forth before answering. "We still don't know how we got home or when. Or why my phone is missing, and your phone no longer works?"

"Maybe Itra or Danae can explain?"

"I've tried to contact Itra and Danae several times. Their phones say no longer in service and their social media has only one group photo of us near the gate at their house from yesterday. What do you recall?"

"It's all kind of hazy," Anton says, running a hand through his hair.

Iana stops pacing and faces him. "Anton, we need new working phones, and we need to get back to Itra's house. Something feels off."

Anton holds up a card. "I found this on your nightstand while looking for your phone." He turns the gold card over, displaying a maze printed on one side. "Do you know where it came from?"

"What twilight world have we entered? I'm packing our bags; we are leaving in five minutes." Iana marches towards the bedroom. She makes it only a few steps before freezing. She squeezes her eyes closed. A reel of memories of dinner with the family, dominos, a hike, the view, and the castle flood her mind. She whirls to face Anton. "Do you remember?"

Anton's face goes from shock to horror in a few moments.

"I remember!" Anton bends at the waist, trying to shake the image of the castle out his ear.

Iana straightens. A new clear image blinds her vision. "Anton! Danae will not understand the danger she is in. We need to go now! I'll explain on the way."

Anton checks the bowl on the counter—no car keys. He runs to the bedroom. He checks the bedside tables, his pant pockets, and the office. "Iana, I can't find the keys." He runs back to the front room. Iana's gone; the front door is open. "Iana?" He hears an echo of footsteps on the staircase below. "Iana, wait!"

Two floors down, she ignores his call and doesn't stop moving. *The garage is just one more floor down.* Iana throws the door open, but their assigned parking spot is vacant. She jogs the row looking for their car. She turns to run back, finding Anton in the doorway.

"It's not here," she says. "We didn't drive home." Her mouth opens again but doesn't make a sound. She finally whispers, "Portal?"

"That explains our mind wipe, missing car, and phone mishap," Anton says. "But now what?" He steps back to let Iana through the door. She takes the stairs two at a time.

"I'll call Nada. Maybe we can borrow her car?"

Iana heads for the home office to use the phone and Anton goes to their bedroom to pack. He pulls a duffle from the top shelf of the closet, and a piece of paper flutters down. It's a drawing of a woman with short wavy hair holding a baby pointing to a clock set to six with one word written: WAIT. Anton thrusts the drawing at Iana as she walks into their bedroom.

"Where was this?" she asks.

"Under the duffle. It floated down when I took the bag off the shelf. Did you put it up there?"

"No." She frowns. "Elis drew a bunch of pictures over the last two weeks." She dashes to Elis's room. Papers clutter his small desk, but the drawings are all nearly identical. She collects the stack, handing them to Anton.

Anton thumbs through the stack. "There are at least twenty drawings here." Anton holds up one. "This one is different." Iana moves closer to see. "No baby, and the clock one minute after six."

"Ugh!" Iana screams in frustration, stomping her foot. "What does all this freaking mean?" Iana slides to the floor. "Kaly, Medusa, Danae."

31

"Ana, is the channel clear?" Altin asks.

"Almost, the last one is nearly out," Ana replies.

"Glendon, drop the dam when Ana calls clear," Altin commands.

"Copy," Glendon says.

"One vessel released a messenger," Vincent says. *"The message says the second, third, and fourth vessels are carrying artifacts from the Library of Alexandria."*

A collective chatter explodes.

"Silence!" Junior yells over the racket. The chatter stops.

"Launch radar to confirm," Altin commands.

"Copy," Berto responds.

"Archers, release markers now," Altin commands.

"Clear!" Ana calls.

"Copy," Glendon responds. *"Dam dropped; the channel is closed."*

"157 sailors," Teuta calls. *"Two in triage for further examination. Total captured 861. We've also detected two*

additional people with Leon and Danae. The portal is blocked. Ivan and I are trying to reopen it."

"Danae!" Itra runs through the conservatory towards the dining hall. He bursts through the door, looking around for Ivan. *"Danae, can you hear me?"*

"What are you doing?" Itra's double asks, following him into the dining hall.

"Radar identifies five vessels are carrying weapons only, and three have large, sealed crates of books and sculptures," Berto says. *"The lead vessel has two unidentifiable devices aboard. Clear to sink the last five."*

"Glendon, do you copy?" Altin asks.

"Copy, on your command," Glendon responds.

"Fire," Altin says.

A loud crashing wave echoes from below, followed by a massive boom.

"Four vessels remain unharmed," Glendon says.

"Berto," Altin calls. *"Search and retrieve."*

"Copy," says *Berto.* *"Deploying units nine and three now."*

"Copy, unit nine lead, over."

"Copy, unit three lead, over."

"No response from Danae or Leon," Ivan says. *"Portals are still closed."*

"Unit ten, stand by, ready for forced entry to the archives," Junior growls.

"Copy, unit ten lead, over."

"Ana?" Itra asks. *"Who is with Danae and Leon?"*

"Unknown, no sight detection of an intruder before or now. Sorry, Itra."

"Itra, come with me," Gjeto calls from across the dining hall. "I may have an alternative to find Danae."

Itra sprints to follow Gjeto with Itra's double at his side.

Gjeto hurries down a corridor, stopping at an entrance. He squats, uncovering a hidden dip on the floor. He presses a release in the dip. A hinged door opens.

Itra leans over and spots the stairs leading down.

"Move quickly but stay behind me," Gjeto explains. "I'll disarm traps as we move." He steps down. "On the fourth step, double tap the center, and the door will close above you. Understand?"

"Got it," Itra's double responds.

Itra follows Gjeto and Itra's double a few steps behind. The door swings shut, and Gjeto taps his light stone. His light illuminates two small corridors. Gjeto disables a swinging machete with a series of stone puzzles.

Itra smiles in recognition.

The stones fit together perfectly in three different shapes.

Itra played with this puzzle as a child with his cousins under the watchful eye of Gjeto.

Gjeto winks at Itra.

They move to a stone wall, a dead end.

Gjeto presses his nose to a stone off-center, and a slot opens revealing a series of stone symbols. He rearranges the order and steps back. He places his right hand over his heart. "Open says me."

The wall slides back two meters.

Itra moves forward to pass Gjeto.

"No!" Gjeto throws his arm in front of Itra. "Not through there, down here." He squats, releasing another hinged door.

"It looks like an oversized laundry chute," Itra says, inspecting the dark tunnel.

"Ready to slide?" Gjeto asks with a twinkle in his eye.

"Game on!" Itra looks back at his double. He is grinning from ear to ear and nods.

Gjeto climbs through the narrow opening, folding his arms; he angles his legs forward, disappearing with a whoosh of air.

Itra eagerly follows.

The tube leads to a dark cavern. The chill of the air seeps through their clothes.

"Where are we?" asks Itra's double.

Gjeto moves to the center of the room, pointing up. Itra and his double follow his gestures. The vaulted ceiling shows their reflections in a mirror.

Gjeto quietly says, "Show me."

The mirror goes dark, turning their reflection into a scene of a bedroom. The back of two figures are standing over another person, lying on a bed.

178

"Leon!" Itra exclaims. "Danae, oh, what's happened?"

"Is that Kaly or Pem?" Gjeto asks.

"I can't tell from here." Itra strains to see more of the room.

"The mirror in the bedroom is one of the escape portals, but it's an exit only. We need Danae or Leon to activate it. If that is Kaly, how did she get in and with whom?"

"Are you asking me?" Itra glances at Gjeto. "Because I don't understand how or why."

"She has been out for too long," Leon says. "We should get someone!"

"She's breathing and her heart rate is normal," Kaly says. "When is the last time she slept?"

"My Kaly would know without asking!" Leon growls. "What did you do to my wife?"

"I'm Kaly, your wife of ten years."

Leon runs two hands through his hair in frustration. "You want to play games, fine." He leaps across the bed, backing her against the wall. She doesn't flinch.

"Somebody's frustrated," Kaly says, kissing his nose. Leon growls in her face. "How did you scratch your cheek?"

"Seriously?" Leon leans close but doesn't touch her.

"Somebody is watching," Kaly whispers.

"Quit stalling!" Leon grunts. "Start talking."

"Leon?" Danae whispers from the bed. "How did I end up here? Kaly, is that you?" She tries to sit up, but the throbbing of her head hinders her progress.

"Danae!" Itra yells after watching her move on the bed. *"Leon!"*

Leon backs away from Kaly, moving to the bed. "You fainted, and your hard head broke the floor." Leon reaches to check the left side of her head. She winces at his touch near her temple. "It's bruised, but only slightly swollen. You may have a mild concussion."

"Itra's calling," Danae says. "Can you get my phone?" Leon laughs—the sound is like a million splinters in her head. "Volume on low, please!" She covers her ears.

"Do you know where you are?" Leon asks, still laughing.

Danae looks around. *The room is not familiar, but Kaly is here.* She focuses back on Leon. "Did you redecorate the farmhouse?"

Kaly laughs.

"Where is Itra?" Danae asks.

"Can you hear me?" Itra asks. "Gjeto, she looks confused. Do you think she's hurt?"

"Itra, why are you yelling in my head?" Danae thinks before speaking to Kaly and Leon. "Not your house?"

Leon sits next to Danae, examining her eyes. "You don't know where we are right now?" His frown lines deepen to a grimace.

"Should I?" she asks. "Where is Itra?"

"Come to the mirror, babe," Itra begs.

She rolls to the side of the bed, slowly sitting up again as the room tilts. She blinks a few times, trying to inhale and exhale through the throbbing sensation.

Kaly is standing on the opposite side of the room, still against the wall.

"Leon, can you help me stand?" Danae asks.

Leon steps beside the bed.

Danae moves her feet to the floor, reaching for his shoulder. "Thanks." She's standing steady enough to walk.

"Good job, babe," Itra coaches. *"Now walk to the mirror."* Itra nudges Gjeto. "How does she activate the portal?"

"Open says me."

Itra's double laughs.

Gjeto shrugs. "Simple is not always a bad thing."

"Now what?" Danae pushes her hair back from her almost purple temple.

"Babe, say, 'open says me' aloud to the mirror."

"Open says me."

Chaos erupts behind Danae. Kaly's reflection leaps towards her, but Leon tackles Kaly to the floor. The room tilts, and Danae is falling again.

<h1 style="text-align:center">32</h1>

"No! Danae!" Leon yells.

"You idiot!" Kaly growls. "Get off me!" She pushes against Leon. "Do you realize the danger she is in now?"

"She is fine, but you're not. Start talking. No games." Leon leans back a little, glaring at Kaly.

"Get off me." Kaly squirms under his glare. Leon leans back further, allowing her to sit up. "Can you just clarify one thing first?"

"Fine. One thing." Leon sits back on his heels.

"Where's Danae?" Kaly pulls her knees to her chest.

"With Itra, I presume," Leon says. "What happened to my Kaly?"

"I'm your Kal—"

"No more lies!" Leon yells. She flinches. "Now, start talking from the beginning. What happened at the old Mokset Castle?"

"I was checking out the bunker on the rise. Danae mentioned its use in the Communist era after their first trip to the remains a year or so ago. Someone knocked me out by force at the bottom of the stairs. When I came to, my wrist and ankles were bound and tied behind my back." She pauses, pulling up her sleeves slowly to show Leon the red marks on her wrists. She leans to show him her ankles, but he stops her.

"Who is Pem?"

"Pem?" Kaly asks. "Leon, Pem has been dead for nearly a decade."

"You know Pem?"

"My dad's twin sister had a daughter, Pem. We were a few months apart in age but could have passed for twins minus her grey patch."

"So Pem is where?"

Kaly frowns. "The last time I saw her was the summer before starting college. She died in a car accident right before you and I met."

Leon nods, but then shakes his head. "How did your cousin come back from the dead, knock you out and fool all of us into thinking it was you?"

"I don't understand," Kaly says. "Pem was here? How?"

"Ivan and Teuta claim the woman who entered here with our group is Pemphredo."

"You thought she was me?"

"I had no reason to think otherwise. We were all slightly distracted by the ember archway, the magic food, and the castle. I need more answers. How did you get untied and in here?"

"Don."

He frowns. "Start at the beginning."

"Beginning as in today or before we met?"

Leon leans forward, moving to mirror her posture. "Interesting. Before we met, if it's related to how you ended up in here today."

"Oh, this is going to take a while." Leon attempts to interrupt, but she cuts him off. "Let me finish. Then you can ask as many questions as you want. Deal?"

Leon nods.

Kaly starts her story. "I'm half Greek, half Turkish. My father's line is Greek, my mother is Turkish. I've talked about my father's story before, but a few details are relevant now." Kaly stands so she can pace. "An artifact was discovered in the early nineties, which led to an official dig commissioned by my father's company. The site was an abandoned castle dating back to 3 or 4 BC, in northern Albania." Kaly looks down at Leon. He remains seated but nods.

"My father carried a logbook everywhere he went. It was mostly field notes, but it was also a diary. His crew reported he lost his logbook, realizing it only after dark when they returned to camp. The next morning, he left camp alone near dawn to search the site for his book. When the crew arrived, my father was dead. His death was labeled an accident because any other explanation was too absurd to consider. They found his body in a newly dug section at the base of a set of stone stairs. Their guess is he tripped down the stairs with a machete in his hands." Kaly shivers at the memory.

"His logbook was never found. It wasn't on him, nor was it at the site. Two years later, my mother was sobbing over a package when I arrived home from school. The package included my father's logbook and a single gold card with royal blue text. The text on the card read, Time."

"Time," Leon repeats. Kaly retrieves a card from the desk. She hands it to Leon. He flips it over. The ink and texture are like messages Vincent and Iana received. "Do you think it is a message from here?"

She nods. "I keep my father's logbook on my nightstand. The morning after you left with Vincent, this card was sitting on top with this." She holds up a gold cube with an ember stone. "I took a chance and snapped a photo of the original card." She holds out another paper.

"Time to Serve." He looks up at Kaly's face. Her expression is nearly manic with animation.

"The message sent to my mother when I was eleven is from this castle." She opens her arms wide. "We're part of this." She picks up additional papers from the desk. "I looked for anything related to time in my father's logbook, but not a single entry was related to time. However, he wrote one name over and over—your name, Leon, documented thirty-two times." Kaly sucks in a big breath before handing the papers over, showing Leon the entries with his name.

"Why would you hide this from me?"

"I've never hidden anything from you including my father's logbook."

Leon stands. "No. Why did you hide all of this?" He shoves the papers to her chest. "You knew all of this before you flew over here!"

"I wasn't sure," Kaly whispers. "After the encounter with Don on campus, I knew it would be better to compare notes in person to make sure I wasn't jumping to conclusions. I thought maybe I was just wanting it to be a connection to my father." She steps back to the desk. "By the time I arrived, the group had already decided to come here for answers. I thought I would wait and get my answers, too."

"Bull shit!" Leon yells. "In ten years, you've never kept finding a new clue or discovery a secret. You've never waited for anything."

She shrugs and picks up one last set of papers. "Take your time reading this. I'll wait for you in the kitchen."

"I'll read it in the kitchen with you," Leon says. "I do not trust you. I still have too many unanswered questions."

Kaly lowers her head before looking back up with a single tear falling down her soft cheek.

Leon nearly shatters at the sight of her sadness.

"I understand," Kaly whispers. She shuffles her way to the bedroom door.

Leon watches her shoulders roll forward and her head lower. He follows, trying to iron out all the details. Too many holes still to fill in.

The kitchen's dining nook is a cozy, almost nautical theme with white plush chairs, blue accents, and a small engraved wooden table. On closer inspection, the engraving is Itra's family crest. The dome over the kitchen provides enough light—the sun appears high, maybe close to noon.

"It's empty," Kaly says, after opening all the cabinets.

"Is a caramel latte, extra foam, one sugar with a white chocolate drizzle: still your go-to drink of choice?" Leon asks, attempting some effort to be kind.

"Yes," Kaly says, grinning.

"Two, please," Leon says.

Two steaming mugs appear.

Kaly gasps.

Leon shrugs and pulls out a chair for her. She sits down and watches him walk around to the opposite side of the table. He sits, taking a sip. She takes a sip, letting out an audible sigh of approval, and the corners of Leon's mouth twitch in response. He shifts in his chair.

Leon tries to focus on the paper, forcing his thoughts of Kaly aside. The bold title reads, *'Be ready. Time is near to view the future start in the rear.'* It is a family tree from Zeus and Mui showing the union of Danae and Itra. The text below the tree reads, *'Illyria ember in time, light the fire at dawn, o'treasure of mine. Illyria ember in time, discover the haze the army will raise, o'treasure of mine. Illyria ember of mine uncover the maze you will embrace all treasures in time.'*

"It's the same poem Unis sent Danae." Leon frowns. "Kaly, are you and Unis working together?"

She shakes her head. "No. The next page is a blood oath signed by our ancestors."

"Blood oath? Our ancestors?" He studies the page. The ancient text is foreign, with two brown stained thumbprints in blood at the end of the passage.

"A translated version is at the bottom."

"Today and now, I pledge my blood to serve and protect Ember's treasures of time. An honor code bound to infinity." Leon pauses. "The thumbprints are labeled Zeus and Phorcys. Who is Phorcys?"

"My ancestor," says Kaly.

"Our ancestors signed us up for a life sentence, times infinity?" He chokes down another sip of his latte.

"How did you find this blood oath?"

"Poseidon and—"

Leon pounds his fists on the table. The mugs rattle in response. He stands leaning on the table and glares at Kaly.

Kaly holds up her hands. "Medusa's father is Phorcys."

"Medusa?" Leon asks. "You said Phorcys is your ancestor. Are you related to Medusa?"

Kaly shrugs.

"When did he give this to you?"

"Bravo," a man calls, slowly clapping.

Leon whirls and faces a man casually leaning against the wall, grinning.

"We haven't been properly introduced. My name is Poseidon. My friends call me Don." He bows towards Leon and Kaly.

Kaly recoils and steps behind Leon.

"You tried to kill my sister and Itra and you stalked my wife. Give me one reason I shouldn't destroy you now."

"The woman you're shielding, I sent her here to seduce or kill you, but she let Danae go. Shame, we must retrieve her later. Come along. We have work to do."

Leon reaches behind him for Kaly but finds only air. He turns to look, but she's gone. Whipping his head back towards Don and now a woman. The woman is not his Kaly, but the white gown and wild hair version he saw earlier.

"How?"

Don laughs. "See you soon."

They vanish.

33

"Danae," Itra says, stroking her hair.

"Hmm?" Danae responds.

"Can you wake up?" He kisses her cheeks.

"Two more minutes?" She feels another person sitting close. She tries to open her eyes. "Who else is here?"

"Dita. She is a healer. You may have a mild concussion."

"Who is Dita?" Danae slides one eye open. The room is dim. There are two figures on the bed and two standing in the doorway near the wardrobe. "Where are we?"

"Dita is family. Let's call her a distant cousin. We're in our assigned bedroom in the castle."

Her eyes fly open at the word castle. She tries to sit up, immediately regretting her sudden movements. "Leon. Where is Leon? Is Kaly here?" She winces in pain, reaching for her temple.

"Whoa! Danae, not so fast." Itra places his hands on her shoulders. "He's still in the archives, and we're not sure if that's Kaly or Pem. Can you tell us what you remember?"

Danae's focus returns.

Itra's double, and Teuta are standing in the doorway.

Itra and Dita arrange pillows to prop her up in a seated position.

She explains the events from the archive living quarters to the mirror.

"A nursery?" Itra looks from Danae to Teuta. "How long were you planning for her to stay down there?"

"We've been strategizing for this invasion and circumstance for centuries," Teuta says. "We were planning for the worst-case scenario. Did the voice in the hall sound familiar?"

"Maybe," Danae stares at Teuta. She's tapping her foot. "Are you anxious?"

"We have two intruders, one with Leon and the other could be just outside the door. I need an answer. Was the voice familiar?"

Danae nods. "It was the same tone and pitch that Don used in my dream and in the clearing."

"Don has breached the archives," says Teuta. *"Activate every available unit."* Then she abruptly vanishes.

"The second intruder: capture or kill?" Altin asks.

Itra and Danae exclaim, *"Capture!"*

"Copy. Unit four take the lead."

"Copy, unit four lead, over."

"Ana, any sign of Don or his men?" Junior asks.

"Not Don," Ana answers. *"But there is a second round coming through the portals in fifteen minutes."*

"Itra," Junior calls, *"stay with Danae, sending unit two to guard the entrance to your suite."*

"Copy, unit two lead, over."

"Geri and Nordi, create a fake army illusion in the clearing," Altin commands.

"Copy," Nordi responds.

"Rudolfi, set the clearing perimeter with the transport gas," Altin commands.

"Copy," Rudolfi answers. *"Gjeto, can you arm the southern line?"*

"Copy," Gjeto responds.

"Archers, take your position," Altin commands.

"Unit four. All clear. The archive hall is empty. Leon has been secured."

"Unit two, in position. All clear."

"Copy," Altin responds. *"Take Leon to Itra's suite."*

Dita returns to the triage near the holding bay.

Danae sits up further in the bed waiting for Leon, but when the door opens, Junior and Ivan walkthrough.

"We need to speak to Leon and Danae," Junior says.

A minute later, Leon bursts through the door. "Danae?"

"All good, bro." She looks him over. He's sweating, his hair is standing on end, and he looks half-mad. "What happened to you?"

"Kaly!" Leon exclaims. "She is with Poseidon."

Ivan and Junior step forward. Leon moves towards Danae protectively before he recognizes them.

Leon throws the papers down on the bed. "That's why he took her, right?" He points at the papers. "She showed me these while pretending to be my wife."

"The blood oath," Junior says, stepping closer to the papers.

"You failed to mention that part," Leon says. "Danae, we're infinitely bound to serve and protect Ember!"

"Wait, we're what?" Danae asks.

Ivan holds up his hand. "We told you there were four bloodlines. We did, however, leave out the part of the blood oath of Zeus and Phorcys. We've had no documentation to prove this long told oath to protect Ember."

"What happened after I left?" Danae asks Leon.

Leon explains his encounter with the imposter and her explanation. He sits down, exhausted from the last hour. "The worst part is that I still don't understand if that was my wife or Pem or both."

Danae moves carefully to Leon's side. "We will figure this out." She places her hand on his shoulder. Her ring feels itchy against her finger. She moves the ring around and up, but her skin looks normal, with no marks. As she slides the ring back down, Ivan walks closer, staring at her hand.

"The stones in this ring, are they a family heirloom?" Ivan asks Itra.

"The middle stone is new," Itra answers. "The side stones are from Gjeto's grandmother. A piece of jewelry given to me after he passed."

"Danae, does your ring ever reflect an orange glow?" Ivan asks.

"Only the day we encountered Don," she answers.

Itra asks, "Why?"

"Ember gave the side stones to my son," Ivan says. "We have embedded the stones in several pieces of jewelry over the centuries. The setting is lovely, Itra." Ivan admires the ring. "Have you had any other sensations while wearing it here?"

"Twice," Danae explains. "When Don lunged towards us in the clearing, it felt like the ring was warm, but our sprint down the ridge distracted me. I don't know how long the sensation lasted. I believe that when Kaly lunged towards me as I exited via the mirror, I had a similar sensation. Now it feels itchy, like a sunburn."

"When Ember gifted the stones," Ivan says. "The card attached said one word, 'Protection.' It's written in the logs dating back to the eighth century."

"This is fascinating and all, but can we get back to the woman I just encountered?" Leon asks, watching the men stare at Danae's ring. "Is she my wife or an imposter?"

Ivan and Junior look at Leon with blank, unreadable stares.

"She was likely your Kaly," Ivan says, clearing his throat. "You mentioned her father was Greek earlier?"

"Yes. She immigrated to the states with her mother and uncle in the late nineties."

"There is a slim chance that she is related to Phorcys," Junior states.

"But it is possible," Ivan says.

"What does this mean for Kaly's safety?" Danae asks.

"Is my wife in danger?" Leon growls, standing abruptly.

"We're making assumptions, Leon," Ivan says. "We all need more facts to assist with this query."

A whirling wind rattles the window in the room. Junior and Ivan move towards the window.

"Trap jammed in the northeast corner," Gjeto calls. *"Two broke through."*

"Archers, fire," Altin commands.

"Two targets collected," Rudolfi says.

"Ana, any other known threats or rogue intruders?" Berto asks.

"Getting two unknown marks, wavering in and out of the archive hall," Ana says. *"Unit four, can you sweep the hall once more?"*

"Unit four, do you copy?" Altin asks. There's no response. *"Unit five, do you copy?"* He calls. *"Does anyone hear me?"* A clatter of chatter starts.

Junior shrills a high-pitched whistle. The chatter cuts off. Itra, Leon, and Danae jump back in surprise because his whistle was audible in the room and in their heads.

"Unit seven, double back to the archives," Junior commands. *"Unit two, standby."*

"Unit seven lead. We've found units four and five. Alive, but unconscious. There's white and purple powder dusting the entire space. Two of my men are down, over."

A massive suction sound erupts beneath the castle.

Dita calls, *"Mayday!"*

"What's happening?" Junior demands.

"The holding bay and triage unit are gone." Teuta calls. *"They've been sucked out of the cavern."*

"What do you mean, gone?" Junior asks.

"The actual bay, triage unit and all the people are physically gone," Teuta answers. *"I believe they have ambushed us from the inside."*

Itra's double and Junior promptly leave the suite.

Ivan faces Itra, Leon, and Danae. "All is not lost. I'm sealing this room with Ember's will. Do not open the door under any circumstance. Do you understand?"

They answer with a collective, "Yes."

"Teuta will be the only one able to penetrate this room. If anyone else enters, defend and protect Danae at all costs." Ivan leaves after receiving a nod from Itra and Leon.

Itra slumps next to Danae.

Leon begins pacing the room.

34

Nada knocks on the apartment door.

Anton opens it. "Hi Nada," he says. "Thanks for coming so quickly."

Iana doesn't move from the kitchen table to greet Nada.

"What's happening?" Nada whispers. "Is she okay?"

"I don't have time to explain, but Danae and Itra need us as soon as possible. Do you need the car back this evening?"

"No, tomorrow is fine."

"I will have my old roommate, David, drive it back first thing tomorrow morning. Is that okay?"

"Yes. Good luck." Nada backs towards the door, waving goodbye.

Anton picks up their bag. "Iana?" He walks over to Iana when she doesn't respond. "Babe?"

He drops the bag to reach for her, but the sound of the bag hitting the floor startles her. Her head snaps up. Her gaze searches the room before meeting Anton's eyes.

"What did you say?" Iana glances at the bag at Anton's feet.

"Nada just dropped off the keys. We need to get moving."

"Elis, where is he?"

Anton lowers down to her level. "Iana, are you okay?"

Iana's eyes fill and several fat teardrops fall, but her expression is blank. "What's happened? What's going on? Why do I feel stuck to this chair?"

"Thirty minutes ago, you had a panic attack after a vision about Danae and Kaly. I moved you from the hall outside of Elis's room to the table." Anton searches her expression for any sign of clarity or recollection. Her face remains blank. "Nada dropped off her car so we can drive up and go help Danae and Itra. Danae may be in danger. Elis is with my parents." He looks at Iana with concern, then he hesitantly removes the maze card from his back pocket. "Iana, you said it was urgent."

The phone rings in the office. Anton straightens quickly and jogs to answer.

"Elis?"

Static

"Hello?" Anton asks with a sigh.

Static

"Who is this?" Anton asks more sternly.

"Elis is the compass," two children say in unison. "He will guide us. Bring him to the ember archway tomorrow at dawn." The line disconnects before Anton can respond.

Anton slams the phone down, cursing. He bolts out of the room to Iana. He explains the call.

Iana nods and stands. She stares through Anton wordlessly. Her eyes glaze over. Anton waits for her to regain her thoughts. Two full minutes pass before Iana exhales a scream so loud Anton steps back, falling over a chair and lands hard on his back.

Iana looks down at Anton. "They're the only answer to the beginning and the end." Iana states in a monotone voice Anton has never heard.

"Who's they?" Anton slowly stands back up, assessing his ribs and back for damage from his fall.

"Time," Iana states solemnly. "We need Elis."

"Elis is safe," Anton pleads. "Can we leave him with my parents?"

"No," Iana says, gulping loudly and then swallowing a sob. "Time will need Elis as a guide. I have seen it all, Anton. He is there. We are there. I don't know how to unsee these events."

"We can't put Elis in danger. There must be another alternative or person. He is six, Iana."

"I know how old our son is, Anton, but it is the only way we can stop—"

"Stop what?"

"Exposure," Iana says.

35

Danae's stomach growls so loud, Itra jumps in surprise. "Sorry. My appetite's on max volume." She grins and shrugs at their jaw slack expressions.

"Seriously?" Leon says, glaring at her and the tray that appears.

"Can you two go pace in the living room?" Danae says, waving her spoon at Leon and Itra.

"And leave you alone?" Itra shakes his head.

"I'm not alone—I have my grilled cheese."

"How are you even joking right now?" Leon glares at her.

"Sorry, brother, I'm using humor as a defense mechanism. How are my punch lines?" Leon turns in disgust. She nearly chokes on the crust with laughter, seeing his expression.

"Nice, real nice. My wife could be in danger, and you're enjoying a grilled cheese sandwich."

Itra gives her a warning glare. She realizes she may have pushed it too far.

"Oops, sorry."

Itra kisses her forehead. He opens his mouth for a bite. She extends her sandwich but snatches it back, finishing the last bite with a wicked grin. Itra shakes his head.

"Tease!" Itra's stomach growls. "Leon, when is the last time you ate anything?"

"Last night in the dining hall," Leon says.

"We may not get another chance—"

"Ribeye, medium rare, mashed potatoes, grilled veggies, a shot of bourbon, and apple pie with vanilla bean ice cream," Danae says. "Times two." Leon's head flies up to glare at her, but he can't hold his glare. "Love you too, brother." The food arrives on separate trays on the bed. "Can we stretch out in the living room?"

Itra nods. "After you, wife."

Leon follows them to the table.

A steaming mug of chai appears a few seconds later for Danae.

The clink of forks creates a melodic accompaniment to the space.

"How is it?" Danae asks when Leon looks in her direction.

He shrugs in response.

"Are you giving me the silent treatment?" she asks with a bark of laughter.

"Altin!" Junior shouts.

"Copy," Altin responds.

"They have knocked out our standby units with sleeping powder."

Leon and Itra stop chewing and set their forks down. Danae sits back pulling her knees up to her chest.

"Ana?" Junior asks.

"The vision is changing every few minutes," Ana says.

"Were any of the captives wearing jewelry?" Vincent asks.

"Several had small pendants," Teuta growls. *"Why?"*

"Ember shards gathered in a small, condensed space could create a portal," Vincent says. *"A possible explanation for the holding bay and triage unit."*

"Not sure how relevant this is, but the police had an evidence bag of ember shards stolen about a week ago," Danae says.

"How big of a bag?" Ivan asks.

"Maybe eight ounces," Danae answers.

Danae looks from Leon to Itra. Their postures suggest that they're ready to pounce. She takes a long, loud sip from her mug. The sound breaks their concentration, but only Itra relaxes.

Danae sets down her mug. "Leon, was Kaly wearing any visible jewelry?"

Leon looks at her blankly before responding. "A gold chain, but I don't recall any details."

"Can you describe the device she showed you?" Itra asks.

Leon takes a small sip of bourbon. "It's a small box, maybe three-by-three inches, gold or gold plated, with an ember stone."

"The clearing is full," Altin calls. *"The previous captives are armed and are now marching towards the castle. Bar every entry, now!"*

Itra and Leon spring to action. They bolt up and sprint in different directions, checking the windows and doors in the suite.

"Clear," Leon calls from the bedroom.

"All good in here." Itra shakes the balcony door for good measure.

The warmth of the mug nearly scalds Danae's white-knuckled grip. "The last count Teuta gave of the holding bay was just over 900. We're entirely outnumbered, even with the support units." Nausea rises as a bitter acid taste fills her mouth. She sprints to the bedroom, surprising Leon as she shoulder checks him in the doorway, trying to move past him.

"Danae?" Itra follows her retreat, but she slams the washroom door in his face.

Itra and Leon whisper outside the door, but she can't make out their conversation. After rinsing her mouth and face, she closes her eyes, taking a slow deep breath in to settle her nerves and stomach. She opens her eyes to pitch darkness. "Elis." His face glows to life. He's busy licking an ice cream cone. "Elis, can you hear me?"

Elis shifts his posture. "Danae! I have chocolate and vanilla because I was a good boy. I didn't leave grandma or grandpa once today." Elis grins, taking another small lick before lowering his brow. "Medusa is coming, but I'll be there at dawn. Wait for me."

"Elis, wait!"

Total darkness surrounds Danae. She closes her eyes, inhaling once before opening them. She's staring at her pale reflection and her temple is now a deep purple. "Shit!" she mutters.

"Danae?" Itra asks as she opens the door. "What's wrong?"

The scowl on her face deepens as she relays the message from Elis.

"Iana would never bring Elis here!" Itra stomps out of the bedroom back to the living room. "There are too many risks. How do we warn her?"

Danae wraps her arms around his waist to comfort him, but also to find comfort herself. *"Ana, I received a message from Elis. He says he'll arrive here tomorrow at dawn and that Medusa is coming."*

"Medusa?" Junior asks.

"Elis is a kid!" Ana exclaims. *"Why would they bring him here?"*

"Hey, I'm just the messenger," Danae says. *"Can we contact Iana through your gift to make sure they stay far away from here?"* Danae squeezes her arms around Itra tighter.

"I'll try, but my gift is short-circuiting. I see one vision on a loop, replaying an event over and over."

"What is the event?" Berto asks.

"A battle at dawn, the castle domes shattering, and the protective barrier destroyed, exposing the Castle of Teskom to all dimensions."

"Illyria ember in time, light the fire at dawn, o'treasure of mine." A choir of voices sing in unison.

Altin whistles, pausing the escalating chatter. *"Focus, they're actively surrounding the castle, just beyond the barrier. Geri and Nordi are creating illusions of our army standing, weapons drawn. At their first move, our archers are ready to fire, but only warning shots. There is no secondary holding bay to portal too. Junior, at your command."*

Glendon shouts, *"We have tracked the holding bay location to a cavern near the Mokset Castle in the future dimension."*

"Do you have the exact coordinates?" Teuta asks.

"Yes, sending now," Glendon says.

36

Anton dials Ermal from his new phone while unloading the car. Iana climbs the front steps with a sleeping Elis. He was snoring ten minutes after they picked him up from Anton's parents.

"Detective Ermal," Ermal answers.

"Hey Ermal, it's Anton." Anton drops the bags in the entry before stepping back outside. "Any chance you're free to swing by Itra's place this evening?"

"Is Itra home? We received information from the tech team about the recording software uploaded to their phones, and there is some bad news I need to share."

"Danae and Itra aren't home. That is part of the reason we need to chat. Do you recall your hike with us yesterday afternoon?"

"I was where?"

"You hiked to the old Mokset Castle remains yesterday." Anton sucks in a breath. "You most likely woke up confused this morning?"

"Ha! Well, you're right about the confused part. I thought I went out drinking." Ermal laughs. "Is my car parked at Itra's house?"

"Yep, right next to mine. I had to borrow a car from a cousin to get back up here."

Ermal laughs. "I nearly—well, I almost—oh, they would've had my badge." He wheezes out one final chuckle. "I almost filed a stolen car report. I'll have a buddy drop me off within the hour."

"Great. See you soon."

Iana joins him on the porch. "Elis is sound asleep. Is Ermal coming by?"

Anton wraps his arm around her. "Yes. He was just as confused as we were this morning."

"I bet," Iana says.

Anton feels a frigid chill run down his spine. "I hope we're doing the right thing by bringing Elis up here."

Iana wraps her arms around his middle. "I still don't know what we should do. I'm hoping to get an additional vision or message."

"Ermal said he had an update from the tech team, including some bad news," Anton says into Iana's hair.

"Bad news is not what we need," she says, squeezing Anton once more before returning inside.

Anton leans forward on the porch rail, searching the Mokset hills for any motion. Daylight is narrowing to dusk, ominously outlining the ridge. A shiver of anxiety from his neck to his toes makes him release the rail and head inside.

Anton finds Iana standing next to the kettle reading a tablet. "Pemphredo is known for alarm and shock," she explains handing Anton the tablet. "My vision showed Kaly lunging towards Danae." She pulls her ponytail loose. "Was it Kaly or Pem? Why would either harm Danae?"

The kettle whistles, causing them to jump.

"Do you want coffee or tea?" Iana asks.

"Tea," Anton says, turning the screen towards Iana. He shows her the family tree from Pemphredo to Medusa.

"Medusa," Iana whispers, walking to the porch.

Anton follows her and they sit on the new bench. They gaze out at the hills and sip quietly awaiting Ermal. Dusk falls to a cloud-filled night, with no stars or moon visible.

"Headlights," Anton says, pointing down the narrow road. "I'll go open the gate." Iana watches as he gently sets down his mug.

Her gaze moves over him to the Mokset hills. She shivers, taking a small sip of hot tea to shake the chill.

A squad car pulls up the drive, and Ermal hops out, waving goodbye to the officer. The officer makes a three-point turn to get out of the crowded driveway. Anton closes the gate and turns to jog back. He stops mid stride noticing a small envelope in the grass barely visible under a few solar lights. He bends to pick it up, and the parchment immediately feels familiar. He jogs up to Ermal and Iana.

"Message received," Anton says, holding up the envelope.

Iana nearly drops her mug in surprise.

Ermal frowns. "Can you two fill me in here?"

"Come inside." Iana waves. "Are you on the clock?"

"Not tonight."

"Beer, wine, or whiskey?" she asks. Ermal's eyebrows shoot up. "Never mind. This will require whiskey for all of us."

Ermal and Anton follow Iana to the kitchen. She opens the liquor cabinet, pulling out the whiskey and three low ball glasses. "Ice?"

"No," Ermal and Anton answer in unison. She pours a generous three fingers of whiskey in each glass, handing off theirs before taking hers. Iana clinks her glass against each of theirs, taking a long swallow.

"This can't be good," Ermal mutters. "Bad news first. Unis Beard is no longer in custody. He was taken or escaped overnight."

Anton and Iana stare at Ermal.

Iana finally blinks and takes a long drink, finishing her generous pour. "Anton, can you replay the events of today while I go check on Elis?"

Anton responds by taking a large swig and refilling their glasses. He hands Ermal the card with the maze.

Ermal's eyes go wide, and his jaw falls open. "It is real," he whispers. "Holy shit."

Anton explains their confusion in the morning and the events of the day. Ermal compares his morning and notes he found his phone.

Iana overhears his last statement as she joins them at the table. "You got to keep your phone?"

"Keep is relative—it was wiped clean," Ermal says. "All my messages and contacts have been deleted." He sighs and takes a long sip of his whiskey.

"What was the other news?" Anton asks.

"The tech report came back this afternoon. The software uploaded to Itra and Danae's phones recorded every sound within proximity, including texts, key swipes, usernames, passwords, and web pages visited over the last two weeks. The data was stored on a massive hard drive recovered at Unis's home. He also had a secondary backup on a cloud server. They're still attempting to trace that server, but I wanted to share one file with Itra and Danae that we found on the hard drive." Ermal pulls out a thumb drive from his pocket. "Do you have a device I can plug this into?"

Iana brings the tablet to the table and replaces each glass with water before sitting down.

"Where is the envelope?" Iana asks Anton. He holds it up.

One word 'Now' is written in blue cursive handwriting and sealed with the family crest.

Ermal turns the tablet towards Anton and Iana.

"The maze," Anton whispers.

"It's a three-dimensional map of the entire castle, including the maze," Ermal says. He double taps to zoom back out. "Before you showed me the card this evening, I thought this may have been an elaborate video game mockup. But now I recognize the conservatory and the steps from memory."

Iana leans forward, wordlessly. She touches the screen. It zooms in to the plants near the entry and even the hidden door in the center to the dining hall. She double taps, and it zooms out. "Wow."

"It's really high tech. The team suggests that the program is one of a kind. No trademarks or patent signature markers, so essentially no known or licensed software, application, coding, or programming. I knew Itra would want to see it."

"May I?" Iana asks.

"Sure." Ermal hands over the device. "We found other evidence that the attorney's office is reviewing additional charges against Beard. The judge had denied Beard bail because of his available funds. He had over three million in cash available to withdraw. The last known tax record for Beard was over a decade ago, so the revenue officers are eager to get their greedy hands on him."

Anton whistles. "Three million is a heavy chunk of change for a rainy day. He could be anywhere by now."

Iana holds up the tablet. "It's here! The treasure. You can see it." Anton and Ermal nearly collide heads looking at the image of a large stone chamber with statues, chests, and framed art leaning against one wall, and bars stacked along another wall.

"Are those gold bars?" Anton asks, tapping to zoom it in further.

"Teuta's treasure," Ermal whispers. "I need to call the station and lock this file down." He leans back, dragging his phone out of his pocket, nearly dropping it from his shaking hands.

"Who do you think has seen this?" Iana asks.

Ermal holds up one finger. "Hey Rudina, is Twyla or Red still in?" Iana can't hear her response. "Hey, Red. I need to lock down the files from the Beard case. Block all access! Can we do that?" Ermal pauses. "The Castle of Teskom file. I want a report on my desk twice a day if someone attempts to access it. Do you understand?" Ermal pauses again. "Great. Do you know of any other copies of this file?" After another pause, Ermal stands and pounds his chest with a fist. "Not good. Keep me posted. Thanks again. Bye."

"What's not good?" Iana asks.

Ermal shakes his head. "The firewalls of our data center shows a potential hack around five this evening. They're attempting to identify the point of access and recover any lost or stolen files. Every file related to Beard's case has been flagged as potentially hacked. The report will take another hour to complete and understand the extent of the breach." Ermal sits and sighs. He drains his water. "We will be royally screwed if this leaks to the media. Every museum, scholar, treasure hunter or pirate, and nearly every damn citizen, will try to scale the ridge and access this fortune." Ermal points at the envelope. "What's in the envelope?"

Iana doesn't respond right away. "Sorry, that's a lot of information to process all at once." She turns the envelope over, breaking the wax seal. They lean back. No dust explodes. She removes the gold card with cursive writing in royal blue ink. She reads the card silently at first glance.

'Tomorrow at dawn, the veil will fall.
Arrive as a pawn or fail them all.

Tomorrow at dawn, Ember calls.'
Iana's vision goes dark.

"Iana?" Anton shakes her shoulders. Her eyes are open but not blinking. Her face is a mixture of grim and wonder.

"What's happening?" Ermal stands. "What did the card say?"

Anton reads it silently before passing the card to Ermal.

"Veil, what veil?" Ermal asks.

Elis bounds into the kitchen. "I'm ready for the hike. We need to go soon."

Ermal and Anton jump in surprise.

Iana faces Elis. She blinks a few times and smiles at him.

"We need to beat the sun, right, mama?"

"Right, baby," Iana says, standing. "Let's get something to eat and prepare food for later. We have two hours to prepare."

"Wait a minute," Anton says. "What's going on? It's dark. There isn't a smooth path up there. We can't go tonight."

"Dad, Ember will light the way," says Elis. "Duh!"

"Iana, a word in the hall, please," Anton says, moving towards the door. Ermal follows.

"Be right there," Iana says. "Can you get eight slices of bread out?" She hands Elis the bag of bread.

"You got it!" Elis sings.

Iana closes the door to the kitchen, motioning Anton and Ermal out to the front porch.

"Elis is the pawn at dawn," Iana says. Anton attempts to speak, but she shakes her head. "He's the key to keeping the Castle of Teskom veiled to the public. According to my vision, Elis is the compass to time. When he steps under the ember archway, he can move and slow time in a specific direction. This will give our side enough time to disarm a mechanism meant to harm the veil hiding the castle. Teuta has been training him for the last few weeks."

Anton runs a hand through his hair.

Ermal sits down, rubbing his face.

"Iana," Anton pleads. "We can't take him up there. The hike alone is risky in the daylight, but at night. We have no guarantee he'll be safe."

"Ember will shield him," Iana says, softly. "I promise. I've foreseen these events with and without him. If we do not arrive with Elis at dawn, our world and the dimensions beyond will erupt into chaos. The five dimensions will all see the castle at once. Beyond the treasures, the knowledge will bring massive wars and destruction. We have to do this." Iana takes Anton's hand. "Please trust me."

"I will guide you to the ember archway," Ermal says. "I think the path is scorched in my mind. I can literally see it. How did that happen?"

"Ember has a sense of humor," Iana says, trying not to laugh. "She is lighting the path through, Ermal."

Anton says scornfully, "You can laugh? How?"

"I wish I could share the vision. The outcome is clear. It's peaceful."

"Ugh!" Anton stomps his foot. "I trust you, but I'm mad that this has to involve Elis. Am I allowed to be mad?"

"Of course!" Iana kisses his cheek. "Ermal, do you have hiking gear, or do you need to borrow Itra's pack?"

"Let me check what the fairy left in my ride." Ermal bounds down from the porch and unlocks the rear of his SUV. "It looks like I'm all packed and ready to go." He isn't joking. He pulls out a fully stuffed pack and a pair of hiking boots. "Teuta?"

"Or Ember," Iana laughs. "I'll prep the food and fill the water bottles. Do either of you want coffee before we go?"

"Yes," Ermal and Anton say in unison.

Iana retreats inside.

Anton and Ermal stare at the hills.

"Ermal, do you really think you can navigate that trail at night?" Anton asks.

"If you would have asked me an hour ago, I would have said no. But ever since I read the latest message, the path to the archway appears clearly in my mind."

"Hmm," Anton responds.

Elis's laughter from the kitchen breaks the moment. Ermal takes his pack and shoes to the porch for further inspection. He pulls out four headlamps, a jacket, a clean shirt, pants, two pairs of socks, a water canister, three granola bars, and two apples. Ermal scrutinizes the clothes and food. After repacking the bag, he checks the lights on each headlamp before clipping them to a carabiner.

Anton watches him repack. "Are the clothes yours?"

"Nope, never seen them before, and there are no labels on the clothes or the granola bars."

"Coffee is ready." Iana calls from the kitchen.

"Ready for the first part of the adventure?" Anton asks.

Ermal tilts his head to the side.

"Iana's coffee is strong and almost guaranteed to make your heart pound out of your chest."

"Ah, something good to balance out the whiskey." Ermal winks.

Anton laughs as they enter the kitchen.

Iana and Elis have an assembly line of bread, peanut butter, and jelly on the kitchen counter. Iana motions to the two mugs at the far end.

Anton takes a small sip and winces.

Ermal smiles, taking his mug. "Cheers." He takes a small sip and nearly chokes. "Strong brew Iana." She turns and lifts an eyebrow. "Seriously, thanks!" He lifts his mug in a toast. She nods.

Anton picks up the tablet. "I think we should review the map while they finish prepping. I want to know all entries and exit points before we arrive." Ermal joins Anton in the living room as they tap their way through the castle floor plan.

"Mom, did you know that Danae is having twins, a girl and a boy?" Elis hands Iana the last sandwich.

"How do you know she is having twins?"

"Emit and Ora told me while I was napping in the car," Elis says, hopping down from the stool. "Be right back!"

Iana brings Ermal and Leon a sandwich and tops off their cups with fresh coffee. "Elis just told me Danae is having twins, a boy and a girl."

"Wait," Anton says, shaking his head. "What? How could he possibly know that?"

"Emit and Ora told him on the drive up here," Iana says, shaking her head. "We're done with the food prep. I'm going to change and get Elis ready. We should be ready in a half-hour. You two good with that?"

"One second," Ermal says, holding up the tablet. "Can you point out the treasure again?"

Iana points to a room below the maze.

The map reacts, showing a large, long room with shelves, but the treasure she showed them earlier no longer displays.

"That's odd," Iana says. "It was here below the maze earlier." She zooms the map in and out. She hands back the tablet in defeat. "Sorry."

Twenty minutes later, they're lacing up their boots, snapping on their packs, and locking the front door.

Ermal packs his sidearm and police radio.

Anton and Iana, already worried, find the addition oddly comforting.

Beyond the porch and solar lights in the drive, the darkness of the night is intense. The shuffle of noise from the sheep next door and a distant bark of a dog are the only sounds as they start their ascent.

37

Kaly wakes to the commanding voice of Don.

"We need to maintain our lines," Don says, pointing to the highlighted marks on a hologram map. "Each position needs to be precise, or else the mechanism will not fire."

"Yes, sir." The man salutes before leaving the cave opening.

"What mechanism?" Kaly asks as she stands rubbing her head. A three-dimensional map of the ridge's topography and a floor plan of the Castle of Teskom hovers above the table.

Don's eyes travel the length of her body, draped in a white gown. He answers in a low, throaty tone. "My Queen's future." He reaches to touch her bare shoulder.

Kaly instinctively steps out of reach. "Medusa's future? My husband and sister-in-law are inside these walls." Kaly points to the lower level. The map reacts, zooming in to the archive living quarters.

"The future is now." Don presses himself against Kaly's back.

"Back off!" Kaly stomps on his foot, elbowing her way away from him. "What mechanism? Where are we?"

"Feisty like Danae!" Don holds his foot. "The mechanism is classified. I can't share any details yet, but we plan to share the knowledge stored here with every dimension."

"Who's 'we'?" Kaly asks, holding up air quotes with her hands.

"Your Queen Medusa, and I," Don says. "You'll sever Mui's tie to Ember as payback for giving away Medusa's location to Perseus."

Kaly barks with laughter. "You think I'm a Grey Sister?"

"We know you are!"

"You're insane! Which one? Or do you think I'm all three?"

"We killed Deino last century, leaving Pemphredo and you, Enyo." He makes a hand gesture over the table. A new holographic map hovers with glimmering lights, shapes of buildings, movement from cars, and flying vessels.

"Where is Pemphredo?" Kaly asks. "And what happen to Unis?"

"Right where they need to be."

"You really expect me to believe any of this?" Kaly waves over the hologram. She edges around perimeter of the table, putting distance between her and Don. She observes the various landscapes. The mountain and ridges suggest its northern Albania, near Itra's home. However, the city landscape matches nothing she's ever seen outside of a science fiction movie. The buildings appear to be liquid and move with the atmosphere. The moving vessels, on closer inspection, are floating, not flying. "What is this?" Kaly stops, breaking her gaze from the display to look at Don.

"Bajze, Albania," Don states with a grin.

Kaly's eyes go wide. "When are we?"

"Smart and beautiful," Don smirks. "The year is 2284." Don watches her expression go from curious to shock. "Like I said, the future."

Kaly sits gracefully on the cold, stone floor before her knees give out. "It's 2284? No way. No freaking way. Leon. How am I going to get back?" She pushes her head between her knees, attempting to slow her rapid breathing.

Don kneels to her level. "Good news! You're likely a widow. So, you can let go of that pompous notion of being married to that lug of a wannabe warrior."

His cocky tone ignites a fire down Kaly's spine. She straightens and looks into his eyes, sucks in a breath, and screams.

"Ah!"

The sound echoes around the cave, causing a commotion just outside. A few heads dart around the corner to find Don on his knees, covering his ears.

Kaly inhales, screaming again.

Don cringes, closing his eyes.

Kaly bolts up, swipes the cube powering the map, and sprints out the same way the soldier left.

Don notices a moment too late, and he rushes out into a sea of men and women dressed in blue tunics. He rolls to his toes, seeking Kaly. *Nothing, no ripple in the crowd.*

Don pushes people away. "Move! Out of my way! Move!" Space is tight, hindering his progress.

Kaly watches him wade through the crowd. She made a hard left just outside the opening, finding a small divot in the stone wall. She flattened herself to the wall after glaring at the men nearby with a fierce warning. They resumed their conversation as if she had never arrived.

Don barrels out of the cave into the evening sun.

Kaly stays low, finding a discarded blue tunic. She discretely removes her white gown and hides the stolen hologram cube in a low knot in her hair. She hunches her posture and gait to appear small. She weaves around a few groups until she can see another opening a few paces ahead.

Kaly creeps forward and takes her chances following a woman heading in that direction. The space widens just past the opening, but the darkness further ahead suggests it may be a dead end or turn.

The woman slows and Kaly steps on the woman's heel.

"Excuse me," Kaly says. "Sorry."

The woman turns to Kaly, letting out a startled cry of surprise. Kaly immediately cups the woman's mouth, pushing her against the wall.

"Speak another word, and I'll break your neck. Nod if you understand."

The woman nods.

Kaly removes her hand, staring at the woman. "Do you know a second way out of here?"

The woman points to her mouth.

"Fine, speak, but softly."

"There's another opening down a flight of stairs around the next bend. Hop the spring at the bottom and walk the wall until you feel the opening."

"Where does it go?"

"It's a portal. The time is unpredictable."

"I'll take my chances," Kaly says, looking over her shoulder towards the crowd. "If that big man returns, scream snake as loud as you can!"

The woman nods.

Kaly stays low and moves deeper into the cave, towards the bend. She loses nearly all light once she turns. The darkness hinders her speedy escape. Nearly falling twice, Kaly feels her way carefully around stalagmites. A rush of frigid air moves her tunic to her right. Kaly moves towards the chilly air. *A dripping sound further down?* She reaches through an opening. She gently extends her foot out—only air, no floor. She squats down further and feels the ground. She blindly takes a step down. She finds solid footing; she tries again, another step. Not exactly evenly spaced, but she descends. Her eyes slowly adjusting to the darkness.

A clatter of noise echoes down into the stairwell. She listens for Don but hears only a commotion of footsteps. She quickly clears the last few steps. The dripping is a trickle of water feeding a narrow stream. She hops the stream and starts feeling the wall until her arm slips through. She pats the surface assessing the space for width and height. It's taller than her, but tight for any human. She blows out all of her air before she sucks in a breath and steps in the passageway.

38

Leon begins to pace the suite's living room. Itra slides a protective arm around Danae as they sit on the sofa and wait for the next call for action.

"Fire to warn, wound, or disable," Junior commands. *"No kill shots."*

"Our illusion defense is weakening," Geri calls.

"What is your location?" Teuta asks.

"East tower with Berto," Nordi responds.

"On my way," Teuta says.

A moment later, the tower door opens. Teuta hands two gold cuffs with embedded ember stones to Geri and Nordi.

"Enforce the illusion now."

Geri concentrates on the construction of an army standing their ground. The illusion forms, creating an army three layers deep, causing the new opponents to back away.

"It's working," Berto says. "Nordi, can you add a few arrows when the archers release their bows to confuse the targets?"

"No problem. Can you have five archers raise their bows but have only one fire?"

"At your command."

"Fire."

Eight arrows split off one arrow and land a few inches from the frontline.

"Perfect!" Berto states.

Teuta whirls around, exiting the tower. *"Ivan, can you meet me in the dining hall?"*

"On my way," Ivan says.

Leon's anxious pacing has moved on to pushups.

Danae curls her legs up on the couch. She leans against Itra. His chest falls into long breaths. She feels her eyelids sag before spiraling down to a welcome darkness.

"Hi, mama," a small voice calls.

Danae searches the darkness. "Who's there?"

"It's me, Emit." A small boy with brown eyes and dark, wavy hair appears. He reminds her of Itra, but his nose is smaller, less pronounced.

"Hi, Emit," Danae responds.

"Ora, are you coming?" Emit asks. A second later, a little girl appears. She has long brown ringlets, hazel eyes, and a heart-shaped face.

"Here," Ora says, smiling at Danae.

Her smile makes Danae gasp. *She looks like me.* The two children are both dressed in blue tunics with white flowing pants.

"Hi, Ora." Danae's voice is shaking. "Are you two lost?"

Ora and Emit giggle.

Emit says, "How can we be lost? We're with you."

"With me?" Danae asks, as her pulse pounds in her ears.

"Mom, wake up!" Ora says.

Danae wakes with such a jolt she accidentally elbows Itra in his stomach. Itra is groaning in pain. The light is gone outside.

Leon is snoring on the adjacent sofa.

"Did you have a nightmare?" Itra's gravelly voice makes her think they've been asleep for hours.

"I remember curling up next to you," she pauses, unable to find the words.

"We fell asleep," Itra says. "No big deal." He stands to stretch. "I wonder what time it is?"

Danae excuses herself. She replays the dream as she splashes cold water over her face. She dries her face with a towel, but the room is dark when she pulls the towel away.

"Elis?" Danae asks the darkness.

"We made it!" Elis sings. "We hiked at night. It was kind of spooky." The image shows him wrapped inside Iana's arms in a hammock. "We're ready to see you at dawn."

"Elis, no, wait—"

He's gone.

She closes her eyes and takes a few deep breaths.

Danae opens her eyes at the sound of an urgent, familiar knock. "Coming," she says, unlatching the door.

"Can you order breakfast?" Itra asks, hustling past her.

She nods and leans against the window in the bedroom. The cool glass feels soothing to her bruised temple. The maze is shadowed by the walls. She sighs.

"Ana," Danae says. *"I just had a conversation with Elis. They're here, near the archway. He said he would see me at dawn."*

"Danae, we'll need you in the east tower in thirty minutes," Altin says.

Itra bolts into the bedroom. "Why didn't you tell me about Elis? You can't go up there."

"I was going to tell you over breakfast. And I want to tell you about my other dream."

"Danae, did you hear me?" Altin asks.

214

"Copy, yes," Danae says.

Leon fills the doorway. "Like hell."

"Look, you two. There are a lot of players in the next few hours, and I'm one of them. Deal with it."

They glare at her but resign and nod.

"What was your other dream?" Itra asks.

"Two children called me mom, a boy named Emit and a girl named Ora. They even looked like us." She cradles her stomach and feels a wave of recognition. "I think we're having twins."

"Twins?" Itra's expression is half terrified, half joyful. Then the joy half wins, and he's grinning ear to ear. "A boy and a girl? Danae, that's amazing!" He picks her up and twirls her around the room.

"It's just a dream," she says breathlessly. "Getting dizzy."

Itra stops twirling Danae and steadies her as the room stops spinning. She laughs at his goofy grin. She looks over Itra's shoulder to find Leon frowning.

"Leon, are you okay?" Danae asks, stepping around Itra. She hooks her arm under Leon's arm.

"Do you remember the twins down the street when we were kids?" Leon asks as they walk towards the living room.

"Sure, didn't one join the army?"

"Ness joined the Air Force,"

"Ah, that's right, and the other was Nelle?"

"Yes, I think she teaches at the old high school. I failed to keep in contact with Ness over the years."

"Why did your mind go to them?" Danae asks, sitting at the table to a spread of food and warm drinks.

Leon and Itra sit immediately.

Leon answers between bites. "Diversion tactic 101. According to the group therapist, if something triggers a stressful thought, divert the thought to something happy. The word twin triggered that woman talking about Kaly's father being a twin, which made my heart race. My only other happy reference to twins was Ness and Nelle."

"And now Danae," Itra says, over a mouthful of eggs.

"Manners," Danae scolds Itra.

39

"What the actual—" Kaly says, breaking through a gooey substance. *Was that jello?* She wipes the sludge from her arm. Then she catches movement ahead and drops to the ground. The darkness makes any recognition of her surroundings impossible. Her gaze follows a dark, pacing figure. She attempts to crawl away quietly, but the cube flares to life, bathing her in light. She tries to cover the cube, but it's tangled in her hair.

The figure is moving in her direction.

Kaly panics and shouts, "Stop!"

The figure stops.

"Who are you?"

"Ermal. I'm a local police officer here in town. Are you British or American?"

"Neither," Kaly says. "What year is it?"

Ermal laughs. "2020."

Kaly sighs in relief. "Ermal, it's me, Kaly."

Ermal laughs and moves his hands through his hair. "How did you end up here?"

"Would you believe me if I said I walked through jello from the year 2284?"

Ermal laughs louder. Catching his breath, he says, "Tonight, I will believe just about anything. Come, we have a small camp just around the bend near the archway."

"Who is… we?"

"Anton, Iana, and Elis."

"Why are they here with Elis? Have they lost their minds? He's six!"

"I'll let Iana fill you in on those details. I'm just the guide." Ermal motions for her to follow. As they walk, he explains their expulsion, confusion, and the card about the pawn at dawn.

A small lantern back lights two adults standing over a hammock. The noise of their steps startles them, and one moves protectively in front of the other.

"It's Ermal and a friend."

Kaly, almost in tears, cries out, "Iana?"

Iana peeks around Anton.

"Kaly?" says Iana. "What happen to you?"

"Wait," Anton exhales. "It could be Medusa."

Iana stiffens.

"Are you Kaly, Pem, or Medusa?" Iana asks, narrowing her eyes.

Kaly walks forward towards the lantern, so the light touches her face. "I'm Kaly, Leon's Kaly. I was knocked out and tied up at the old Mokset Castle. When I came to, I was alone until Don arrived." Kaly shakes her head. "He's certifiably nuts."

"How are you here now?" Iana's posture is rigid.

"I came from the future in a portal passageway in a cavern wall near a stream. Ermal was pacing nearby."

"Were you followed?" Anton asks.

"I don't think so." Kaly holds up a small cube. "I took this from Don."

"Mom," Elis says, sitting up in the hammock. "It's time. Hi, Kaly."

Anton assists Elis out of the swaying hammock.

"Did we wake you?" Iana asks, patting his wild curls down.

"No," Elis says. "Ember did."

Elis turns to Kaly. "Did Don show you his plan?"

Kaly lowers to Elis's level, ruffling his hair. "Not exactly but I did overhear Don giving orders about setting a perimeter to align a mechanism."

Elis extends his hand. "May I please have the cube?"

She places the cube in his tiny palm.

Elis sets the cube on a smooth rock. He stands back and whispers, "Open says me."

A hologram map lights up, hovering above the cube.

Elis moves the map with practiced ease, each adult staring speechlessly.

"Here, correct?" He highlights a perimeter with eight bright spots.

"Yes," Kaly says.

"Mom, can you contact anyone inside?"

"Let me try," Iana says. *"Ana, can you hear me? Danae or Itra?"*

A roar of sound ignites before the isolation of one genuinely concerned and pissy brother rings over loud and clear.

Itra growls, *"Tell me you're not near the archway with Elis."*

"Sorry, brother. It's hard to say no when you receive an invitation with the option to arrive or the world will end. I need to get a message to Ana."

"I'm here," Ana answers. *"I can see a map. What are the eight bright spots?"*

"We believe these are the points Don has set up for a mechanism." Iana pauses and turns to Elis. "She can see the map and the designated points. Elis, what else do you need?"

"I need Danae in the east tower when I enter the archway. We'll connect as I guide her time to each of the eight points until they disable the mechanisms. I'm the compass for her to slow time."

Iana nods.

Anton and Ermal wordlessly stare at Elis.

Ermal begins to shift side to side.

Anton kneels to Elis's level.

"Danae is on her way," Berto says. *"How did you get this map?"*

"Kaly took it from Don in the future," Iana says. *"She found an opening in a cavern near the clearing."*

218

"That could explain how Don attacked Danae and I," Itra says.

Iana almost screams in panic. *"So, he could be here right now?"* She follows up aloud. "Don used that opening when he attacked Itra and Danae."

Ermal takes a defensive post after turning off the lantern. Elis deactivates the map, pocketing the cube. The sky lightens as the group falls silent and watchful.

"It's time." Elis turns, walking purposely towards the ember archway. Iana follows after taking Anton's hand as he stands.

"We're coming," Iana calls. *"Please protect my son at all costs."*

"Wait, what are we supposed to do?" Kaly asks. "What about Leon?"

"Stay, watch, and listen," Elis says. "You'll know when you're needed." He barely finishes the last word before walking with confidence through the ember archway.

40

Pemphredo fights her restraints in the darkness. "I did what you wanted! Let me go!"

"It's just the beginning," says Medusa, sauntering into the bunker.

"Ember will destroy you!" Pemphredo spits.

"She'll never see it coming before it's too late." Medusa laughs. "I will take the very thing she wants to protect the most."

"Kaly is smart. She'll stop all of this before it's too late."

"You have faith in the professor?" Medusa asks. "Why?"

Pemphredo ignores her questions and continues to fight the restraints.

"That's amusing." Medusa moves back towards the door.

"Wait!"

"Graveling doesn't suit you," says Medusa. She leaves the bunker, closing and locking the door behind her.

"Unit four, defend Elis's position in the archway," Altin commands.

Elis hops up on the old hitching post near the archway to view the clearing. Dozens of men and women in blue tunics run in every direction as arrows descend from the castle.

Iana places a protective hand on Elis's shoulder.

"Mom, is Danae in place?"

"Elis, I'm here," Danae says. *"Can you hear me?"* A very anxious Itra is shuffling behind her. She mutters to him, "Stop pacing!"

"Hi, Danae," Elis says. *"Ana, can you point Danae towards the western mark?"*

"Copy," Ana says. *"Ready."*

Elis hops down. *"Danae, repeat after me."* He keeps one foot on the ember at the base of the archway and one foot on the grass. He raises one arm, pointing west.

"Time will bend. Ember will descend."

Danae repeats the phrase. *"Time will bend. Ember will descend."*

A cloudy haze descends over the western mark—movement slows to a crawl under the veil.

"Move the unit in now!" Elis calls. *"Remove any jewelry or metal-plated objects."*

Altin commands, *"Unit one, go."*

Anton taps Iana. "What's happening?"

Iana points to the west. "Our son is bending time with Danae." Her lips curl upward—his face reflects her own.

"Ana, move Danae to the next point, east of the last," Elis says. *"Repeat the phrase with me."*

Elis and Danae chant in unison, *"Time will bend, Ember will descend."* A second cloudy haze falls over the next mark. *"Altin, now."*

"Unit seven, go," Altin commands.

"Unit one, one device recovered a small gold cube with an ember stone. We identified no other jewelry. Restrained fourteen men, seventeen women, over."

"Elis," Junior calls. *"Altin has the other units ready. Just say go after you're in position."*

Elis and Danae repeat the phrase six more times. Each unit recovers a gold cube with one ember stone. Elis utters his final, *"Go."*

The sun crests the eastern mountain range in harmony with Elis's final command. The light changes from a dewy morning glow to full sunrise, highlighting the true nature of the battle.

Arrows litter the ground. The few intruders not under the veils of slowed time escape through the future archway. No blood, just a slow-motion choreographed sequence of capturing and disarming the opponents.

"Ana, can you scan for any outliers?" Junior asks.

"Copy," Ana says.

Elis spins to Anton with a huge grin. "Dad, we did it!" He jumps to high-five Anton.

As Elis's feet leave the ground, a wave of air blasts through the clearing. Anton catches Elis as the force of the impact propels everyone up and back before free falling.

Anton gasps on impact. Air slowly returns to his lungs with a sharp pain.

"Elis, are you okay?" Anton grunts, patting him over. Feeling the rise and fall of his chest against him provides some relief. "Hey Elis, wake up." Anton shifts to look back. "Iana!"

A few of the unit four men slowly rise to a seated position, looking around disorientated. Anton catches the men's attention. "We need help!" A few of the men crawl over to Anton. "Check Iana first. My son is breathing."

"Sir, Iana's gone," the unit man says.

Anton twists and grunts with pain to look for Iana. "She's gone?"

The man points to the ember archway.

Elis stirs, drawing Anton's gaze away from the archway. "Elis," Anton says, "can you hear me?"

"Dad?" Elis whispers.

"Are you ok?" Anton stifles a cry. "Does anything hurt?"

Elis whimpers. His eyes are squeezed shut.

"It's ok. I've got you!" Anton cuddles him closer despite the pain in his ribs.

"Ember heals those that protect and serve," Dita calls, running up to Anton. "He may be sore for a minute or two, but she'll work her magic."

"Where did Iana go?" Anton asks.

"Mom?" Elis asks, a little more alert.

"The blast threw her back through the ember archway," Dita says. "I have two medics going through now to check on her. Can I assess Elis?"

Anton nods, looking back at the two medics as they vanish under the archway. He winces when he moves, giving space for Dita to look Elis over.

"Anton, are you injured?" she asks.

Anton nods, pointing to his ribs.

"Assess his ribs." She calls out to another medic. Dita quickly examines Elis. "Elis is okay."

"Looks like just bruising maybe a fracture, but no broken ribs," the medic reports Anton's injuries.

"Anton, do you want to stay with Elis or go to Iana?" Dita asks.

Itra runs towards Anton. "Anton, go! I'll stay with Elis."

Anton lets a tear fall, unable to weep in fear of the pain. Itra helps him stand.

"Thank you." Anton leans on Itra. "What happened?"

"Our best guess is the second that time stopped bending. Ember descended, pushing everyone out and away from the barrier. But that is only speculation."

Anton carefully bends over Elis, gently kissing his cheek. "Be good for Itra. See you soon, buddy. Love you!" Elis mumbles something with his eyes still closed.

Danae and Leon run towards Anton and Itra.

"Is he ok?" Danae asks, kneeling next to Elis.

"Yes," Itra says. "Leon, can you go with Anton and check on Iana?"

"Of course, I also need to find Kaly."

Itra narrows his eyes at Leon. "Take a weapon or ten if Don is there waiting—you may not have a chance."

Leon pats Itra's back and jogs over to a unit commander. He returns, weapon in hand.

Danae hugs Leon and Anton. "See you soon." Anton and Leon nod and vanish under the ember archway.

"Rise and shine, buddy," Itra sings. "It's breakfast time!" Elis stirs, but still doesn't open his eyes. "Elis, we can have chocolate chip pancakes with hot chocolate."

One eye pops open. Elis takes a minute to focus. "With marshmallows?" he exhales with a ragged cough.

Itra looks to a medic nearby in alarm. The medic gives a wink and small grin before moving on to another injured man.

"Of course, buddy!"

Elis slowly blinks a few times. After a few deep breaths, Elis turns around, searching for Iana and Anton.

"Your mom and dad are okay. Danae and I will look after you until they return." Elis's eyes fill with tears. Itra picks him up. "You did great! They're so proud of you!"

"It's my fault," Elis stammers between a sob. "I meant to keep my feet grounded until it was time."

"Hey, buddy, it's not your fault," Itra whispers, smoothing down his curls. "You did everything right."

"Elis, we did it," Danae says. "We bent time."

Elis sniffles and sighs into Itra's shoulder. Itra shifts Elis as they climb the first step.

Ana comes down to join them. "Elis, my dear," Ana says over his sniffles. "You were fantastic! Come inside. We have so much to show you, plus we have breakfast waiting."

Elis peeks out from Itra's shoulder and catches a glance of Ana. His expression goes from joy to confusion.

"Are you my mom, too?" Elis asks, reaching out to stroke her cheek.

Ana clasps his hand on her cheek, kissing his palm, an action Itra has seen his sister do hundreds of times.

Elis launches himself at Ana. She catches him without missing a beat, burying her nose in his neck.

The image is strikingly familiar. Danae catches Itra's gaze; his eyes are glassy with tears.

"Do you like pancakes too?" Elis says somberly into her hair.

"Sure do," Ana laughs. "But only with chocolate chips."

Elis giggles. He leans back to look her in the eyes. "Me too!" He climbs down. "Last one to the table is a rotten egg!" He bolts through the large entry but skids to a stop. "Wow!" He spins in a circle, stopping to examine the waves on the floor.

A noise from the conservatory distracts Elis. He strolls in, picking at some leaves, smelling others, and stops to touch the elephant waterspout.

Itra reaches over and pulls the elephant ear forward. Water gurgles out, surprising Elis. He splashes and laughs loudly before the door to the dining hall opens—Itra's double steps through, grinning.

"Elis, you should see the size of my hot chocolate," Itra's double teases.

"Two Uncle Itras? So cool!" Elis runs towards him. Itra's double sweeps him up.

"Hope my brother plans to run off Elis's sugar high," Ana says. Itra and Danae laugh.

The noise level rises with intensity as they join the others at the table. An argument between Teuta, Ivan, and Junior seems to be in full swing.

"He reminds me of you, Itra," says Gjeto. "His posture, his walk, even the giggle." Gjeto smiles with love towards Elis.

"Iana always says he is a mini-me," Itra says and laughs at Elis's expression after he uncovers his breakfast. His squeal of delight nearly silences the room.

"Any idea what the argument is about?" Itra asks Gjeto, gesturing towards Junior.

"Itra!" Elis laughs. "Look at the size of this pancake!" He motions with his hands outstretched on either side of his head. Elis has the floor; all eyes turn towards him. He takes a long, loud sip of his hot chocolate. "Mmm, that's so good! I'm never leaving this table."

Laughter fills the space, cracking the tension in the hall.

Junior, Ivan, and Teuta leave the hall for Ivan's study. Ivan slides the door closed.

"The ship artifacts recovered from Alexandria are staying," Ivan says. "They're mostly relics related to the Illyrian era, nothing significant enough to turn over to Cairo authorities. End of discussion. My primary concern at the moment is what triggered the blast."

"Fine," Junior sighs. "But the devices in today's attack came from the same vault where we plan to store these items. We need to establish a new vault and increase layers of security. And what if those devices triggered the blast?" He narrows his gaze at Ivan and Teuta. "We could be dealing with a betrayal of huge consequence if we failed to protect and serve."

"Let's not jump to any accusations," Teuta chides.

Junior stomps. "No! Ask questions now or else." He barges out of Ivan's study without another word.

Teuta and Ivan follow Junior out to the dining hall.

The noise has simmered to the clink of silverware against plates and a contagious round of yawns.

Junior stands at the head of the table. He picks up a vacant chair and slams it down, causing several people to shout in response.

"Good, now that I have your attention. We know that a member of this family is responsible for the attack against Ember. This betrayal may very well sever our blood line with the Castle of Teskom. If anyone here knows anything about these devices," Junior says, holding up a gold and ember cube and scanning the table for anyone refusing eye contact. "Step forward now."

"Who are you?" Elis innocently asks. Itra places a protective arm around him as Junior locks eyes with Elis.

"My name is Mui Junior or just Junior, to most here."

Elis cocks his head and smiles at him. "Ember said you would be angry, Mr. Junior. My name is Elis." He never breaks eye contact with Junior.

Junior mimics Elis's posture. "Ember said I would be angry?"

"Yep." Elis takes a long sip of hot chocolate. "If you examine the vault, the real cubes are in a trunk with a red eagle. The object you're holding is a fake. The ember stone is only real on one."

Junior looks down, turning the cube over, then looks to Ivan and Teuta and back to Elis. "When did she tell you this?"

"About two minutes ago, before you came charging through that door."

"Altin, please escort Ivan to the vault to verify this information." Junior commands.

Altin stands wearily at first but straightens, joining Ivan as they head towards the door.

Elis yawns.

"Elis is ready for a long nap," Vincent says.

Itra yawns. "I second that."

41

Kaly involuntarily whimpers with fear as she watches Anton and Iana walkthrough after Elis. Exhausted, she asks, "What kind of cryptic crap was that?"

"The object of this puzzle is just to stay vigilant," Ermal says. "Everything else is a gamble."

"I love to gamble." A deep booming voice startles Ermal and Kaly. Ermal turns, frantically trying to locate the sound of the voice.

Don rounds the bend. "I see you found my portal."

Kaly moves behind Ermal.

Don pounds his fist into his palm. "You took something and someone from me." Don retrieves a large dagger from his boot and leaps two steps, covering a distance too impossible to comprehend.

Ermal fires his sidearm, hitting Don square in the chest.

Kaly screams, crouching and holding her hands over her ears.

Don stumbles back, looking down at the red stain forming in the center of his chest. "How?" His face turns blood red as he charges towards them again, dagger raised, but Ermal fires again, landing a shot just above Don's right eye. His slow fall is almost graceful.

The thud of his weight shakes the earth just as the sun meets the eastern horizon.

Ermal lowers the sidearm, placing it back in the holster before his knees give. "What have I done?"

"Thank you," Kaly whispers, touching Ermal's shoulder.

He pulls away.

"It's okay, you're in shock."

Kaly turns towards Don's prone form but quickly turns away, bending at the waist, heaving in response.

"Ugh," Kaly mumbles.

Ermal hands her a canteen from his pack.

She rinses her mouth and secures fallen strands of hair behind her ears. Her voice is still shaky but she says with confidence, "Ermal, you did the right thing. It was the only thing you could've done."

Ermal kicks the dagger away from Don's body. He kneels to check Don's pulse but finds only air. He quickly stands and steps back, looking down and around.

"Where did he go?" Ermal asks.

Kaly points up.

Ermal looks up to find transparent droplets moving up towards the sky from the spot where Don's body was moments ago.

Kaly steps up beside Ermal. "The moment you moved the dagger away, his body melted into water flowing up like rain. There's that old saying 'ashes to ashes, dust to dust.' Guess it's different for the god of water."

Ermal steps back, his face pales, and sits hard on the ground.

Kaly bends to examine the dagger—a leaf-shaped blade, a round bronze pommel, a wide hide wrapped grip, and a straight bronze cross-guard. She hesitantly wraps the hilt with her tunic, and she shifts the blade in the morning light. Finding the right angle, she stops to read the engraved text—ὕδωρ.

"This means water in ancient Greek," she says, pointing out the text to Ermal.

"Kaly?" a voice calls from behind them.

Kaly whirls around to find Leon jogging towards her. A few other figures are kneeling behind him just outside the archway. He stops, staring at the dagger in her hand.

Kaly drops the dagger, realizing how she might look—raising her hands, showing Leon no other weapons.

"Kaly?"

"Yes," Kaly cries out. "Don is dead."

"He was here?" Leon asks, drawing his weapon and looking around for a body.

Ermal raises his hand. "I shot him twice."

"Is he dead?" Leon asks.

Ermal nods.

"Where's the body?" Leon asks.

"Evaporated," Ermal says. Leon raises an eyebrow. "No really, he melted into water when I kicked the dagger away."

Leon shakes his head and lowers his weapon.

"Where's the rest of the group?" asks Ermal, straining to make out the people kneeling by the archway over Leon's shoulder. "Is it over?"

"Elis is with Itra and Danae," Leon says, pointing to the archway. "Iana's injured. Anton and the medics are with her."

"Iana, shit, how bad?" Kaly asks. She starts to move towards Anton, but Leon holds her back.

"Let them work," Leon says.

"How was she injured?" Ermal asks. "What happened?"

Leon explains the blast after dawn and turns to Kaly. "How did you end up here with Ermal?"

Kaly explains her escape from the future. He motions for her to stop talking.

"I need a few questions answered before you go any further," Leon says. Kaly nods. "Who released you after you were tied up at the old Mokset Castle?"

"Don."

"Where did he take you from there?"

"To another bunker."

"Was anybody else there?"

"Yes, Unis Beard—"

"Unis?" Ermal asks, interrupting Kaly. "How?"

"He claims Don took him from jail."

"And who else?" Leon asks.

"Don said she was his Queen," Kaly says with a frown. "Medusa."

Leon and Ermal step back in surprise.

"Who are you?" Leon asks.

"Kaly."

"When is the last time you saw me?"

"The archive living quarters."

"That was you?" Leon asks.

"Kind of," Kaly says, lowering her head. "It was my projection. I could see, feel, talk, and hear you and Danae, but I was still bound in the bunker."

"I tackled you!" Leon grunts.

"I think I was projecting through the woman you called Pem," Kaly says.

Leon shakes his head. "You kissed my nose."

"Not my physical lips, just my conscious thought of kissing you," Kaly says.

"Shit," Ermal whispers.

"What the actual—you really think we are that gullible?" Leon says, lowering his tone and steps within a foot of her. "How did she enter the archives?"

"The gold cube," Kaly says. "Don bragged about the portal device before leaving the bunker."

Leon narrows his eyes. "And the shimmering magic she pulled off?"

"Assuming she has some sort of trinket like mine," Kaly says, pulling a gold chain with a snake coil charm from under her blue tunic.

Leon reaches for it, but Kaly steps back.

"If you remove this," Kaly whispers. "I turn to stone. Medusa placed it around my neck when my wrists were still bound."

Leon steps closer but doesn't touch her. "You're real. My Kaly?" She launches herself into Leon's arms.

Leon stiffens at her embrace.

"Do I smell like home?" Kaly whispers.

Leon sighs in relief. He picks her up, allowing her to wrap herself around him.

Ermal turns away to give them a moment and starts to walk towards Anton and the medics.

"Iana!" Anton shouts.

Ermal sprints towards him.

"Oh, no!" Anton yells.

Leon untangles from Kaly and they run towards Anton.

"What's happening?" Kaly asks as Leon kneels next to Iana.

"She…" Anton cries. "They can't find a pulse." He sobs. "She stopped breathing."

One medic administers chest compressions, but the other medic vanishes under the ember archway. Leon assists the medic, taking over with chest compressions.

"How long without a pulse?" Leon asks the medic.

"Almost three minutes," the medic replies. He checks her airway to start mouth to mouth.

The other medic and Dita appear at a run towards Iana.

Leon stands to defend but recognizes Dita and steps back.

Dita kneels at Iana's side.

"Clear!" Dita calls, placing her hands on Iana's chest.

Iana's chest rises and falls once.

"How is she doing that?" Ermal whispers.

"Dita's a healer, remember?" Leon whispers.

Dita checks for a pulse. She shakes her head. "Clear!" She calls again. She checks her pulse again and examines Iana's eyes. She shakes her head. She continues her attempts to revive Iana.

After nearly thirty minutes. She sighs before wiping her tears and sweat away.

"Time of—"

"No!" Anton cries. "Keep trying!"

Kaly holds Anton back from lunging towards Dita.

Dita stands. "Anton, I'm so sorry."

Anton shoves Kaly aside and drops next to Iana. "You have to keep trying!" He sobs. "I need her. Elis needs her! Do something!"

"Leon!" Ermal yells.

Leon looks up to find Kaly, frozen to stone. The snake charm and chain are laying on the ground.

"Kaly!" Leon grabs the chain and fumbles with the clasp, trying to place it back around Kaly's neck. "The clasp is broken. Help!"

Dita manages the clasp and places it around Kaly's neck.

"Kaly!" Leon cries. Her stone eyes stare back. He screams, "Medusa!"

42

The unit near the archway draws their weapons when Dita steps through holding Don's dagger.

"All clear," Dita says.

Vincent quickens his pace towards her. Tears are falling down his face.

"Is she really gone?"

She nods.

"My dear niece," Vincent cries. "Gjeto and I will break the news to Itra and Danae. Is Leon staying with Kaly?"

"Yes," Dita says. "I tried to convince him to come inside, but he refused to leave." She shakes her head. "Ermal has arranged a chopper to transport Iana, Anton, and Elis back to the valley. Anton needs Elis."

"Of course." Vincent nods. "We have another problem," he says. "They found one major item missing." He turns to walk back towards the castle.

"Wait," Dita says. "You can't just drop a bomb like that and walk off." She jogs, catching up with Vincent.

"A painting of Medusa on a bronze shield."

"It's not over?"

Vincent shrugs as they reach the giant stairs. "Can you help this old man up?"

Dita climbs up the first stone, reaching for his hand. She explains the events in the clearing as they amble up the last step and inside.

A giant force of air rushes through, knocking over a few plants.

Bang

They duck down in alarm. The large wood and iron entry door is closed, and the iron bar across the door is secure.

"What the—" Dita mutters. "Where are Itra and Danae?"

"In their suite," Gjeto says from the dining hall door. She nods.

Gjeto and Vincent head towards the rear of the conservatory.

"Sister, a word," Junior calls from the open dining hall door.

Dita enters the dining hall and follows Junior towards Ivan and Teuta.

"Dita," Ivan says formally. "We just need to ask a few follow-up questions."

Dita says nothing, waiting on the first question.

Teuta asks, "Did Kaly mention Don?"

"Don is dead." Dita lays Don's dagger on the table.

They exchange wide eye looks of shock.

Ivan asks, "Did Leon kill Don?"

"Does it matter who did?" Dita asks in return.

"No," Junior responds, "well, maybe. Where's the body?"

"Floating in the atmosphere." Dita looks at their blank faces. "He melted into water when they moved his dagger away from his body."

"You saw this happen?" Teuta asks.

"No, Kaly and Ermal did," Dita answers.

"So, Leon did not kill him," Junior states. "That's good."

Ivan folds his hands behind his head and loudly exhales. "Well, the other missing artifact is a problem. The Medusa Shield. Da Vinci painted the shield, but the bronze shield itself is the relic, not the painting. It holds the castle's mirror shield together. It appears the perimeter set up was a ruse."

"Seven of the devices were fake," Junior says. "The only working device is homemade. The expulsion of air that flattened the grounds was Ember's alarm."

234

Dita's skin prickles with a warning.

"We're using illusions to maintain the shield, but Geri and Nordi can only do so much. We have failed. The castle appeared in all dimensions for nearly an hour."

Dita exhales a breath, looking at the worry on their faces. "And none of us saw this coming?"

Teuta flicks her wrist. An image hovers above the table. A woman dressed in a white gown with long dark curly hair opens a door, walks in, takes a shield-shaped object from the room, and vanishes. The image flicks again from a different angle, showing the woman's face.

"Is that Pem or Medusa?" Dita steps closer to the image. The image vanishes and a third appears. The same woman is wandering in the archives. "When was this last clip taken?"

"Almost six hours ago," Ivan replies.

"Can you zoom in?" Dita asks. "What's hanging around her neck?"

Teuta zooms in on the image.

"The chain hanging from the woman's neck is different from the one Kaly was wearing before—she wasn't," Dita says. "And the first image of the woman in the vault?"

Teuta moves her hand flipping the image back.

Dita points. "No chain."

"The woman in the archives and vault wasn't Kaly," Dita says. "So, it is either Medusa or Pem." She explains what Kaly told Leon about her encounter with a veiled woman Don called Medusa.

Suddenly, a glow emerges. A blinding light covers the entire dining hall.

They freeze in response.

"Illyria ember in time," a voice sings, "light the fire at dawn, o'treasure of mine. Illyria ember in time, discover the haze the army will raise, o'treasure of mine. Illyria ember of mine, uncover the maze you will embrace all treasures in time."

Junior coughs loudly, unable to hold a choking curse.

"Who has the shield?" Ivan asks.

"Her reflection to behold is not so old, but her disguise will cause a rise," the voice sings.

The room falls dark for a moment before the natural daylight streams in from the dome above.

They stand, blinking several times to adjust to the light.

"Ember has spoken," Teuta says. "The disguise will cause a rise?"

"Pem's disguise of Kaly?" Dita answers.

"Maybe?" Teuta responds.

"A rise of the shield?" Ivan asks.

"We need to recover the shield," Junior says. "Is there a way to track any portals used here or in the vault?"

"I will check the library and archives," Ivan says, walking briskly to the library entry. He pauses before going in. "Junior, we need an update from Berto on a longer alternative to hold the illusion shield."

Junior nods. *"Berto location?"*

"East Tower," Berto responds.

Junior abruptly turns and walks through the conservatory door.

Dita relays Anton's request for Elis.

"Is he medically clear to transport?" Teuta asks.

Dita nods.

"It's the least we can do," Teuta says with a frown. "Tani."

"Will you come with me to the future cavern?" Dita asks.

Teuta nods.

Gjeto knocks lightly on Itra's door.

Itra stiffens when he opens the door to Vincent and Gjeto.

"May we come in?" Gjeto asks.

Itra opens the door wider, gesturing to the living space. Elis is snoring softly in the middle of the large bed.

Danae stands from the couch as they enter. She notices Itra's grim face and tears immediately fill her eyes. "What's happened?"

Gjeto motions for them to sit.

"Iana," Gjeto struggles to keep his tone even. "She's gone."

Itra stands. "What do you mean, gone?"

"The blast threw her under the archway," Vincent explains. "Iana suffered a major head injury and—"

"No, not possible!" Itra exclaims.

"Itra," Gjeto says, "they tried to revive her, but Iana's gone."

Danae stands. "Why didn't they move her back inside the archway. Ember is a goddess. She can do anything, right? Bring her back, bring her back to life!"

Vincent and Gjeto shake their heads.

"Anton has asked Teuta to transport Elis to him so he can break the news," Vincent says.

Itra sprints towards the bedroom.

Elis is gone.

Itra crumples to the floor. "She can't be, she can't."

43

Elis appears near Anton's feet just before they are about to board the chopper.

Anton scoops him up.

Elis mumbles, "Mama." Anton pulls him closer. Elis sighs and then snores.

Leon nods towards Anton as they board the chopper.

Anton mouths two words out the window. *"I'm sorry."*

Leon shakes his head and watches them take off from the clearing. He shields his eyes from the dust kicked up and turns away, walking back towards Kaly.

He kneels at the base of her stone figure. His tears fall in quick succession. He pounds his fists into the ground until they are numb and bloody.

"Why her?" Leon asks, looking up at her sculpted face.

A small snap of a branch has Leon on his feet scanning the area.

"Who's there?"

"Unis."

Leon can see him stepping out of a few thorny bushes further down the path. He snags his jail issued scrubs on the bramble.

"You did this!" Leon points to Kaly's frozen form.

"No!" Unis raises his hands in protest. "Don took me from jail and placed me in a bunker. He brought Kaly there. Medusa placed the gold chain around her neck."

"And let you live?" Leon says through clinched teeth.

"Right," Unis whispers. "About that. I am a ticking time bomb."

Leon draws his borrowed weapon.

"Wait! If Medusa reclaims the Castle of Teskom, Kaly will return to life."

Leon levels his weapon to Unis's chest.

"Seriously, I was only a last-ditch effort if Poseidon and Kaly failed to persuade you and Danae to sever the ties with Mui's line." Unis steps back slowly.

"Don't move another step," Leon commands. "How would I sever the ties with Mui's line?"

"Time," Unis whispers.

"She wants my sister's unborn child?"

Unis nods.

Leon fires the weapon to the left of Unis's feet.

Unis yelps in surprise.

"Try again."

"Look," Unis whimpers. "I'm only telling you what I know."

"You seem to be in the know," Leon says, "when you were harassing my wife and sister."

"I was blackmailed."

"Ha!" Leon scoffs, aiming for his head.

"I swear," Unis says, holding up his hands. "I was sent anonymous tips with specific instructions. If I completed the task, I would receive a lump sum payment. If I failed…they would withdraw the payment amount instead."

"You were paid?"

"Yes, but only because I was being blackmailed," Unis says. "As a blogger I don't make much. I never knew what was at stake here."

"What is your actual name?"

"Unis Beard."

Leon fires to the right of his feet. "Last chance."

"Earl Eunice McCoy." He closes his eyes and covers his chest.

"Earl?" Leon scoffs.

He nods.

Leon steps nose to nose with him. "If I find out you're lying, I'll slit your throat ear to ear."

"Not lying," he stutters. "I swear!"

"Where is Medusa?" Leon asks, stepping back and raising the weapon.

"Inside." Earl points to the ember archway. "She returned to the bunker with a shield and gave me my very own death trinket." Earl slowly raises his right pant leg. A live snake is wrapped around his ankle. "If any harm comes to her, it'll bite. According to her description, my agony will be long and painful and will ultimately end in death."

"How did you get here?" Leon asks.

Earl holds up a small gold cube with an ember stone. "She set the coordinates. I felt the ground fall from under me, and I landed in that bush."

"Why did she send you here?" Leon asks.

"Only a guess," Earl says. "She knew Kaly was stone, and you wouldn't leave her side."

Leon yells, "Danae!"

44

Itra and Danae make their way down to the dining hall. Junior stands at their arrival, expressing his condolences.

Itra and Danae nod.

Junior gestures towards the table, and they sit.

"Where is Leon?" Danae asks.

"Leon is alive," Junior says. "But Kaly was turned to stone just outside the ember archway."

Danae and Itra explode. "What!"

Junior explains the events in the clearing starting with Kaly's encounter with Medusa. He moves on to the missing shield, the blast, and how Kaly ended up as stone.

"Where is Leon?" Danae whispers.

"He is in the clearing with—"

Danae shoves the chair back and turns for the door.

"Wait!" Junior calls.

"Like hell!" Danae jogs to the front entry. It's still barred. "Open says me!"

The door remains closed.

She calls louder and with more authority, "Open says me!"

The door doesn't budge.

Itra jogs up beside her. "Danae," he whispers. "The rest of the family is gone."

"What do you mean, gone?" Danae asks turning her focus to Itra's face. His brows come together.

"We failed."

Danae flinches.

"The family failed to protect and serve," Itra whispers.

"How?" Danae asks.

"The shield has not been recovered," Junior says, walking towards them. "Chapter Nine expelled Ivan and the family back to their homes and timelines. They will have no memory of the events here or the battle."

"Why are we still here?" Danae asks.

"The blood oath," Teuta says stepping out from the future cavern stairwell.

Danae whirls around to face Teuta. "Did you lock us in?"

"No," Teuta says as she flicks her wrist. She frowns staring at the door. She flicks her wrist again. "Ember?"

45

The falling feeling slams into Danae's gut before she collides with Itra.

"What the hell was that?" Danae asks, looking around. They're standing in the maze. She spins, looking up to the windows and balconies, feeling the eyes of someone watching. She stops, finding a veiled woman at a window looking down.

The woman nods just slightly.

Danae feels an icy chill down her spine.

"Danae," Itra says. "The statue is moving."

Danae turns away from the window and watches statue move unveiling a set of stairs.

"Stay here," Itra says. "I'll look for another exit." He runs through the maze trying to recall the routes he traced from the card sent to Iana. He hits a dead end and doubles back. "Dead end, trying another," he calls. He mutters a curse after hitting the second dead end. He returns to the center. "Danae, I think we need to go down."

Danae scans the rest of the windows and balconies.

The setting sun shifts the castle in a slow rotation towards the east.

"I think I saw Medusa in a window, but she's gone now."

"Yep, we are going down," Itra says, striding down the first three steps, reaching his hand for hers. "We aren't waiting around for her to return."

She grips his hand hard with a squeeze, and he squeezes back a gentle response.

The stairs are all stone, mostly even, making progress easy. Darkness falls and suffocates the air around them.

Danae stops. "Itra, I think the opening closed above us and I feel cold to my bones."

Itra taps his light stone, making them blink several times.

Their eyes adjust to the illuminated space.

"It's okay," Itra says. "I don't think it goes too much further. Stay close." He kisses her quickly before taking another step down.

The stairs abruptly end to a long doorless corridor. A small light further down indicates maybe it turns or curves.

They jog forward.

Itra feels a prickle run down his spine; he stops to look back. The entry to the stairwell is gone.

"Danae!" Itra whispers.

Danae slows and turns around. "Open says me," she calls loudly, surprising Itra.

A wall shifts a few steps away.

Danae laughs. "Hey, I didn't think it would work. I was just trying to remain calm."

"Good to know practical thinking is part of your calm strategy."

They creep close to the opening, listening for any movement or voices.

He stretches his neck out long enough to look inside. He turns back, frowning. "Don't kill the messenger?"

"What?"

He winks. "More stairs."

"Ugh!"

"Was that a yes or no?"

Danae shoves him towards the opening.

The stairs are uneven, making their progress slow and methodical. They smell musty air before finding a rough cave opening. They duck inside and find no other visible entries or openings. He holds her hand as they move around some giant stalagmites.

"Limestone?" Danae asks after touching the surface of one large pillar near the middle of the space.

He nods. "Open says me."

A rumble of rocks closes the opening they came through and the ground splits.

They scramble back.

After the dust settles, Itra creeps towards the new hole in the ground. He rolls to his toes to peer down into the pit.

"There's a light on down there. No stairs, but a small ramp."

She exhales. "Ask permission first?"

He almost laughs, but he complies. "We mean no harm. May we enter?"

A warm glow grows brighter.

Itra takes a tentative first step to test the surface. *Stable*. Another step. *Good*. He nods back to her.

Danae moves carefully behind him, reaching eye level with the room.

She pauses, taking it in. "Whoa!"

It's not a room, but an endless space: the ceiling is nearly thirty stories high, maybe higher. The room is full of countless barrels, crates, trunks, even metal shipping containers further down, a few vehicles, and a prop.

"Is that a plane?" Danae asks.

He follows her line of sight. "No idea, but I think that's a tank." He points down on the opposite side.

She turns. The cavern extends behind the ramp.

"What is this place?" Danae asks.

"The vault?" Itra asks.

46

Teuta screams, "Let me out!" She attempts to portal. The darkness prevents any clue to the room or space. She attempts to portal again and fails.

"You can't possibly think that is part of the plan." A voice calls from a distance.

It echoes like a cave.

"What did you do to Junior?" Teuta asks.

The voice laughs. "That old piece of rock?"

Teuta identifies the tone and pitch to be possibly female.

"Tonight will be spectacular."

"Who are you?"

"The better question is, what are you? Messenger, fairy queen, or pirate?"

"You created a trap specifically for me, pretty sure you know exactly what I am." Teuta pounds on the walls.

The voice laughs.

"Who are you?" Teuta calls.

"Goddess of Stone."

Teuta squeezes her eyes shut, losing her patience.

"Speechless," the voice teases. "How very odd?"

"You're insane," Teuta says.

"Maybe, but thanks to the blood oath, we're here to claim my blood right and share the knowledge with the world."

“The blood oath is to protect and serve, not to share.”
“Ha!”
“Ember will reign down over you.”
“Not if I control her time.”
“Ha, you think you can control Danae?”
“I have seen the future, Teuta. Your end is near.”
“By Ember’s hand only.”

47

Danae leans over a white hovering sphere shaped craft, but steps back—her ears prickle.

"Itra, do you hear a pulsing sound?"

"Huh? Sorry, what did you say?"

"Do you hear a rhythmic pulsing sound?"

"No," Itra says, pointing to a red and black box nearly as tall and wide as him. "Did you see the label on this?"

Danae walks over and reads the label. "Soldier XII."

"Do you think it's a robot or artificial intelligence?"

"We found a book about artificial intelligence in the archives. It listed a northern Albanian, Nik, as one of the first programmers in AI." She nods at his surprised expression. "What do we do now?"

Itra shrugs, walking to a cluster of paintings and sculptures.

Thump, thump, thump

"Itra, it's getting louder!"

Itra turns, holding a small painting. "Sorry, I hear nothing."

Danae feels the pulse pulling her.

Thump, thump, thump

The sound swells with each step. Danae's ring burns and pulls on her finger. "Itra!"

Itra drops the painting and runs towards her.

Danae is fighting her own hand, which is reaching for a blue velvet box. It clamps down like a magnet. As she tries to pull it away, the box follows. "What do I do?"

Itra attempts to pull the box away, but he's propelled back and lands hard against a few wooden crates.

"Itra!" She runs towards him.

He stands and holds up his hands. "Stop!"

Danae skids to a stop, eyes wide.

"I don't think I can touch or be near it. Can you open the box?"

Danae blinks back a tear. She nods. She turns her hand over and opens the box. An ember stone—the size of a bottle cap on a gold chain—pulses out at her.

The gold chain lifts from the box and clasps around her neck so quickly that neither Danae nor Itra have time to react. The box falls from her hand.

Danae blinks rapidly.

"Danae!" Itra claps in front of Danae's face. *Why isn't she responding?* "Please come back to me!"

Danae loudly exhales.

Itra sighs.

"We must free Teuta," Danae whispers.

"Free her from what?"

"Medusa has taken Teuta."

"And Junior?" Itra asks.

"Gone." Danae swallows hard. "Medusa claimed her blood right when she took the shield from the vault."

"Why are we still here?" Itra points to Danae.

"My bond to the blood oath. Ember needs our help to restore order."

"How can we restore order?"

"This amulet," Danae says, reaching to touch the ember amulet resting on her chest. "It will protect me and my blood from any harm."

"You know all of this," Itra says. He steps closer. "How?"

"Ember."

The falling feeling punches Danae. She lands erect on her feet, this time on a step outside of a large wood and iron door. Itra lands a second behind her. He bends at the waist, trying to stop the spinning of his insides.

"You good?" she asks after finding her breath.

"Not sure that's what I'd call this feeling, but alive, yes."

"Open says me," Danae calls.

The large door swings open.

Danae whispers, "The present cavern."

They cautiously move inside.

An image is playing. Leon is standing in the clearing with a weapon drawn, glaring at a man.

"Leon!" Danae calls and stumbles forward.

"Is that Unis Beard?" Itra asks.

"Leon!" Danae repeats.

Leon turns to look for her. "Danae, where are you?"

Unis steps back in surprise, looking around the clearing at Leon's response.

"In the present cavern," Danae says.

"Danae," Leon whispers. "Is Medusa there?"

There is a noise coming from a large box sitting near the cliff opening.

Itra turns in defense, moving in front of Danae.

Teuta cries out from inside the box, "Medusa is here!"

"Ruin the surprise, why don't you?" A woman saunters out of the darkness in a white flowing gown, her face hidden by a hood and a veil.

"What do you want?" Itra says, scowling at her as she approaches.

"My chance to rule with Poseidon, my pet, by my side."

Leon shouts. "Poseidon is dead!"

"You're wrong!"

"He melted into water after they took his dagger," Leon says, keeping his eyes on Unis.

"How?"

"Two gunshot wounds," Leon says smugly. "One to the chest and the second to his stupid head."

The woman smothers a cry. She moves several steps closer to Itra and Danae.

"What do you want?" Danae asks. She can feel the amulet grow warm against her chest.

250

"Full control."

"Full control of what?" Itra asks, keeping his body in front of Danae.

"Time," the woman says. "Danae will sever her ties to the Castle of Teskom and Ember shortly after she gives birth to Time. Time will serve me."

"You're crazy to think that is even an option!" Danae scoffs.

Itra rolls to his toes, ready to charge. "Never!"

"Wait!" Leon shouts.

"For what?" Itra mutters.

"If you harm her," Leon says, "she will kill this fool, and Kaly will remain stone."

The woman nods. She raises the veil past her chin.

The amulet vibrates against Danae's chest. She moves in front of Itra in one swift step, surprising Itra and the woman.

The woman hesitates long enough for the amulet to lift from Danae's chest.

A powerful force pushes the woman's body out of the cavern opening. Her screams fading to a whisper as she falls to the rocky shore.

"I'm so sorry, brother," Danae whispers to Leon.

Clap, clap, clap, clap, clap, clap

"Bravo!" a woman calls from the shadows.

Teuta screams, "Ember!"

Danae and Itra land in the clearing next to Leon. Leon swings the weapon in their direction.

"Danae!" Leon cries.

"Leon!" Danae exclaims.

Itra catches his breath. "It wasn't Medusa under the veil."

"What?" Leon and Danae yell in unison.

"Her hood flew back. I saw a grey streak near her temple. It was Pem."

"If Kaly is still stone and he is not dead." Leon points towards the very pale face of Unis Beard. "Then, is…"

Itra and Danae whisper, "Medusa."

48

"You fool!" Medusa growls.

Teuta laughs.

"You think you are so clever?" Medusa says, walking towards the box.

"Ember will protect Danae," Teuta says with confidence.

"And who will protect you?"

The walls of the box slowly move inward.

Teuta attempts to portal again but fails.

The space narrows making it harder to breathe.

"Where is your mighty Ember now?" Medusa teases.

The walls suddenly stop moving. Teuta sighs.

"Here."

Medusa spins, searching the space.

"No, over here."

Medusa mutters a curse and scans the cavern, slowly turning. She removes her veil.

"My word you haven't aged a day," the voice whispers in her ear.

Medusa screams and jumps back in alarm.

"You think you are the only one that figured out how to project over the last thousand years?" the voice echoes in the space.

"Medusa," Teuta whispers, "you're finished here."

Medusa turns to glare at the box. "You want to play games?"

Medusa takes a step towards the box.

"I wouldn't do that," the voice whispers.

Medusa takes another step and a blast of air slams her against the opposite wall. She slides down in a heap.

The box opens just wide enough for Teuta to portal out of the present cavern.

"We can't leave Teuta in there with Medusa," Danae says.

Leon and Itra glare at her.

"What?" Danae glares back.

"Danae, we were just booted out by Ember," Itra says. "I think we are exactly where we need to be."

"So," Danae says, "we just walk away and pretend everything is okay?" She shakes her head.

"Danae," Leon says, "she already killed Iana and turned Kaly to stone."

Danae's eyes fill with tears. "I'm so sorry." She sniffles. "But can we really just let her win?"

"It's too late," Unis says, groaning in pain. He collapses on the ground. The snake is uncoiled but still attached to his leg by its fangs.

Leon carefully aims and shoots the snake.

The snake stops moving, but Unis begins to shake.

"I think he is having a seizure," Leon says, kneeling to roll and hold Unis on his side.

Unis gasps for air.

"If any harm happened to Medusa," Leon says, looking up at Danae and Itra. "The snake was triggered to bite Unis."

Unis goes rigid and releases a quiet exhale.

Leon rolls Unis to his back.

Danae squeaks in horror.

Unis's face and neck are swollen beyond recognition.

Leon checks for a pulse. He shakes his head.

"It was a long-nosed adder," Itra says. "Even if we had an anti-venom to inject, he would have had a very slim chance of surviving that bite."

Danae turns away and buries her face in Itra's chest. Itra kisses her head gently.

Leon clears his throat.

Itra and Danae turn towards Leon.

He is pointing past the ember archway. They can see the castle.

"We are so screwed," Danae whispers.

"What happened in there?" Leon asks.

Itra explains the missing shield, the blast, and the vault to Leon.

"Unis said Medusa brought a shield back to the bunker he was in," Leon says, checking Unis's pockets and holds up the cube.

"Can you reverse engineer the coordinates?" Danae asks Itra.

"Maybe," Itra mutters. "But if not, I know someone that can."

49

Teuta appears between Leon and Danae.

They scramble back.

"You should come with a warning bell!" Leon scolds.

"Who is that?" Teuta asks pointing to Unis's corpse.

"Unis Beard," Danae says.

"Actually, his real name is Earl Eunice McCoy," Leon says.

"Earl?" Itra scoffs.

"Why is he here?" Teuta says.

"Don used him to send messages to Danae and Itra," Leon says.

"Was he the man in the bunker with Kaly?" Teuta asks, recalling Dita's explanation of events after the blast.

"Yes," Leon says.

"What happened to Medusa?" Itra asks.

"She is still alive," Teuta says with a shiver. "Ember broke me out of that tiny box. Do any of you know where the Medusa Shield is?"

"A bunker somewhere in Mokset, but when is not clear," Leon states, explaining his conversation with Kaly and then Unis.

"He came here with this." Leon hands Teuta the gold cube.

Teuta turns the device to inspect the ember stone on the cube and taps a corner. The box unfolds into a flat square. A message hovers above the surface. Teuta uses her finger to scroll through the message. "Got it!"

"Got what?" Itra squints over her shoulder, attempting to read the lines of numbers.

"The last known coordinates in Mokset," Teuta says.

"But is it in this year, our universe or…" Danae asks.

"Or," Teuta says. She turns to Leon. "Catch!"

Leon flinches as a large staff appears falling from the sky. He catches the staff with ease and grins.

"Ember's gift to you," Teuta sings. The top of the staff glows with an ember orange. "Double tap the staff."

Leon holds the staff out and follows her instructions. The staff transforms into a scythe. The blade is translucent.

"Tap once more," Teuta instructs. Leon taps and the scythe brightens with an ember glow. "Good, now release the staff."

"Let it go?" Leon questions.

Teuta nods.

Leon releases the staff and winces for a brief second. He rolls up his sleeve. "What is this?" Leon glares at Teuta as he shows Itra and Danae a new tattoo of the ember staff.

Danae covers her mouth in surprise and Itra steps closer to inspect the new art.

"So impatient," Teuta chides. "Think of holding the staff."

Itra scrambles back as the staff appears in Leon's hand again.

"It will always be with you now," Teuta says with a smile. "Ember needs Leon and Danae to guard the clearing and the castle's entrance until the shield has been returned. They are the only ones blessed by Ember to protect and serve at the moment."

"Excuse me," Itra says, pointing towards the castle. "Medusa is still alive and in there."

"Ember has a sense of humor," Teuta says and giggles. "Medusa is alive inside a stone statue."

Danae and Leon say in unison, "Nice!"

Itra smirks.

"I'm staying with Danae," Itra states.

"Not possible." Teuta flicks her wrist.

"Wait!" Danae screams.

Itra vanishes reaching towards Danae.

"You could have at least given us a moment." Danae glares down at Teuta.

"No time," Teuta states.

"What about Kaly and this guy?" Leon asks, pointing down to Unis.

"Kaly will remain here," Teuta says. She frowns, looking at the statue. She glances down and sings, "Tani."

Unis's body vanishes.

"Where did you send his body?" Danae asks, looking at the bare ground.

"On the lake shore near a patrol unit," Teuta says and twirls to walk back towards the ember archway.

"Follow or make a run for it?" Danae whispers.

"I can hear you!" Teuta chides.

Leon grunts and double taps his staff. "I could, you know." He winks with a wicked grin.

Danae shoves his shoulder.

Leon releases his staff and pulls her in for a hug. "We've got this," he whispers into her hair.

"For Kaly," Danae whispers.

Leon's chest shudders and he pulls Danae in closer.

RECOVER OR YIELD

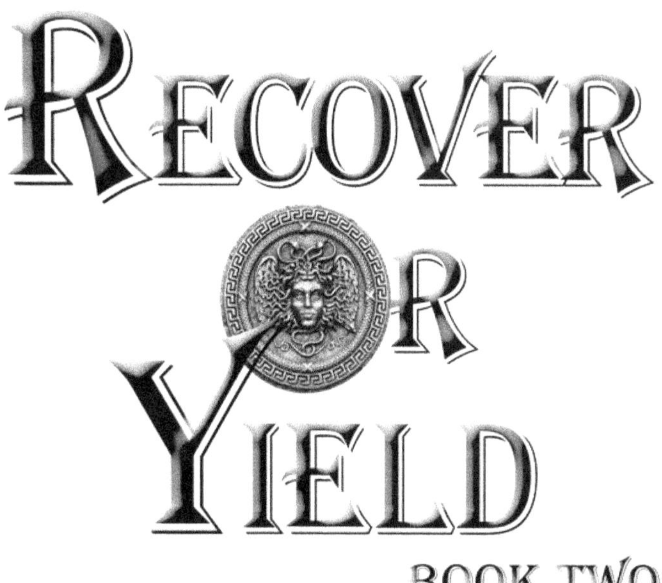

Preview

1

"Leon, we won't stay at the Castle of Teskom forever," Danae says, arching her back. "I'm not giving birth here, that's for sure." She shifts from side to side and looks past him.

The Castle of Teskom foreboding presence seems to hover at the far side of the clearing. The towers are nearly hidden in the clouds descending from the evening sky.

Leon nods and turns his back to the castle. He glares at the archways.

"I won't leave my wife as a stone statue for eternity!" Leon says, kicking a small rock across the clearing. "Hell no!"

Danae winces. "How are we supposed to defend the castle and the goddess Ember?"

The ember amulet around Danae's neck lifts away from her chest billowing her top. She presses her palm against it.

Leon nods to Danae as her jaw slackens and her eyes go wide. "What is it?"

"It's vibrating," she says, lifting the amulet out from under her top to examine it.

Leon moves closer and reaches to touch it.

"Wait!" Danae steps out of his reach. "When Itra tried to touch it, he was propelled back. I'm not sure what it will do to you if it did that to my husband."

Leon raises his hand in surrender. He calls his long wooden staff, a gift from Ember. The glow from the top creates a halo of light over them.

"Should we wait out here or in the castle?" he asks.

She turns in a circle, looking at the clearing, the archways, and back to the castle. "I hesitate to stay out in the open after watching the battle this morning. Castle?"

Leon responds by turning towards the castle, but he pauses after a step. He glances once over his shoulder to the archway where Kaly's stone figure remains.

Danae loops her arm through Leon's and nudges him forward. He stiffens but softens under her arm after he releases a long, ragged exhale.

"We'll try everything we can to bring her back," she whispers.

He swallows hard before trudging towards the castle.

They walk quietly on the worn path up to the enormous steps. He bounds up the first and extends his hand to her. She takes his offered hand, and they climb up the next three giant steps together.

Standing at the top, they look back out over the clearing to the five archways. The last of dusk falls surrounding them in darkness.

A cool breeze slithers a wave of chills down Danae's spine. She rubs her forearms and notices a slight shiver run through Leon as well. She abruptly turns back towards the castle, longing for the warmth of the conservatory just past the foyer. She stumbles to a stop.

"Leon!"

Leon whirls, double tapping his staff, transforming it from an ember glow to a long, shimmering scythe.

"What's wrong?" he asks, scanning the entry.

"The blue and gold waves on the mosaic tiles are gone." Danae kneels to examine the entry floor.

Leon taps his staff back to an ember glow and lowers the light towards the floor.

"It's a mural of us standing here and now," he states, stepping back.

"But how?" asks Danae.

"It's a reflection," Teuta says, appearing in the archway leading to the conservatory.

Danae and Leon are startled by her sudden, but tiny, appearance. Teuta stands barely half as tall as Danae and a third of Leon's height.

"Teuta, where is Itra?" Danae asks, placing a hand on Leon's arm.

"Itra is with Elis and Anton," Teuta says.

"Hmm," Leon mocks with a scowl. "And what else does the great and mighty castle messenger bring us?" He rolls to his toes. "More bad news? Or are you sending another loved one away with a single word?"

Teuta frowns and twirls to enter the conservatory, but pauses. She turns back and tosses two light stones towards Leon and Danae.

They catch the small stones and activate them by tapping the center. The light hovers just above their heads, illuminating the entry.

"Come along. We have much to discuss." Teuta dances forward past the first row of plants.

The warm air lifts the chill Danae had felt moments before. She nudges Leon along as they follow Teuta to a curve in the path lined with rows of plants. She pulls back the climbing vines and pushes open a door.

Teuta gestures to the open door.

Danae and Leon enter but hesitate a few steps in.

The warm yellow walls of the dining hall are now a vibrant purple and the glass dome, dark by the night sky, has a few new panels of shapes that are currently shifting.

"Whoa?" Danae whispers.

"How?" Leon asks.

"Ember." Teuta states. "When a new bloodline is assigned to the castle, the old traces are removed."

"Itra's line is essentially erased?" Danae asks.

"Yes, precisely," Teuta says.

Danae scans the hall. The long table and chairs appear nearly the same, minus the crest carving on the back of the chairs. A new swirling pattern is engraved in the wood. The design across the mosaic tiled floor reflects the castle as it was originally built surrounded by a valley of trees and the mountains to the east.

Teuta skips across the hall to the side with three doors and stops outside the furthest one on the right. She pushes it open.

Danae recalls Itra attempting to open this door during their first visit. It had been locked.

Teuta walks through the door and the light above her expands.

Danae follows Teuta, but stops at the threshold.

"Where are you taking us?" Leon asks, running into Danae.

"To your living quarters and war room," Teuta sings.

"Our what room?" Danae whispers.

Leon nudges Danae forward.

Teuta twirls around the large hall draped in ruby red silks with bold purple walls.

Danae's mouth falls slightly ajar taking in the ancient white marble furniture in contrast of the vibrant silks. The glass dome above has several painted figures of Greek Gods. Zeus, Athena, and a few others they don't recognize.

"What in the—" Leon whispers.

Danae drags her finger along a side table. The entire hall is pristine, no dust or cobwebs.

"This is the family war room for Zeus and his descendants," Teuta gleefully sings. "Preserved only for your return."

Danae sighs and shakes her head. "Teuta, we can't stay."

Teuta's smile falls when she faces Leon and Danae. "You two must stay and find the Medusa Shield to protect the Castle of Teskom."

"How?" Danae asks.

"Using this," Teuta says. She holds up the gold cube that the blogger, Unis Beard, had used to transport to the clearing outside of the archways before he was killed. "Leon said the blogger saw Medusa bring a shield back to the bunker before she sent him to the clearing."

"Yes, but—" Leon says, shaking his head, "why us?"

"It is your duty by blood to protect and serve," Teuta says.

"That didn't exactly work out for my sister-in-law, Iana," Danae says, narrowing her eyes.

"We tried to save Iana," Teuta says.

"But you didn't succeed!" Danae exclaims. "Elis is without his loving mother. I refuse to risk any more of my family, especially Leon, who just lost Kaly."

Leon bites the inside of his cheek.

Danae turns for the door. "Figure something else out. We're done."

The door to the dining hall slams shut before she reaches the threshold.

Leon double taps his staff and swings the scythe towards Teuta. She vanishes before the arc of his flaming blade can make contact. She reappears on the opposite side of the room, unphased and smiling.

"As a descendant of Zeus, you will protect and serve," Teuta sings and waves her hand. "Read and learn."

Two books appear on the large marble table before she vanishes again.

"Son of a—" Leon shouts. His voice echoes back.

Danae curses and kicks the door. She walks over to the table and picks up a book. She looks at the cover. It reads 'OPEN.' She picks up the second book and holds it up so Leon can read the cover.

Leon squints and says, "Medusa Shield."

Danae nods. "The OPEN book booted me out through a protection portal when Itra and I found the castle."

"Great! Try that one first," Leon says. "What chapter was it?"

"Chapter nine," Danae says, bracing for the stomach drop sensation of transporting as she cracks open the book. Nothing happens, but she feels an overwhelming compulsion to sit and read.

"Danae, what is it?" Leon asks, watching her eyes narrow on the page.

Danae lowers herself into the chair and doesn't answer his question.

"Danae!"

Danae looks up and blinks.

"Sit," she says in a monotone command. "Read. We don't have time."

Leon gapes at her expression and response. He releases the staff, and it vanishes. He rubs his forearm where the new staff tattoo holds the essence of his gift from Ember. He plops in the chair next to Danae and opens the other book on the Medusa Shield.

Recover or Yield, Book Two, is available in eBook, Paperback, and Hardcover anywhere books are sold online.

Acknowledgments

This book and the inspiration for this series came from Art, my husband, and his desire to explore Albania, his home country. I've enjoyed being along—sometimes far behind—for the ride. He provided a stress-free environment to create and write. Thank you for the support and encouragement, and for making sure I always come down the mountain.

My thanks also to my faithful friend and lifesaver for this project, my editor, Jenny Leonard. Her wisdom transformed the manuscript. You're a beautiful new mom, an amazing friend, and the best editor a new author could ever dream of—THANK YOU!

About the Author

Kim Malaj resides on a vineyard and homestead in northern Albania with her husband, Arti, author of Northern Albanian Folk Tales, Myths and Legends. Although she is a Show Me State (Missouri) lady at heart (Go KC Chiefs and Royals!), she loves her life at Homestead Albania.

When she's not writing, she tends to the garden, orchard, vineyard, and livestock. She's also brews up batches of raki and wine, and other sweet and savory treats made from the fruits and veggies produced in the garden. She is an avid photographer, an active blogger about the homestead, and a hobbyist drone pilot, learning the art of aerial photography and filming.

Visit the blog: www.HomesteadAlbania.com
For publishing news: www.KimMalaj.com